# FELIZ NAVIDAD

Raul paused, looked at her, then reached up and cupped her face, the leather of his glove soft against her cold cheek. "I would like nothing better than to spend tomorrow with you. I just need to run by the office early in the morning."

She smiled, joy surging through her at the knowledge that they would have another day together. "That's . . . great. Well, what are we going to do now?"

He glanced around, grinned, and leaned in close to whisper into her ear. "I'm getting a little cold and tired. A nap in front of the fire might be nice before we have to brave the family. Don't you think?"

Rebecca grabbed the front of his parka and shifted upward to nip his earlobe. "Sounds perfect."

He raised his hand in the air and let out a loud whistle, which hailed a cab for them in a second. She smirked and shook her head. "You don't waste any time, do you?"

Raul snagged the handle on the door, pulled it open, and held it out for her. As she slipped in, he said, "Not if that time involves you, *querida*."

# FELIZ NAVIDAD

## Caridad Scordato

**PINNACLE BOOKS**
Kensington Publishing Corp.
http://www.encantoromance.com

PINNACLE BOOKS are published by

Kensington Publishing Corp.
850 Third Avenue
New York, NY 10022

All Kensington Titles, Imprints, and Distributed Lines are available at special quantity discounts for bulk purchases for sales promotions, premiums, fund-raising, and educational or institutional use. Special book excerpts or customized printings can also be created to fit specific needs. For details, write or phone the office of the Kensington special sales manager: Kensington Publishing Corp., 850 Third Avenue, New York, NY 10022, attn: Special Sales Department, Phone: 1-800-221-2647.

Pinnacle and the P logo, Encanto and the E logo Reg. U.S. Pat. & TM Off.

First Printing: October 2001
10 9 8 7 6 5 4 3 2 1

Printed in the United States of America

*To all my nieces and nephews—Jonathan, Lauren, Brendon, Erika, Peter, Deanna and, Desiree—for all the love and joy they bring into my life.*

*To my dear friend and movie buddy, Grace, who is forever young. I am so happy we got to know one another and have been able to share this time together.*

# One

"*Mami,* don't worry. I'll definitely be home by Christmas Eve," Rebecca said reassuringly, cradling the phone to her ear while she slipped a suit out of her closet and ripped off the thin plastic bag from the dry cleaners.

"*Mi'ja. Noche Buena* is less than a week away. I don't understand why this couldn't wait until the new year," her mother complained, and quite frankly, Rebecca didn't know how to counter that. She wished her trip could wait as well, but when a major client—especially one who was responsible for placing her on the radar screen with her ultra-conservative, chauvinist bosses—said "jump," Rebecca did just that.

For that reason, she spent another minute or so trying to placate her mother. After she finished on the phone, she resumed her packing, all the while thinking about just why she was headed to New York City. It was never one of her favorite places to visit anyhow. She had been there on more than one occasion for business meetings and conferences, but Rebecca found the city and its inhabitants just too hard and demanding.

She much preferred the friendlier, less harried pace in her Miami hometown. Not to mention the Miami weather.

New York City in the dead of winter was a nightmare. The cold, rain and snow made the already crowded and bustling metropolis even more inhospitable. Sidewalks became slippery slopes ready to dump unsuspecting pedestrians on their butts. Their umbrellas added to the mess, creating a walking obstacle course along those precarious sidewalks. And of course the taxis, always a strange concept to her, were never to be found when the weather was bad. In Miami a car was both a necessity and a status symbol. Rarely did one use a taxi.

She wouldn't even think about New York's idea of mass transit for dealing with situations when above-ground travel became impossible. Her one subway ride during a conference several years earlier had been a noisy, crowded abomination during which she'd had her pocket picked.

New York was definitely not Rebecca's number one winter travel choice, especially with the holidays just days away as her mother had reminded her only moments ago.

But she had no choice. The rumors were flying all around the law firm. She was next in line, her name at the top of the list of hopefuls for partnership. That was an amazing feat in itself. It wasn't often that the other partners at RLL, one of Miami's premier boutique firms, allowed someone into their vaunted ranks.

It was even more of a surprise considering her age, sex and ethnicity. If the rumors were true—and in a firm the size of RLL the office grapevine was incredibly accurate and speedy—she would be the youngest partner, chosen at the ripe old age of thirty. To make that accomplishment even sweeter, she would be the first woman and Latina. Quite a coup and one which she wasn't about to mess up.

Besides, she had brought this client into RLL with a lot of hard work, and the client had treated her well. They had started off slowly, testing the waters and when her abilities and dedication became apparent, they had gradually shifted all of their legal work to her and her colleagues at RLL. Because of that, she felt she owed them this one unreasonable demand, namely, snagging the rights to a hot new technology just before the holidays.

CellTech, a small New Jersey biotech company, had

recently gotten FDA approval for a gene therapy to help counteract the effects of certain types of auto-immune nerve diseases, and patents for both the therapy and the vectors used for transport. Her client already held the license to one of CellTech's other genetic mapping procedures and had hinted to CellTech that they were interested in the rights to these properties. In deference to her client's size and their past relationship, CellTech had entered into a gentleman's agreement of sorts whereby her client would get first crack at acquiring the rights.

Rebecca knew CellTech's current attorney was both savvy and determined. He had negotiated the earlier patent license agreement, and she understood that he would tolerate only so much, especially when his client's product was already in hot demand. In light of that, the draft Rebecca had prepared and was ready to discuss with her client in the morning was a little more giving than the standard licensing arrangements.

As she packed, adding one more dark-colored suit to those already on the pile on her bed, she considered the team that she would take with her to provide support during the negotiations. Andrew Waverly had the necessary technological expertise and he was excellent at licensing arrangements. Sheila Smith, a paralegal they both shared on various projects, would help with the assorted tasks they might need done over the course of the next few days. Rebecca was confident they could handle the sensitive negotiations and obtain what her client wanted, as well as make it home in time for *Noche Buena* and the holidays that followed.

She finished setting out her clothes on her bed and packed them up into her bag. By tomorrow afternoon she would be on a flight to New York, and the draft of the agreement would be on its way via fax to CellTech's attorney. After that. . . .

She flipped on her television and surfed through the

stations until she hit one of the channels offering weather information. Waiting until they gave the report for the Northeast, she flinched at the freezing temperatures and at the weather front the meteorologist said would surely skip the area.

Rebecca was normally a trusting individual, but when it came to meteorologists and their forecasts she was always skeptical. The weather front in question was a slow one, according to the expert, and had already dumped light snows throughout the Midwest. In her mind's eye, she pictured that front slowly getting bigger, growing until it filled the entire area over the Northeast with a large, angry mass of snow.

Rebecca shuddered, drove that image from her mind and instead convinced herself the weather reporter was right and the storm would be a small nothing that just skimmed over the area and did little damage. But just in case, she added her one and only pair of snow boots to her bag. Now nearly a decade old, they had been used only a half-dozen times or so on those reluctant trips up North.

She hoped they would see no service during this trip.


Her client had been pleased with her proposed strategy for obtaining the licenses. They approved her choices for the maximum amounts to be offered as payments and royalties as well as the remaining terms of the agreements. Rebecca had made a point, however, of playing devil's advocate and identifying the most likely terms and requirements to be requested by the other side given the unique nature of the product. The client considered her comments and they settled on a strategy for interim responses. Many of the responses to the possible scenarios Rebecca had proposed would require approvals from the upper levels of management.

Rebecca returned to her office, sure she would be able to accomplish everything and actually looking forward to heading to New York that afternoon for the negotiations. If all went as planned, she would be in her hotel room in Manhattan in time to have a late supper, a nice long bath, and a full evening's sleep so she'd be ready for sitting at a conference room table all the next day.

Determined to get on her way, she sat down at her desk to take a last look at the agreement for CellTech, as well as check for any upcoming deadlines she would have to deal with before she went away. Satisfied with the contracts, she asked her secretary to fax them over to the CellTech attorney. Then she reviewed her mail and the files docketed for the next two weeks and quickly dictated letters to be typed and sent to her contacts in various countries.

There was only one file in the pile that might demand more than just a routine follow-up. She had commenced a legal action against a counterfeiter in Argentina and her local attorney had been unable to serve the offender with the court papers advising him of the action. It didn't come as a surprise that the counterfeiter was making himself hard to find.

After being told by the local authorities about the possible illegal goods, Rebecca had hired her own investigator to get information and samples. Her client, a large multinational entertainment company, had confirmed that none of the T-shirts bearing dozens of different cartoon characters and related trademarks was legitimate.

Hoping to resolve the matter amicably, Rebecca had sent a cease and desist letter requesting that the goods be turned over to her Argentinean counsel, who would then donate them to a local charity to be given to the less fortunate. She had also asked that the counterfeiter agree to not produce any more goods with her client's trademarks and copyrighted characters in exchange for not taking any legal action.

Apparently that hadn't sat well with the man, who had ignored the letter and continued selling the illegal products.

Rebecca had been forced to file a legal action to shut him down, and now they had only another week to notify the counterfeiter about the action, otherwise they would have to petition the court to allow the seizure without his presence. The infringer would lose thousands of dollars, but she felt no sympathy for him. Her clients and the people who they licensed to use their properties lost millions to counterfeiters. Unfortunately, people seemed not to be bothered by buying bootleg tapes, compact discs and T-shirts.

Dictating the comments for her Argentinean attorneys, she thereafter gave detailed instructions to her paralegal on what steps to take over the next few days. She knew her assistant would handle the matter and contact Rebecca only if it became absolutely necessary, so Rebecca could concentrate on her negotiations.

Finished with her work, she shut down her laptop and packed it into her briefcase along with a hard copy and backup disk with the CellTech documents. She called and left messages with the licensing expert and the paralegal who would be going with her to New York.

Rebecca checked her watch. She had a few hours to go before her flight and was more than ready. She was about to tackle the review of an affidavit and its exhibits which were due when she returned, when her telephone rang. The display told her it was Simon Langleis, the latest Langleis to carry on the tradition of lawyering in the family firm. Rebecca immediately picked up, not wanting to keep a senior partner waiting.

"Yes, Mr. Langleis. How can I help you today?" she asked deferentially.

"I'd like to discuss this CellTech agreement you're working on, Rebecca. Please come to my office." His tone brooked no disagreement.

"I'll be there shortly," she answered. He responded with, "Make it sooner rather than later, Rebecca. I'm a busy man."

"Yes, sir," she said, only to find that she was saying it to a dead line, for he had already hung up.

She muttered a curse under her breath and placed the phone gently into its cradle, although she would have gotten some small measure of satisfaction from slamming it down.

Simon Langleis might be one of the senior partners of the firm, but Rebecca had never been impressed by him in the few rare contacts they'd had. It was common knowledge that his grandfather had pressured him into becoming a partner. His father had chosen not to go into the family business and was quite happy running a small real estate empire in Miami's trendy South Beach area.

Langleis had migrated toward the patent side of the firm's business, which meant that more often than not, he was dealing with papers and inventions. When dealing with patents, he was apparently quite good, for he had the kind of mind suited to drafting claims and detail work.

Rebecca rose and headed for his office, which was on another floor of the building along with the rest of the patent staff offices. She stopped in the anteroom of his office and waited while she was announced. It came as no surprise when his secretary, a pleasant, middle-aged woman, gave her an apologetic smile and told her to take a seat and wait, as he would be busy for a few minutes.

Rebecca nodded and made herself comfortable on a chair in the anteroom, smoothing the skirt of her black linen suit as she sat there, trying to not let his obvious power play bother her. She was thankful that she didn't need to work with him on a regular basis. Besides, as a partner he had a lot of clout. If the rumors were true and she was being considered for partnership, now was not the time to anger him in any way. Not even if it grated to have to suck up to him and humble herself. Sometimes that was part of a lawyer's advancement on the career track at RLL and so she sat and waited.

And then she waited some more.

# Two

Twenty minutes later, Langleis buzzed his secretary and told her to let Rebecca in.

Rebecca entered and approached Langleis's desk, waiting for him to motion her to sit. When she did, she sank into the low-slung chair, which forced her to look up at the man behind his very large desk. Although she'd been in his office before, she didn't recollect the chairs being so squat and the desk so massive, and wondered whether it was just her imagination working overtime or if he'd made some changes. His next question confirmed her impressions.

"Are the new chairs comfortable?" he asked. His tone was amiable enough, but she sensed an ulterior motive behind the question.

"Plush, but a little low," she responded, and tried to shift upward so that she was level with him, but it was difficult. The cushioning on the chair gave too much for her to maintain that position.

"Mmm," was all he replied, and he leaned forward, resting his elbows on the spacious and nearly empty top of his desk. His position forced her to gaze up at him, like a groupie staring up at her idol on a stage. Now she realized the reason for the new chairs. She'd heard of tactics like this for intimidating one's opponents. Keep them low and looking up, make yourself seem physically larger and you supposedly had an unconscious mental advantage.

Rebecca knew just how to whittle away at it, and took the lead in the conversation, becoming the one asking rather than answering. "Why do you want to talk to me about the agreement for Pharmavax?"

Langleis was surprised by her taking the initiative and sat up straighter, blinked quickly a few times as if jump-starting his brain. "Yes, yes. While Pharmavax has become one of this firm's more profitable clients—"

"Thank you. That's good to hear," she interrupted him. "I worked hard to land them as a client."

His blinking increased slightly, but he didn't hesitate to parry her comment. "While we appreciate your work in bringing them in and cultivating their business, I must personally express my reservations about their latest endeavors and this agreement with CellTech."

Rebecca shifted to the edge of the chair and found that by sitting on its frame rather than the fluffy upholstery, she was able to level the physical playing field. "I'm rather confused by that comment, given that Pharmavax's stock price has been increasing steadily as has their business due to good press releases about the company and what it's doing. Thanks to that, the work they've given us in various areas has likewise increased."

"Yes, but sometimes more work isn't the issue, Ms. Garcia. Not if we are representing people or companies of whom we do not approve," he intoned seriously.

Rebecca had to give him some credit. At least he wasn't willing to represent just anyone in order to earn the almighty buck, but she failed to see how Pharmavax fell into the category of unsavory clients he was talking about. "Pharmavax is a leader in its field, Mr. Langleis. It has been written up in various journals and the patents we have secured on its behalf in the last two or three years have been—"

"Widely publicized and in some instances criticized," he retorted and reached for a piece of paper from the edge of his desk which she noted was a printout from the firm's records system. Without delay, he began to read off the titles of some of the latest patents. "Gene sequence for. . . . Adenovirus vector for gene therapy. . . ."

Rebecca was both surprised and confused by his statements. While primarily a trademarks expert, she had a master's degree in biochemistry and had flirted with the concept of going into patent law at one time. In light of that, she had worked closely with the patent attorneys at the firm who had actually written and secured those patents for Pharmavax along with dozens of others. She knew how hard it had been due to the increased scrutiny given to such requests by the Patent Office.

"Pharmavax spent years and millions of dollars to research those sequences and therapies—"

"But there are grave issues here as to just what should be patentable. Human gene sequences are just that. Human and part of the greater scheme of things. There are those who say biotech companies such as Pharmavax are becoming genome brokers in order to profit from things which belong to all," he stated hotly, his zeal for the issue all too apparent and bordering on scary.

"There are those who rushed to the forefront and secured patents on sequences without any understanding of what they did and without any useful purpose, precluding others from using said sequences for other endeavors. Because of that, the Patent Office tightened their examination procedures. For each and every one of the patents we secured for Pharmavax, we were able to prove that they had not only mapped the sequence, but found something novel and useful from that sequence," she responded calmly. She harbored no guilt or contriteness for her client's actions. They had worked hard and invested substantially. She was convinced that their discoveries would one day help save lives. Like any company inventing a similar product or drug in a new category, they were entitled to patent protection.

Langleis steepled his fingers, tapped them together slowly and then settled back into his maroon-colored leather chair. "Do you consider yourself religious, Ms. Garcia?"

Rebecca thought of the upcoming holidays and all that they meant to her. Some would say that Christmas had become a season of trappings and secularism. She was to some extent guilty of becoming too concerned with the material aspects of the holiday, but deep down inside she tried to keep the spirit of family, love and her religion alive. She glanced up at Langleis and softly said, "I have my beliefs, Mr. Langleis."

He nodded and motioned his hand in a dismissive gesture. "Then as you're sitting in that conference room bartering over a piece of humanity, try to remember those beliefs. Try to remember that this is a season about celebrating those things that make us unique and can't be reproduced by man."

Rebecca hesitated, considering his words and finding that for the first time, she had some measure of respect for him for taking a stand. In all the time she had known him, he had never impressed her as a man of conviction. This brief conversation had changed that. She rose, stood before him for a second and said, "I thank your for your comments, Mr. Langleis. I will keep them in mind."

When she left his office, she shut the door behind her and met the inquisitive glance of his secretary, who asked, "What's with him?"

She shrugged, looked back at the closed door as if she could look through it to the man inside. "Just a touch of the holiday spirit, I think," she answered.


The flight to New York was on time and relatively smooth. Only a few bumps and jostles marred their descent into Newark Airport, compliments of a small storm that the pilot advised was sending a light drizzle onto the New York metropolitan area.

Rebecca and her colleagues entered the relatively new,

clean and well-kept Continental Airlines terminal. It was spacious and airy, and getting to the baggage claim was easy even with the large number of passengers coming and going in anticipation of the Christmas holidays.

At the entrance to the baggage claim, a limo driver stood holding up a placard with the RLL name. Andrew Waverly waved to the man, who came over, took their claim checks, and asked them to come with him to point out their luggage. Fortunately, their bags were among the first on the carousel, and as the driver grabbed two of the bags and Andrew another, they exited the terminal to the short-term parking area where the driver had stationed his car.

"Sorry to make you folks walk, but this is the fastest way to get outta here," the short, rotund man said, huffing slightly from the weight of the bags.

"Do you need help with those?" Rebecca asked, and pulled the shoulder strap of her briefcase up higher as it slipped down due to the added bulk of her laptop.

The man shook his head and then stopped abruptly behind the bumper of a sleek, black, stretch Lincoln Town Car. With a grunt he dropped their bags onto the ground and popped open the trunk. Rebecca glanced at Sheila and gave her a pained smile.

"Nothing fragile in there, I hope," Sheila mumbled beneath her breath as she leaned close to Rebecca.

Rebecca gave a quick laugh and nudged the other woman playfully. "At least it's not too cold," she said and exhaled forcefully, watching as her breath misted before her face.

Sheila nodded. "Still above freezing."

The driver turned to them as he slammed the trunk shut. "But not for long. My bones tell me we're in for a turn," he said, rubbing at a spot right above one knee.

"The weatherman says the front's going to miss us," Rebecca replied, and followed the driver around the side of the car. He opened the door for her and she thanked him, but after they were all seated in the back of the large limo, the conversation about the weather resumed again.

"Now I know they've got all that fancy stuff nowadays. Radar and doppler and everything else, but seems to me they're usually more wrong than right," the driver declared as he looked around to back out the large car from the parking spot.

After he had maneuvered out of the space, he finished with, "My knee hasn't been wrong as long as I can remember."

Rebecca glanced at Andrew, who gave her one of those "humor the old guy" kind of smiles and shrugged. "We'll be home before Santa takes off from the North Pole, Becca," he teased, knowing her concerns about making it back to Miami in time for the holidays.

She peered out the window and her breath frosted the inside of the glass, making it impossible for her to see more than a passing blur of lights in the dark winter night. She wiped at the glass with her hand, managing to clear it enough to be able to view the hazy skyline of lower Manhattan. The World Trade Center towers were barely visible in the gloomy night sky. As they drove up onto an elevated portion of the New Jersey Turnpike, more Manhattan landmarks came into view. The unique slanted roof of the Citicorp building, bright white against the gloomy night. The steely, ornate top of the Chrysler building and the Empire State, its long spire obscured by low hanging clouds. In observance of the Christmas holiday, the lower portion of the building was bathed in green lights, while the extreme top, up near the observation deck levels, was bathed in red.

"Pretty, isn't it?" Sheila said, the awe apparent in her voice.

Despite her dislike of New York City, Rebecca had to confess that tonight it gleamed in the dark, a unique man-made jewel sparkling with vitality. "It's a nice place to visit—"

"But you wouldn't want to live there," Andrew finished for her and they all chuckled.

"No, I wouldn't," she replied quickly and shuddered as if chilled. "Give me a Miami winter any day."

"Yep, and all those palm trees trimmed with lights, fake silver icicles and glass balls," Sheila reminded her facetiously.

Rebecca shook her head and smiled. "Okay, I give on that. In a one-season town, the holidays are well . . . different. But it's the spirit that counts, Sheila."

"That's right, Sheila," Andrew joined in. " 'Tis the season regardless of the weather."

"Pardon me for being a cynic, but being a transplanted New Yorker, I always find it hard to get into the Christmas spirit when it's seventy degrees and the sun is shining," Sheila responded. "I still miss the smell of wood burning in the fireplace and the crisp, clean air after a fresh snowfall."

Rebecca tried to picture those things in her mind, but having been raised in Miami, her sensory associations about Christmas were totally different. Not to mention that being Cuban, Christmas Day was secondary to Christmas Eve, or *Noche Buena* as it was called, and to the Epiphany on January 6th—*Los Reyes.*

Rebecca always knew *Noche Buena* had arrived when she awoke to the smell of the garlic- and citrus-scented pork slowly roasting in the oven. Her *mami* would wake at three or four in the morning just to get the large leg of pork cooking so that it would be so tender, the meat would literally fall off the bone. Not to mention the smells of candles and incense, heavier in the humid Miami air, as she and her family attended Midnight Mass.

"Well, Sheila, I have to admit that my Miami Christmas is way different, but you know what?" Rebecca prompted.

"What?" both Andrew and Sheila responded in unison, mimicking New York accents so that the word came out like the "wa" Joe Pesci used when playing a wiseguy.

She laughed as they intended and shook her head at their playfulness, which reminded her of why she had chosen the two of them to accompany her. Besides their professional abilities, they always managed to alleviate any tension with humor. "Regardless of everything else, the holiday is about our memories. About our families and love and sharing the season with those we care about."

"Damn," Andrew said, but the word lacked any sting. "You had to go all maudlin on us."

"Yes, Becca. Keep up this serious side and you're going to be just like all the other stuffed-shirt partners at RLL," Sheila kidded. Andrew immediately spoke up. "Rumor has it they're going to make your stuffed shirt-ness official any day now."

It wasn't news to Rebecca, but she wouldn't bank on it until it became official. Especially considering today's conversation with Simon Langleis. If he got others at the firm thinking negatively about her client and her ethics in representing them . . . She wouldn't think about it. She had too much else to worry about and couldn't let those thoughts distract her from what was important right now, namely securing the rights for Pharmavax.

"Let's table that discussion," Rebecca advised and from her tone, there was no disputing that it was the boss talking and not the friend of a moment before.

Andrew grinned at Sheila and replied, "Don't want to jinx yourself, Becca?"

"Andrew, you don't know how to quit sometimes," Rebecca replied in jest, but worried that Andrew didn't really understand how the game was played in most larger firms.

Andrew had no hesitation about owning up to it. "Yes, I don't, Becca and neither do you. I still don't get how you put up with all the bull at RLL."

Rebecca stared out the window and realized they were heading into the tunnel that would take them from New

Jersey into Manhattan. Once inside, there was just one way to go and she acknowledged that she had followed a similar path at RLL. She had put herself in a kind of tunnel, looking only straight ahead at her destination—a much desired partnership. She'd avoided anything that might distract her, concentrating on one path, one destination. Nothing to move her in any other direction.

Her parents and family called her single-minded and determined, and, nearing thirty, she had almost reached her goal. And yes, she had put up with a lot along the road, but that was typical in the legal profession. You had to play the game. "RLL is no better or worse than most," she replied, but her declaration lacked conviction even to her own ears.

Andrew looked at her sharply as did Sheila, and Rebecca wondered how two people could be so in synch. "You two really need to consider getting involved, you know. It might give you something to worry about besides me."

"Andrew and I admire you, Rebecca. You're smart and capable and one of the few humans in any position of authority," Sheila answered on their behalf.

"I appreciate that, Sheila, but becoming a partner at RLL isn't going to change me," she asserted.

Andrew and Sheila again exchanged a conspiratorial look, and Rebecca was spared any further discussion when a taxi cut them off and the limo braked to an abrupt halt, as they started to turn onto 42nd Street from the tunnel off-ramp. "Sorry," the driver apologized. "Some of these guys are lunatics behind the wheel."

But as he said that, he transformed, his hands clutching the wheel and his driving becoming much more aggressive as he battled traffic. Seconds later, he whipped around a stopped taxi with his tires squealing from his speed, his horn blaring the entire time. Rebecca was grateful when he finally pulled up in front of their hotel.

As she stepped out onto the curb and waited for the driver to deposit their bags with the Grand Hyatt bellman, a blast of wintry air blew up under the hem of her skirt and she shivered. Grabbing the lapels of her overcoat, she pulled them tight and glanced up at the night sky.

There was a fine rain drizzling down, and the heavens were heavy with dark, threatening clouds. She remembered the weather report and hoped the man had been right. Supposedly this front would do nothing more than bring some colder weather and rain as it slowly moved across into the ocean.

Another blast of cold air whipped down 42nd Street, seeping through the heavy wool of her coat and stinging her pantyhose-clad legs. Rebecca shivered. It was if she had been warned not to take the weather for granted.

# Three

Rebecca closed the door as the room service waiter left, and walked over to the table by the window where he had set out the light supper she had ordered. Lifting the lid on the main plate, she eyed the cottage cheese and fruit salad platter and, knowing it would keep, opted to take the hot bath she had been craving since the chill of the Manhattan night had crept into her earlier.

Rebecca returned to the bathroom, where the large tub was already partially filled with steaming water scented with the bath salts the hotel provided for its patrons. She trailed her fingers through the water, enjoying its fragrance. Slipping free the knot on the terry cloth robe, also provided as a compliment to the hotel's patrons, she took it off, tossed it onto the seat of the toilet, and eased into the heated water in the tub.

It was deliciously decadent, she thought, sliding down until the water was covering her shoulders. She leaned her head back against the edge of the large tub, closed her eyes and let her normally busy mind wander aimlessly. Thoughts came of the myriad gifts she had just finished wrapping the night before and packed in bags to take to her parents' home for *Noche Buena.*

*Dios,* but she couldn't wait to get home. It was something that always restored a sense of balance in her life, reminding her of those things that were important. Things like the warmth and love of her family and friends. She wondered which of their many relatives and acquaintances would be there for dinner and who would come by the house to pass a moment afterward.

Friends and family were good, she thought, reducing it to its most elemental state as the water lulled her mind. But of course, since every good invariably had a bad to counter it, she wondered if her matchmaking parents would sneak a prospective suitor amongst the group that would be sharing the *Noche Buena* meal or dropping by after for coffee, desserts, and the never-ending Cuban chatter and dancing.

Her mother, in particular, was tireless in her endeavors to get Rebecca married off like her brother and sisters. It didn't matter that between the three of them her mother already had a like number of grandchildren, one from each of her siblings. As the eldest child, Rebecca was supposed to already have been married and procreating happily, which in theory was fine except if one wanted a career.

It was ironic in a way, she thought, as she reached for a thick washcloth, soaked it and squirted some of the scented bath gel into its plush folds. All her life her parents had stressed the importance of an education and proving oneself worthy of being in America.

Rebecca had taken that to heart, and was quite comfortable that she had held up her end of the bargain. She had gone to college on a scholarship thanks to her grades and decided to stay on for a Masters in Biochemistry thanks in part to a federal grant funding the research with which she had assisted. After a change of heart when she realized research wasn't her thing, she had decided to go to law school. There had been no question of her acceptance, thanks to her LSAT scores. She had done well, earning a spot on the Law Review and a summer internship at RLL. The work during the internship had resulted in an invitation to join the firm after graduation, and now she could almost taste the partnership.

It was a rich taste, that of success. But the yin/yang of it reminded her of the bitter price she had paid—namely that of being the eldest in her family with no prospects of either marriage or children in the imminent future, much to her parents' dismay. The success they had preached and wanted for their children had both its rewards and consequences.

As Rebecca passed the soapy washcloth over her body, scrubbing the lather onto her skin, she paused and again wondered which young man her mother had arranged to be around in the hopes that the sparks would fly and Rebecca would finally find the man to complete her life. In her mother's mind, no woman's life was complete without husband and home.

The last man her mother had invited, a distant *primo* named Luis, had been very attractive. Rebecca would give her mother that much credit. She had an excellent eye for men which was obvious from her own choice of a husband. Even at fifty-five, her father was a handsome man who still turned women's heads when he walked into a room. Dark-haired, with just a touch of silver at his temple to give him that mature, distinguished look, he had flashing dark green eyes, and a smile that lit up his whole face. He was quick to bestow that smile for he was carefree and loving.

Luis, unfortunately, had not had a personality to go along with those good looks. Petulant and conceited, he had spent more time talking about himself than finding out just what she was interested in. Not to mention that if he had stopped to look at himself just one more time she might have screamed. He had even stopped to straighten his tie in the side view mirror of his Mercedes after the valet had brought it around when their one and only date was over.

Rebecca had called her mother the next morning and read her the riot act about any more potential suitors miraculously showing up. Her mother had been respectful of Rebecca's position at first, but by the end of the conversation Rebecca had been apologizing for her ungratefulness. She had managed to negotiate a truce of sorts in one of the hardest deals she had ever brokered. Her mother would have made a fine lawyer.

There had been no repeats since then, but with the holidays upon them her mother was certain to think that all truces were off and that Rebecca was once again fair game.

She shuddered, both from that thought and from the chilling of the water in the tub. She glanced at her wristwatch and realized that she had been soaking for close to an hour. Time to get out.

Stepping from the tub, she quickly towelled off and slipped on the terry cloth robe. Her feet were cold against the icy tiled floor, so she alternately placed one over the other, trying to heat them up as she ran a brush through her shoulder-length hair. The ends were slightly damp from the water, but she wouldn't worry about styling it now. She was taking a shower in the morning anyway.

Padding out to the main room, she slipped on some thick socks she had brought along to keep her feet warm and then headed over to the table where her meal sat. She grabbed the remote for the television, pointed it at the set, and turned it on.

She sat and removed the cover from her meal, poured herself a cup of the hot tea which by now was both strong and a little tepid from sitting for so long. She didn't mind. She liked her tea almost as black as coffee and it was still hot enough to warm her, especially when mixed with the milk she had asked room service to heat as well.

As she nibbled at the fruit and cottage cheese, she idly flipped through the stations on the television, finding little of interest until she ran across the *Biography* program on the A&E channel. It was the start of one of their theme weeks centering around the creators and stars of the holiday classic *It's a Wonderful Life*. Tonight's episode, which began the week, was on Jimmy Stewart. Similar episodes followed for Donna Reed and the director, Frank Capra. The fourth episode was on all the other players in the motion picture, and on Christmas Eve they would air the picture itself. She made a mental note to tape it since she would be at her parents'—

That thought stopped her short and she gazed out the window, taking in the rain that was still coming down. It was a delicate rain, visible only because of the lights from the hotel and nearby buildings, which turned it into a silvery mist. Occasionally the mist grew agitated, twirled around in the gap between her hotel and the Chrysler building across the way, probably by a blustery gust of wind.

Rebecca tore her gaze away from the window, turned her attention to the show on Jimmy Stewart and finished her light dinner. Pouring another cup of tea, her last if she wanted to sleep that night, she headed for the bed, placed the cup and remote control on the nightstand and turned down the bedspread.

Returning to the chest of drawers on the opposite wall of the room, she opened one drawer, grabbed a pair of newly purchased flannel pajamas and headed to the bathroom where she slipped them on. On her way back to the bed, she detoured to her briefcase, pulled out the book she had started on the plane and which was one of her few guilty pleasures. She might not have any romance in her real life, but the novels she read certainly did.

The sizzling story, about stars who meet on a movie set and find love, dragged her mind away from the cares of her career and its pressures. She especially loved the way she could identify with the heroine's struggle to define her identity and to break out of the role in which the hero sees her in order to win his love. In her life, Rebecca had often faced similar challenges as a woman in what was still predominantly a boys' club.

As for romances, Rebecca had been teased more than once for her reading choices. After all, she was an intelligent woman and therefore well above romances, but she paid those critics no mind. Reading a romance was no more stupid than reading a spy thriller. Anyone who thought otherwise was just being a chauvinist.

So she settled in, engrossed in both the *Biography* program and her novel, her attention occasionally distracted by the weather visible from the windows of her room. Slowly she began to grow drowsy, from both the tea with hot milk and the long day of travel, and eventually she reluctantly placed the book aside, shut off the light, and set the alarm.

Snuggling down into bed, she was asleep within minutes, dreaming of nothing but finishing up her business and getting back to her family and the Miami warmth.


She was a creature of habit, both at home and on the road. The alarm went off at 5:30 a.m. and by the time the phone rang with a wake up call fifteen minutes later, Rebecca was already up. She brushed her teeth, splashed some cold water on her face, and ran a brush through her dark brown hair.

By six she was seated at the table by the window once more, nibbling the continental breakfast that room service had brought up, and skimming over the daily paper. She was only half-listening to the television she had snapped on as soon as she awoke. Like always, she tried to look for upbeat things in the paper, avoiding the grisly details of another brick attack against a pedestrian on a midtown street and the pictures of three young boys killed by their mother in a murder-suicide ritual. As always, the good things in the paper were slim pickings, and she set it to the side, rose, and after rummaging in her briefcase, pulled out the agreements she had faxed to CellTech's lawyer the day before.

She returned to the table by the window, slipped her feet up onto the chair across the way from her and drank from her second cup of coffee as she perused the contracts. The preambles were standard, a recitation of the parties, the corporate addresses and the rights they either were acquiring or owned. Nothing out of the ordinary there.

Turning her attention to the meat of the documents, she was satisfied that they would give them a sound foundation with which to begin. After all, it was fairly similar to the agreement already in place with CellTech for the use of another patent involving a computer program and lab techniques for gene sequence mapping. Pharmavax had already used that technology with great success, for they had been able to map several gene sequences and identify the products of those segments. The result had been the granting of several patents. Additional work was already underway by Pharmavax to develop gene therapies of its own based on the discoveries.

Rebecca was as convinced as Pharmavax that the new gene therapy designed by CellTech would have far-reaching impact, so she understood their haste in trying to secure the rights. In addition, the various patents involved in the therapy included one for a lipid-based vector which allowed for transfer of the genetic materials to the patient. Lipid-based vectors were usually not as effective as virus-based ones, but safer since they contained no active viral material to infect the patient.

CellTech had somehow improved the transfer capabilities and efficacy of their lipid-based vector, and therefore the technology for that alone had great benefits, especially if Pharmavax could use the CellTech vector to deliver the gene-based therapies it developed in the future.

The announcement of an upcoming weather report on the television intruded into Rebecca's thoughts, and she put aside her papers and glanced out the window. It was still dark outside in the winter morning. The silvery mist of the night before had grown thicker, more defined, but was not yet snow.

The weather reporter came on, describing it as a freezing rain and advising on the slow-moving weather front that was headed their way. Jokingly, he lapsed into song. "I'm dreamin' of a white Christmas," he began, crooning in a horrible imitation of Bing Crosby's famous rendition of the song. As his cohorts on the show teased him into silence, he gave his five-day forecast which included the upcoming Christmas holiday, and predicted that the New York metropolitan area would have at least some snow as ground cover for Christmas, but not much.

Rebecca breathed a sigh of relief and flipped to another station just in time to catch the beginning of that report. Here the reporter was calling the current precipitation sleet, and it made Rebecca think of something that someone had once told her about Eskimos having over a hundred words for snow. New York weather reporters might not be so different with all their varied terms for the same cold, semi-crystalline stuff coming down in ever steadier amounts outside her window.

This reporter was at odds with his colleague on the other station. "All you kids wishing for a snow day and those adults who are kids at heart will be disappointed this Christmas," he said, and proceeded to display the radar picture of the front and how it would miss the area entirely.

Rebecca was inclined to hope the second reporter was right, especially with Christmas Eve only days away.

The phone rang, jolting her attention from the television. She grabbed the phone, glanced at her watch, and realized she was running late and needed to head into the shower. "Hello," she answered and Andrew responded with his own jovial greeting.

"You want us to come by your room at 8:45 to get you?" he asked and she confirmed it, repeated her room number and quickly hung up, intent on getting into the shower.

Just for good measure however, she flipped to one last weather station and watched. Then she wished she hadn't.

This station was predicting that a major storm would hit the area within two days. By Wednesday night at the latest.

Rebecca shut off the television, refusing to accept that forecast and in imitation of the first weatherman, began her own off-pitch crooning of "I'll be home for Christmas" as she headed into the shower.

# Four

At 8:45 A.M., Andrew and Sheila came to her room as promised, and they headed to the main lobby of the hotel, a large, multi-level affair complete with waterfalls and multiple stairways and escalators that led to scattered areas along 42nd Street. Taking the lead, Rebecca headed down one of the escalators and out through the main revolving doors to the sidewalk. They were protected there from the worst of the weather by a large overhanging structure that was part of the hotel. It extended all the way to the curb, where a bellman was busy getting taxis for the long line of hotel guests waiting beneath the structure. She hesitated for a moment, wondering whether to get a cab for the short two block walk, and was quickly jostled by someone trying to get by her on the crowded sidewalk. There was no apology, no "Excuse me" as the man barrelled past, his face hidden by the umbrella that he had up in deference to the lousy weather.

Rebecca glanced back at her two companions and noted that they were as prepared as she for the weather and had umbrellas in hand. "I guess we walk," she said, hit the button on her small umbrella and when it was up, headed eastbound on 42nd Street. She was no great distance beyond the protection of the hotel's awning when the wind kicked up, nearly yanking the umbrella from her hand and driving stinging pellets of frozen rain against the small portion of her legs that was not covered by her long, wool overcoat. The chill was immediate and she burrowed deeper into the folds of her coat, scrunching her shoulders to cover as much of her neck as she could against the cold. She made a mental note to buy a scarf somewhere when she had a chance.

Trudging to the curb, she kept her pace slow since her pumps were slipping against the thin layer of slush that was slowly accumulating on the sidewalks and streets. At the curb she gingerly stepped past the growing pool of liquid, but was not so lucky at the far side of the street, where a clog somewhere had resulted in a body of water too large to go around, especially with the crowd of people trying to negotiate the corner on their way to work.

Rebecca stepped into the water's edge and prayed her pumps would hold up on the walk to her adversary's office.

At the corner, she glanced over her shoulder, noticed Andrew and Sheila were right behind, but conversation was impossible beneath the protection of their umbrellas and the crowd that occasionally came between them. As they crossed the broader width of 42nd Street to get to the southern side of the street, the wind whipped down the thoroughfare angrily, stronger now that it was free of any obstacles. The handle of the umbrella rattled in her hand, shifted back and forth as she fought to keep it upright. Again at the curb there was a freezing puddle to step into and again her pumps bore the brunt of the burden.

For some reason the wind remained stronger on this side of the street, and Rebecca was forced to drop the umbrella down and walk blindly into the wind behind the thin protection of the nylon that kept the freezing pellets from driving into her face. The umbrella wasn't enough however to protect the bottom third of her legs, nor the gap between her wrist and the fine leather glove she was wearing. The wind stung that small little slip of skin that was exposed as she carried her briefcase.

She cursed under her breath, berating New York and its weather, wishing her client had exercised the sense to let her conduct the negotiations via fax rather than in person. As one final puddle got the best of her, soaking nearly all of one foot as she sank into it at the last intersection, she vowed she would charge a new pair of pumps to her expense account to replace the pair of Gucci shoes that were certainly ruined beyond repair.

At the revolving doors to the CellTech attorney's office building, she quickly pulled her umbrella closed and jumped into the rapidly spinning doors being driven by the people impatient to get into work and out of the bad weather. She barely cleared the opening of the revolving door before it disgorged Sheila and then Andrew, in nearly as bedraggled a state as she. In the short two block walk, their coats were wet and glistening with the icy drops which clung to them, and their umbrellas were dripping onto the carpets which had been laid on the marble floors of the lobby, apparently in anticipation of the precipitation.

Rebecca gave her umbrella a shake, driving off most of the moisture, turned and glanced around the lobby for the elevator banks. She found them quickly, but paused to appreciate the uniqueness of the building.

Walking over to a large, circular rotunda lined with midnight black marble, she was followed by her two colleagues. In the center of the rotunda area was a large hole at least thirty or more feet in circumference. It was surrounded by brass railings and in the middle, filling the entire rotunda, was an enormous brass globe.

Andrew pulled open his coat and suit jacket, and quickly glanced at his shirt. Lifting his gaze, he teasingly said to Sheila, "What happened, Lois? There's no big, red S on my shirt."

Rebecca joined Sheila in her laughter, and pulled at Andrew's lapel. "It's 'cause you left your big red cape back in your hotel room, Superlawyer," she kidded back, thinking that many a visitor to the building had likely had the same reaction.

Once the home of the *Daily News,* the building had

earned its fame as the home of a "greater metropolitan newspaper" during various scenes in the first *Superman* motion picture. Now the offices were leased to a number of different tenants and Rebecca wondered whether they even noticed or cared about the globe or the large clocks along a far wall which were the remnants of former tenants. As she glanced around, noticing the harried looking workers scurrying through the lobby without even picking up their heads, she doubted it.

Typical, she thought, failing to understand how New Yorkers in general could be so oblivious to the unique things around them. Was it that there were too many of them and they had become desensitized to it all, or was it that the pace and pressure of their daily lives had eroded any desire to just take the time to enjoy those things around them? Regardless, she was glad she wasn't in the same boat as them, for as far as she was concerned, that ship was named the *Titanic* and sinking quickly.

She'd take the pace and substance of her life back home, which still allowed for some civility and appreciation of life.

"Come on, team. We need to hit the road before we're too late," she said, realizing that with the weather and their playing tourist in the lobby, it was almost nine o'clock. Her adversary would be waiting for them and she hated to make a bad impression by being late.

The elevators were broken into two different banks. One which serviced the lower floors and the other which serviced floors above twenty. The offices of Adamson, Fuentes & Santos, the lawyers for CellTech, were located on the 33rd floor, so they boarded the express elevator to the upper stories along with a large number of others.

Inside the elevator, the smell of wet wool and leather permeated the interior, as did the acrid scent of cigarette smoke from those who had hastily had a last puff before entering the building. As in a number of cities, many New York offices had no smoking policies which meant smokers were driven out in front of their buildings to satisfy their nicotine cravings. Rebecca and her colleagues had already passed another building this morning where a large congregation of smokers were huddled underneath the canopy of the building's entrance, puffing away and creating their own kind of air pollution for those trying to get into the building.

The elevator rose quickly, but then became a local as it made numerous stops on its way to the 33rd floor. By the time they got there, the elevator was nearly empty.

The hallway by the elevator banks was wide and quite clean. Polished mahogany panels lined the walls of the hallway and the firm's name was elegantly done in gleaming brass letters mounted onto the deep, reddish brown panels of wood. Floor-to-ceiling glass doors closed off the firm's space from the elevator hallway.

A receptionist was visible through the one set of doors. The others opened onto a foyer where a very elegant Queen Anne couch was visible and what appeared to be a small conference room.

Rebecca walked to the receptionist's area and the well-dressed and elegantly coiffed woman smiled and disengaged the mechanism locking the doors, allowing Rebecca to open them.

"May I help you?" she asked, her head barely visible above the edge of a large mahogany desk. Her tone was cultured and lacked the heaviness of a typical New York accent.

"Would you please let Mr. Santos know that Ms. Garcia, Ms. Smith and Mr. Waverly are here to see him," she answered.

"Certainly. If you'd care to take off your coats or freshen up a bit, I'll get you settled in the conference room and let Mr. Santos know you're here," she said and rose, walked to a closet by the main door and opened it so they could store their things.

"The ladies' room is at the end of the hall to your

right. The men's room is on the far side," the receptionist stated pleasantly and motioned to the doors out to the hallway.

Rebecca and Sheila walked down the short hall and to the ladies room, where they both quickly straightened the mess the wind had made of their hairdos. As Rebecca smoothed her hair into place, she glanced at Sheila. The attractive blonde quickly gathered back her mass of long curls with a scarf that perfectly matched the dark, wine-colored suit she was wearing.

Rebecca glanced down at her own tailored black suit and felt drab, like a pea hen next to the peacock. That was one thing she regretted about working at RLL. They had little tolerance for any deviation from the traditional garb of white shirts and dark suits for their attorneys. That was apparently the proof of their professionalism and even the female lawyers at the firm were expected to follow that dress code.

She tried to do what she could and her designer suits were at least feminine and a cut above the drab boxy men's style suits in which many of her female colleagues were imprisoned. Smoothing the lapels and giving the hem a straightening tug, she consoled herself with the fact that at least it showed off her trim figure as best as it could. Not that it mattered. After all, they were here for business.

Nevertheless, it was hard not to miss the appreciative look that Andrew shot Sheila as they returned to the receptionist's desk.

The receptionist advised them to make themselves at home and that Mr. Santos would be with them in a moment. She also explained that they were free to help themselves from the platter of assorted breakfast breads and pastries, and the coffee urn that was set up on a credenza within the conference room. "That's very kind of you, but I believe we'll wait for Mr. Santos," she advised, even though she noted that Andrew was gazing lovingly at a cheese danish on the platter much as he had been admiring Sheila just before.

Andrew gave her a pained look and she smiled at him, sat at the table and waited.

She was doing a lot of that lately.

Raul Santos grimaced and rubbed his temples, trying to ease the pounding headache as he listened to his mother detail all the plans for the upcoming holidays. Every year, she and his three sisters took over his home, a large brownstone in the mid-60s, and prepared a traditional Cuban dinner for their growing tribe of family and occasionally, some friends.

He wasn't a Scrooge by any stretch of the imagination, but with as much work as he had planned for the next few days, he couldn't devote the time now to deciding who would be sitting where and what new things to try in addition to the traditional pork, rice, beans and other *Noche Buena* staples. "Listen, *mami*. I'm already late for a meeting and I have to—"

"Ignore your mother," she rebuked, but there was a teasing quality to her voice.

"I will call you later so I can ignore you some more," he said, gave her his love and hung up.

Grabbing the amended contracts for the Pharmavax deal, he perused them quickly, rose, and slipped on his jacket, a concession to visits from outsiders. His firm had gone totally casual over three years ago and normally he would not be wearing a suit. The tie was tight against his neck, like a noose on a Death Row prisoner. It was how he had felt for many years as he had worked his way up to the partnership level. Now as the seniormost partner, he had tried to create a firm that had more flexibility than most, and not just in terms of the dress code. Under his leadership, the firm had developed better benefits packages for all the employees, allowed flex time attorneys and made partnerships attainable without the loss of a private life.

All in all, he was happy with his little kingdom, but displeased with being late for this meeting with the RLL people, RLL being the exact antithesis of the kind of firm he had helped create. The suits from there would not take kindly to waiting, even if the suit happened to be wearing a skirt, he thought, thinking of Ms. Garcia and wondering what kind of woman she was.

Her Martindale-Hubble entry had only confirmed that she had gone to some of the nation's top schools and had a Masters in Biochemistry in addition to her Juris Doctor. Not so far fetched for someone who was a patent attorney, although his contacts said that she only flirted with patents and spent most of her time with the trademark end of RLL's business. She was only thirty, still young in lawyer-years, but she had impressed him with the thoughtful and professional way in which they had dealt with each other in the past.

He therefore hurried the short distance from his corner office to the main conference room, knocking on the door to advise them of his entry in the event they were discussing something confidential. When he walked in, they all rose, and while his attention was at first diverted by the attractive blonde in the maroon suit, it was the woman at the head of the table who captured and kept his interest as she turned and faced him.

She was close to his height, maybe five foot five or so, and held herself with a natural grace that was extremely appealing. Her dark brown hair was cut in a longish bob which framed her face. The deep color of her hair matched that of her eyes, but contrasted with her creamy complexion. She was very attractive, and the severely tailored lines of her suit admirably displayed her slim figure.

"Rebecca Garcia, I presume," he said and held out his hand.

Rebecca smiled and took hold of his hand, returning

the firm, surprisingly pleasing grip. "Raul Santos. It's nice to finally meet you."

"Same here," he replied and grinned. His smile triggered a funny little sensation in the pit of her stomach, kind of like a hunger rumble, but not quite. She told herself it was unprofessional to be checking him out, but she still couldn't resist doing so as she introduced him to Andrew and Sheila.

He was just a few inches taller than she, maybe five foot nine or ten or so. His hair was a dark brown, on the longish side and not scrupulously cut like that of some of her colleagues. It had a natural wave which when coupled with its length, gave it a tousled disarray that just called for you to reach out and attempt to smooth it into place. Like many men of his age, he sported a goatee which framed lips just too full and tempting to be on a man. His skin had a healthy tanned look about it, but it wasn't a tan. Physically he was sleek, with broad shoulders that the suit, an Armani if she was any judge of fashion, covered admirably. The fitted structure of his jacket enhanced his physique, displaying his flat midsection and lean hips.

After shaking hands with both Andrew and Sheila, he turned and smiled at her again. There was just the hint of a dimple in each cheek and his hazel-green eyes glittered as they swept over her and he said in a voice smooth as molasses, "I got your fax and as you can imagine, my client and I have some changes."

"Mr. Santos," she began, but he jumped in.

"Raul, please. After exchanging so much paper with you, we should probably be on a first name basis by now."

His tone was sincere and Rebecca had no doubt of his intentions, although she found it ironic to be dealing with an adversary on a first name basis when there were attorneys with whom she'd worked with for years at RLL who still insisted she call them "Mister." She nodded, motioned for him to sit at the table and said,

"Becca, *por favor,* Raul. Do you have a copy of the amended contracts for our review?"

"Becca. I like that," he replied as he handed her a single copy, but promised to bring two more for her colleagues. "I know you'll need to review these. I've made this conference room available for your use. If you need anything, use of a copier, fax, etc., just ask the receptionist."

Rebecca glanced at the amended contracts with the redlining and strikeout highlighting the changes that had been made. It would take them several hours at least to go over them and try to formulate their response. But she was optimistic that by late afternoon, if not earlier, they'd be able to talk it over with him. "Will you be available later to discuss this?"

Raul nodded and rose from the large, mahogany table. "I'm at your disposal. I think we'd all like to wrap it up for the holidays so we can be with our families."

Rebecca and her colleagues stood as well and she nodded in agreement at his statement. "Yes, it would be nice to be home for the holidays. I'm sure your wife—"

"My mother and three sisters," he corrected quickly. "I'm still single and they drive me crazy at this time of year."

"I totally understand," Rebecca commiserated and found herself smiling broadly at the thought that he might be available. "My parents and siblings are the same way."

The hair of his goatee framed his wide, inviting grin. "Well then you understand why we should try to wrap this up as soon as possible. I'll go and let you get to your work," he said and walked out, shutting the conference room door behind him.

Rebecca turned and faced Andrew and Sheila. Andrew gave her a quirky smile. Sheila, an admiring one. "Smooth, Becca. Really smooth," she teased.

Rebecca pointed her manicured nail at Sheila. "Remind me to fire you when we get back," she teased and then issued instructions on what she wanted done as the boss in her resumed control.

But even as she sat down at the table to commence her review, she couldn't help but remember how nice Raul's mouth looked as he smiled.

# Five

Raul returned to his office, the headache he had been suffering from totally gone after just that one short exchange with Rebecca Garcia. *Dios*, but she was one attractive woman. What made her even more interesting was that he knew that beauty was combined with some incredible brains as well. He found nothing sexier than an intelligent woman and couldn't understand the attraction many men had for brainless bimbos.

They could keep you occupied for as long as it took to satisfy you or them physically. On the other hand, a woman capable of challenging you mentally satisfied indefinitely.

In his book, Rebecca was a dangerous package. Brains and beauty, although brains didn't guarantee she wasn't boring. Somehow he doubted she would be boring. Call it intuition. Attribute it to the energy he sensed coming off of her and those working for her. Or from those he had spoken to in advance of this meeting. All held Rebecca in high regard, both professionally and personally.

He shook his head as he settled down at his desk, slipped off his jacket, and loosened the noose around his neck. Sitting back in his chair, he glanced at the photos arrayed across his desktop. His mom and dad, shortly before his father had died. His three sisters, two of whom had a growing brood of kids and one who was very much like him—dedicated to her career.

At thirty-one, his sister Alicia was too busy working

and establishing herself in the world of professional baseball as a sports trainer to give either time or thought to a relationship. Raul had been similar in his earlier years. At thirty-six he now had the advantage of being well-established in his profession and of recognizing that success at a career wasn't everything. In time he intended to settle down. With someone bright and intelligent. Beautiful.

Not that Rebecca was raising thoughts of suddenly becoming attached, but she certainly had piqued his interest. And maybe over the course of the next day or so, he might get to know her better, share a pleasant dinner or drink, but not much more, he considered.

After all, Rebecca was flying back to Miami in two days if all went as planned. And as intrigued as he was, Raul had no need for complicated long distance relationships.

Rebecca sighed and dragged her hand through her hair, pulling it off her face where it had fallen as she had scrutinized the amended contracts. Most of it had been what she was expecting, including CellTech's refusal to grant an exclusive license for the patent on the lipid-based vector. She had assumed as much since an exclusive was the equivalent of owning the patent. CellTech had been too smart up until now to lock up a valuable technology in the hands of someone else.

What she hadn't counted on was the initial payments CellTech had requested. The highest number publicly mentioned for similar rights had been five million dollars. CellTech was asking twenty million for the deals and that was way over what her client was prepared to pay, especially with the lack of exclusivity on the lipid-based vector patent.

There were other little things as well and she reviewed those once more. Sometimes it was the tiniest of things in a clause that was slightly ambiguous which caused problems later on. When she was done, she glanced up and noted that Andrew was still working on his comments while Sheila was sitting at her laptop, busily working on something.

Rebecca stood and stretched, walked over and read the screen over Sheila's shoulder. "How's that affidavit going?" she asked, motioning to the papers she had marked up in the office the day before and which Sheila had brought along to work on in the gaps when she wasn't needed.

"I will be done with it shortly, but do you need something now?" Sheila asked, glancing over her shoulder.

"No, I'm fine. As soon as you're done Andrew, let's take a break for an early lunch. We can talk it over while we grab a bite and then maybe have Raul join us to discuss everything."

Andrew picked up his head from where it had been buried in the papers and nodded. "Just another half an hour or so, Becca and then I'm yours."

Rebecca rolled her eyes and glanced at Sheila as the other woman smirked and gave a short laugh. "Promises, promises, Andrew. Hurry it up. We've got a battle plan to set up," she reminded and took a quick peek at her watch. It was just before eleven and the coffees she'd drunk along with the half of an oat bran muffin had nature calling now that her mind wasn't occupied with the papers.

She excused herself, left the conference room and charged ahead down the hallway, her mind already thinking about all that they had to get done so they could move along the discussions. She was pushing through the door when it opened and she tumbled headlong into the arms of Raul, who was coming through the door in the opposite direction.

She clutched at his shoulders as he lightly grasped her waist. He had shed his suit jacket and was in shirtsleeves, his tie loose and slightly askew. His hair was tousled, as if he had been repeatedly dragging his fingers through it. Again she itched to smooth the wavy locks into place.

"Sorry," she mumbled and pulled away as the heat of his hands penetrated the silk of her shirt and had her thinking all kinds of things she didn't want to be thinking about. Think contract, she told herself.

Think off limits, he told himself as he reluctantly released her and acknowledged that she was slim beneath the tailored jacket of her suit. He had nearly spanned her waist with his hands. "No, I'm sorry. I was just coming in to see if you needed anything. Lunch maybe?" he asked and rocked back on his heels, giving himself much needed distance from her all too intriguing presence.

Rebecca glanced back in the direction of the conference room and he sensed she was uneasy, as if their run-in exposed her in some way. She nervously clasped and unclasped her hands and finally answered. "Having lunch brought in would certainly help save some time. *Gracias* for the offer."

"It would be my pleasure," he replied and linked his own hands behind his back, not trusting himself. "Anything we can do to settle this business and get you back on your way to Miami," he said and winced at his words. They could be so easily misunderstood. He compounded his mistake by saying, "Not that I want you to go, Becca."

Rebecca gave him a tight smile and a chill answer clearly meant to try and restore neutrality. "We'll be on our way as soon as we can reach an agreement that's mutually beneficial to both our clients."

Embarrassed, he glanced down at the shine in his shoes and shuffled back a bit before facing her again. "I'll have my assistant come in and take your order. Call me when you're ready," he said, turned and walked away without waiting for her reply.

Rebecca watched him go, telling herself not to admire his lean hips or the perfect swell of his butt now that his jacket was gone.

She told herself that, but it was a wasted effort. He was just way too tempting.

Just as Raul promised, his secretary came in to take their lunch orders and afterward, some very efficient delivery people removed the remains of the breakfast items and set up an assortment of sandwiches, chips and sodas. As they ate, they discussed the various details of the agreements, Sheila making formal notes on the laptop so that Rebecca and Andrew could discuss them further.

Andrew concurred with all of Rebecca's comments. While that was reassuring, it didn't make it any easier to decide on courses of action. She had her client's instructions and options well-defined and fitting them into the parameters dictated by CellTech's version of the agreements might be difficult.

Nevertheless, she had no intention of failing to get this agreement and in a way that would please Pharmavax. "Sheila, please see if you can borrow a printer and get Andrew and me copies of the comments." Sheila nodded, saved the file and placed the computer in suspend mode so she could close it up to take with her while she went in search of a printer.

When she had left, Rebecca faced Andrew who was busy tapping an expensive Mont Blanc pen against a legal pad. "I don't think it makes any sense for you and me to get to the nitty-grittys when we are light years away on the big stuff."

"Nope," he said but offered no further comment, just continued to tap the pen.

She considered him. Unlike many, Andrew wasn't one to let her founder just to make himself look better. He was a team player as she was. Which could mean only one thing. "You don't think we're going to be able to swing this, do you?"

"Nope," he said. The tapping of the pen increased in

speed and she reached out, laid her hand over his to stop the motion.

"Talk around the office is that you're not aggressive enough, Andrew," she said softly and at that Andrew looked up slowly, pulled his hand away from hers.

"Anybody who isn't following the chum trail those shark hunters toss at us is turned to bait at RLL. Haven't you figured it out yet, Rebecca?" he said and then sighed harshly. "Right, I forgot. You're about to move up the evolutionary chain at RLL. You're no longer a bottom feeder like the rest of us."

She genuinely liked Andrew and so she curbed her anger at his vitriol. "You are a really good attorney who just needs to learn how to play the game. There's nothing wrong—"

"With losing your integrity? Not to say that you have, Becca. It's what I admire most about you. Somehow you've managed to keep your humanity," he said softly and stood, shoved his hands in his pocket and paced.

Rebecca answered softly, "You can too, Andrew."

He halted in mid-stride and shrugged almost as if in resignation. "I'm not sure I want it as much as you, Becca."

She stood before him and laid her hand on the shoulder of his jacket. "I think you do. This is your chance to shine. If we can do this—"

"It'll guarantee your partnership."

"And maybe move you up that evolutionary chain," she kidded, trying to lighten the dark mood that was so rare for Andrew.

Sheila walked in and with that, his whole demeanor changed before Rebecca's eyes. It confirmed to her what she had suspected before and brought sympathy for the man and for Sheila. The ruling order at RLL would never approve of one of their attorneys being involved with a paralegal at the firm. As she met his gaze, comprehension dawned in Andrew as to how transparent he had been.

"Becca," he began and swallowed uncomfortably.

"Don't worry about it, Andrew. I would never betray a confidence," she replied and with that, returned to the head of the table and took the papers from Sheila.

She glanced at them, commended Sheila on the job she had done, and handed Andrew his copy. "Let's get to work, *amigo*."

He smiled at her and nodded, all the tension leaving his body. "Thanks, and yes, let's tackle this. We want to make sure the present under your tree this year is exactly what you want."

"And that would be?" Sheila asked facetiously.

"My partnership, of course," Rebecca answered quickly and without hesitation.

"Right," both Andrew and Sheila confirmed in unison and then they got down to work, trying to craft the compromise which would put the wrapping on the gift Rebecca wanted more than anything.

Besides getting home to open that gift of course.

# Six

Raul and one of his partners were discussing the possibility of opening a new office in Miami and a merger with one of their Mexican associates when his secretary came in to advise Raul that he was wanted in the conference room.

He offered his partner some recommendations on changes and additional comments to be sent to their prospective partner. The other man agreed with Raul's suggestions and indicated he would draft the response for him to look at.

After he had left the room, Raul glanced at his watch. It was nearly two, but he had expected as much. The changes he had proposed were substantial when compared to the contracts Rebecca had sent over. The terms proposed by Rebecca had been very similar to those already in place between the two companies, but she had of course made changes to the initial payments and royalties, in addition to requesting exclusivity on the lipid-based vector patent. That hadn't been enough in Raul's mind. He needed additional protection and benefits for his client on these deals due to the special nature of the patents.

He was also aware that of all the terms proposed by Rebecca, the exclusivity issue was one his client would not budge on for any amount of money. He hoped it wouldn't be a deal breaker for Pharmavax because the rest of what was being offered would really help Cell-Tech to have the funds to continue their research into similar therapies for other diseases.

He had even considered for a moment, a very brief one, to try and convince CellTech to give Pharmavax the exclusivity they desired. The discussions between himself and the four partners at CellTech had been detailed and animated. Plus, he understood their rationale for not doing so and actually not only agreed with it, but admired it from a humanitarian perspective.

Pharmavax could afford to pay the big bucks, but CellTech thought the technology could help spur the development of gene therapies of all kinds by allowing people to use a safer transport mechanism. They wanted to keep it available for others.

Of course, it was a sound decision on a business level as well. Allowing more people to use it meant more in royalty fees from a number of people. The old "not putting all your eggs in one basket" principle was especially sound in business. He'd known of more than one law firm who'd relied predominantly on a single client and found themselves out of business when that client was either absorbed or suffered economic setbacks.

He'd vowed not to let that happen in his firm. In addition to several large clients, he had cultivated a number of smaller ones who had potential, such as CellTech, and possible new business opportunities such as the merger and expansion to Miami.

Regardless, he had to get going, he told himself, knowing his opponents would be waiting for him with their counter-proposal. He grabbed his Waterman pen, a pad of paper and his copy of the agreements and headed to the conference room, where the delivery people were just cleaning away the remains of lunch and setting up some fresh coffee, cold sodas and cookies.

Rebecca wasn't seated at the table. She was leaning on the edge of one of the windows which faced downtown. She had been looking out the window pensively, but turned and smiled as he entered. Motioning to the cookies and other items now gracing the credenza, she said, "Do you treat all your adversaries this well, Counselor?"

He chuckled and shrugged his shoulders. "Not adversaries, Becca. Just on opposite sides for now, until we work out a few things."

Rebecca walked over to the large table, grabbed one of the copies of the agreement they had just finished amending and handed it to him. "I thought we had reached the point where it made sense to sit down and iron these out one by one, beginning with any possible deal breakers."

"I agree." He reached out, took hold of the paper and immediately noted the many changes. He let out a low whistle. "On second thought, maybe you were right about the adversary part."

She walked over to the credenza, placed some chocolate chip cookies on a plate and grabbed a Diet Coke. "Actually, Raul. I'd like to think that any man who can be thoughtful enough to provide an afternoon snack can't be all bad."

Raul smiled at her comment and held out his hand for her to sit at the table. She did, positioning herself across from Andrew and Sheila, and leaving a spot free next to her. Her invitation wasn't clear, but Raul thought it would help on various levels, including the "we're not adversaries" one. He could see now why it had taken so long to choose a round table for the Vietnam peace talks.

He set his copy of the contract down at the spot next to her along with his pen and yellow legal pad. Returning to the credenza, he made himself a mug of coffee and a plate of cookies of assorted types. Mug and plate in hand, he seated himself next to Rebecca and even though she shot him a confused look, he made no overture to move to another place at the table.

"Ready, Counselor?" he asked and sipped his coffee.

"Ready," she acknowledged and they got into it and immediately hit a roadblock on the first contract for the gene therapy.

Pharmavax had offered 1.5 million as an initial payment with royalties which could reap millions for Cell-Tech if the therapy took off.

"It's not in line with what's happening in the industry," Raul advised Rebecca. She in turn questioned how he had arrived at his request of ten million for each deal, in addition to other assorted payments. "Schering paid five million and the terms offered possibilities of upwards of thirty-five million for the patent holder."

Rebecca was well familiar with the deal. "The p53 gene therapy they acquired rights to had the possibility of widespread application. This therapy is limited to some very specific auto-immune nerve diseases," she countered and wasn't surprised when he came back with more of his own facts and figures to support his client's demands, including statistics on the increasing number of cases for various degenerative nerve diseases.

With her science and biochemical background, Rebecca countered Raul's statements with an explanation of the differences in the mechanisms of just one of the diseases he had mentioned and the CellTech therapy.

Raul was impressed with her understanding of the whole process and her knowledge of the industry. "The therapy is, as you noted, not necessarily broad-based enough to work across a wide spectrum of diseases, like the p53 gene. Nevertheless, it isn't specific to one disease either, which is why I suspect Pharmavax is so keen on acquiring this patent."

He leaned back in his chair, adopting a very loose, casual stance. He wanted to defuse the growing sense of confrontation, plus he needed to put space between himself and Rebecca. Sitting this close and leaning near to read as she motioned to spots in the contract was a distraction. She smiled way too nicely, and with his nose nearly next to her cheek, her fine, creamy skin was way too alluring.

Rebecca glanced at him, adopted a similar stance and

let out a sigh. "There's no question my client believes this can be profitable for them, Raul. They wouldn't be going after it otherwise. But since this is about a profit for them, you know how many risks are involved just to get this to market," she responded, and Raul listened patiently as she generalized about the costs of producing the initial product, clinical trials to test it and obtaining FDA approval for their version of the therapy. The last in particular was always an iffy thing and had doomed more than one company.

As Rebecca finished, her colleague Andrew spoke up and gave Raul a more detailed analysis of some of those costs. Raul listened, but was already well aware of the financial risks. It was one of the reasons that his own client was so keen on licensing the patent to generate income rather than trying to do it themselves. CellTech was still too small to become a full scale manufacturer, and in reality, he doubted if that was what they wanted to do. Scientists and researchers by nature, he sensed they liked the discovery part of it better and were more than willing to let someone else deal with marketing and manufacturing their discoveries.

But discovery, like Columbus had realized centuries earlier, demanded a bank roll. Although the arguments and figures Rebecca and her colleague were presenting were reasonable, he didn't want to give up quite so easily.

"I can understand your concerns, Rebecca. If the first payment of ten million is too steep to begin with, what can you do?" he asked and met her gaze. For a moment he was flummoxed as her smile broadened with his seeming acceptance of their position.

"I'm glad we can be reasonable," she said and quickly added, "I may be able to convince them to offer two and half."

Raul shook his head. "No way is my client going to accept that as the total figure for the deal. They probably spent that alone in the last year on trials and approvals."

Rebecca knew she had pressed aggressively, but the meaning hidden in Raul's words was clear. They had a beginning money amount and could work from there. She was, for the moment, exactly where she wanted to be. "Understood, Raul, but I trust you can recognize that my client will also have to spend similar sums to do trials, obtain FDA approval and get the production of this going. It's a big expense with—"

"No guarantee of success. You said that before, but I'm sure your client's marketing people have done their model of what this could make for them, the costs, etc. Do we at least agree on the percentage to be paid as a royalty?" he questioned and when she nodded her agreement, he continued with his proposal and outlined a secondary payment scheme based on Pharmavax's profits.

Raul's proposal was in line with one she and Andrew had discussed before he came into the room. If the therapy was profitable, Pharmavax would make enough to warrant the additional payment. "I think another two and half is more reasonable, but we'll contact the client later and discuss it. At least we have a workable proposal," she replied and looked at the comments she and Andrew had drafted. She chose the next stickiest issue and again, she, Andrew and Raul tackled the details.

As they discussed one point, Rebecca made amendments on her copy of the contract, and when there was some confusion about the wording, Raul shifted to read off her copy of the contract and the notes she had taken. She should have been concentrating on the work, but it was difficult to do with him so close.

Instead she found herself admiring his hands, which were large and well-shaped. Very sexy hands, with just a light smattering of hair visible at his wrist beneath the cuff of his expensive shirt. He had on no rings, but that same wrist sported a very simple gold bracelet that did nothing to detract from his manliness.

When he glanced up to confirm his interpretation of

her amendments and playfully complained about her nearly unintelligible handwriting, his smile warmed her insides and she found herself smiling back and wanting to lean close and savor that smile with her lips. For a moment as his gaze darkened, she worried that he might have sensed her interest, but she quickly quashed her response by sitting back in her chair and somehow answering him. "Counselor, my handwriting is a result of an unfortunate choice of Pre-Med as my undergrad major. I had a 4.0 in bad penmanship. As a fellow convert from the ranks, I thought you would have been able to decipher it as well."

Raul laughed and shook his head. "Guilty, Becca. Who would have ever thought those degrees would lead us here instead."

"Fate," she answered too quickly for as his gaze met and held hers, it was clear it was about more than just their choice of careers.

She coughed nervously, confirmed what the amendments should be and they continued with the remaining review. By five o'clock, they had finished the first contract and were ready to tackle the second.

Raul's back was tightening up from so much time in the seat and he could tell Rebecca was in a similar position from the way she shifted uncomfortably in the leather chair. "Why don't we take a fifteen minute break to stretch, maybe freshen ourselves. Or if that's not good, if you wouldn't mind giving me a few minutes to check on any messages I might have gotten . . ."

Rebecca rose and stretched, and he was hard pressed not to notice how the fabric of her shirt molded itself to her small, but interesting breasts. He forced himself to look away when she caught the nature of his attention and blushed, pulling her lapels tightly closed.

Trying to restore his sense of order, he said, "We'll start up again in about fifteen minutes, or whenever you're ready."

When Rebecca nodded, standing stiffly by the table and flipping through her notes and papers, he didn't wait for any further answer and left the room.

As he stepped out into the hallway, he took a deep breath and wondered how he was ever going to survive the next two days without kissing her.


Rebecca for one was clearly relieved with the chance to move around and to regain her perspective about her adversary. She made a point of reminding herself of that. He was for the moment her opponent, no matter what he wanted to say to the contrary.

His friendliness was likely just a negotiating tactic. One to put her off guard.

The break was therefore good for restoring the much needed formality necessary as a lawyer. Not to mention taking the time to make a pit stop at the ladies room again. "Sheila, do you need to freshen up?"

Sheila looked up from the computer where she had been busy making the agreed upon changes to the contract. "In a sec, Becca. Just need to save this."

"Save it and after we come back, see about getting it printed out and sent to the people at Pharmavax. I think they'll be pleased, but we do need to get their approval on the payment structure we've worked out," Rebecca instructed and after, she and Sheila went to the ladies' room while Andrew likewise took a break.

Once they were standing at the sinks in the bathroom, washing their hands, Sheila looked around and seeing that it was empty, turned to Rebecca and whispered conspiratorially, "So tell me what you think of our Mr. Santos?"

Rebecca didn't look up from her soapy hands, washed them over and over again like Lady Macbeth trying rid herself of her guilt. "He's very capable and judging from our past correspondence—"

"Maybe you have gone over to the ranks of the RLL

partners," Sheila cut in. She shut off her water and walked past Rebecca to reach the towel dispenser, shaking her head the whole time, while muttering to herself. "Capable. Lord, I bet he's capable all right."

There was no doubting that Sheila wasn't referring to his legal skills. Rebecca made a move to quash the conversation. "I thought you and Andrew—"

"Becca, you know the saying. 'Just because I'm on a diet, doesn't mean I can't look at the menu' and if you aren't looking—"

"Looking at the menu isn't what I'm being paid to do at the moment, remember? I'm here to negotiate a contract and distractions are not good," she confessed, comfortable around the other woman. Even though Sheila was a paralegal at the firm, Rebecca genuinely liked her and thought of her as a friend. They had, on more than one occasion, gone to lunch. Rebecca respected the young woman who had struggled hard to finish college and get her paralegal degree.

"At least you can admit he's distracting," Sheila laughed and handed Rebecca a paper towel as she finally rinsed off all the soap and shut off the faucet.

Rebecca playfully yanked the towel out of Sheila's hand. "Okay, yes, so you've pried it out of me. He is attractive. No strike that, handsome."

"You mean, very sexy, Counselor," she teased, mimicking the way Becca had treated him in the conference room. "You do recollect what sex is, don't you? And remember the penalty for perjury, Counselor."

Rebecca chuckled and nodded. "Sheila, you would make a great litigator and unfortunately, no. I don't recollect what sex is since I make it a rule never to undertake that kind of activity. When I do, it is with someone who I care about, and therefore, it is not just sex, it's making love."

"Rebecca stop being obtuse. You know that somewhere in that love part, there's sex. It goes hand in hand, like an assault being an inherent part of a murder," Sheila reprimanded and walked out to the foyer of the ladies' room, where she opened her bag and extracted her cosmetic kit so she could freshen up.

Having no need of such things, Rebecca just smoothed her hair and leaned her butt against the edge of the counter, facing Sheila and away from the mirror. "You're right to compare it to an assault, you know. You never know when love's going to just come out and beat you over the head. And when it doesn't work out—"

"It can be murder," Sheila finished for her and proceeded to open her mouth in an oval so she could reapply her lipstick, an intense wine color that matched the scarf holding back her long blond curls. As she did so, she glanced out of the corner of her eye at Rebecca, her gaze amazingly astute. "I guess you had a not so nice experience."

Rebecca shrugged. "Actually, not so bad would be more accurate. But definitely not the stuff of dreams—"

"Or those romance novels you are constantly reading," Sheila said and Rebecca's face warmed in embarrassment.

"My guilty secret is out. They entertain me and help me to relax. And I think as intelligent women we all know that what we're reading is . . . well, fiction," she confessed.

Sheila finished with her make-up, turned and faced Rebecca. "There is likely no swashbuckling pirate waiting around the corner for me, and thank God for that. I'll take a nice, caring man like Andrew any day, not to say he isn't handsome and exciting in his own way. But Becca, falling in love with Mr. Right isn't always fiction. And romance . . . well, romance is a part of everyday life if you've got the right person with you."

Unfortunately, Rebecca had yet to meet that right person and there were no prospects in sight. Suddenly saddened by the thought, she glanced at her watch. Some time had passed since they had left the conference room. Trying to get a lighthearted mood going once again, she retorted, "It's been twenty minutes, Sheila, and we all know that as love and romance goes, that's about all the time you ever get."

Sheila laughed, turned and walked toward the door of the ladies' room, but not before tossing a quick rejoinder back at Rebecca.

"Becca, when you meet the right man, you won't settle for just twenty minutes."

# Seven

Back in the conference room, Andrew was giving a once over to the document on the screen. Raul had yet to return and Andrew advised that his secretary had come in and indicated Raul would join them in about another ten minutes.

"How does it look?" Rebecca asked, going to stand behind Andrew and reading from the screen as he scrolled along.

"Fine. I'd like to see a hard copy first and then we can send it off," he commented.

Rebecca agreed. She and Andrew left the computer to Sheila who put it in suspend mode and again took it in search of a printer.

As they waited, they both grabbed another cookie or two to stave off any hunger pangs. After all, it was unlikely they would get out of there before nine or ten, which meant a late dinner for them all.

Raul returned as promised shortly thereafter, Sheila in tow behind him with four copies of the draft of the agreement. Resuming their same positions around the table, they all sat down to give it a final read and within half an hour concluded that all the amended sections were as agreed upon. Sheila pulled out a fax cover sheet and handed it to Rebecca.

"I'll need to talk to the client in the morning. Is eleven good for you to resume discussions?" Rebecca asked, and when Raul agreed, she jotted a quick, but clearly written note on the sheet indicating that she would be calling to discuss the contracts at 9:30 and that a draft of the license for the lipid-based vector would hopefully follow later that night.

After Sheila had left to fax the materials, Rebecca turned to Raul and asked, "Ready to tackle the next one?"

He nodded, but she sensed the resignation in that nod, almost as if he was certain that no matter how they tackled this agreement, they would be hard pressed to reach an arrangement that pleased both sides. His next words confirmed it. "I think we both recognize that the single most important term here is one which maybe neither of our clients is willing to budge on."

"The exclusivity clause is one we've gone around on before, Raul," she reminded. It had been a sticking point in the contract they had negotiated nearly two years ago for one of CellTech's genetic testing processes.

"I remember it well, Becca," he began, using the nickname she had given him permission to use. For some reason, it now jarred her a little, for coming off his lips, it was way too intimate and way too friendly given the attraction for her opponent. Maybe because of those wayward thoughts she'd been having but shouldn't have been having. Still she said nothing about it. Acknowledging that the nickname bothered her would give him an advantage which she was sure he would use. Any good lawyer would if they sensed some weakness in an opponent.

"I gave up the exclusivity, Raul," she acknowledged. "But, if I recollect correctly, the asking price went down considerably because of that compromise."

Raul smiled. *Dios,* but she was good. He had no choice but to admit that, well aware of where she was leading with the whole gambit. Still, he wasn't about to budge on the price and he suspected she wasn't about to cave on the fact that for that amount, they wanted total control of the patent. "This is a revolutionary vector, Becca. With your knowledge of the field, you know that as does your client. Even without the exclusivity, the freedom that this patent will give Pharmavax to develop safer therapies—"

"Again, there are no guarantees that Pharmavax will be able to market or protect anything developed using this technology. There are too many variables involved, including the fact that there's more and more opposition to protection being given to these types of inventions," she stressed, Simon Langleis' words of yesterday helping her in a way that Langleis probably could never have envisioned.

Raul laughed harshly. "Just because some woman decides to patent herself in protest or some environmental group joins in with its own campaign doesn't mean that the community at large will not recognize the good that can come about from these discoveries."

"Neither of us can guarantee that, Raul, and I'd be remiss in my duties as a lawyer if I told my client to commit for this sum of money given the current atmosphere," she replied and looked up and across the table at Andrew. "Andrew, do you agree?" she queried, needing to hear his input to maybe break the impasse that was quickly developing.

Andrew took a nervous swallow, aware of the faith Rebecca was placing in him. A moment later he squared his shoulders, rose higher in his seat as if in recognition of the position in which she had put him. "Even in a hostile environment such as the one that is developing, a company could justify certain expenses. But without exclusivity and with this figure, the risk is too great."

"Giving exclusivity is the equivalent of selling you the patent," Raul countered. "My client would reap little financial reward even at this figure while the promise is untold for Pharmavax. There's no way you can pay enough for exclusivity, but even if you did put that high a figure on the table, my client wouldn't accept it," he advised, the tone of conviction so strong in his voice that Rebecca knew there was no way of dissuading either him or his client.

"May I ask why?" she said, intrigued despite herself.

"Call it scientific integrity. Call it humanitarian considerations. There may be many therapies developed which would benefit from using this kind of vector. To allow as many people who are ill to benefit from the discoveries, this particular technology needs to be available to more than one company," he stressed.

Rebecca inclined her head and considered him, trying to read just how committed he was and finding him all too persuasive. She couldn't believe he could deceive her so effortlessly. He wasn't just mouthing the words. He, and presumably his client, were serious in their intentions. And she admired them, for both the humanitarian and business reasons for their decision.

In a time where few gave thought to others, this was a refreshing position.

She knew her client was willing to give on the exclusivity, but only if the price was right. She sensed the time had come to switch tactics. She glanced up at Andrew, inclined her head and when he nodded, she calmly said, "I applaud your client's ethics. My client has similar beliefs, but quite frankly, being able to license a multitude of people is a cash cow, no matter what spin you want to put on it, Raul."

Raul nodded and smiled tightly. "I can't argue that it's a sound decision for my client on multiple levels, Counselor."

His use of "counselor" this time was anything but friendly. They were clearly entering into an adversarial mode. That was good. It made it easier to play hardball. "My client is prepared to walk away if the economics of the deal aren't good. But the loss to CellTech would be great for more reasons than just the loss of the income the deal would generate. Pharmavax is a recognized leader in this area. Entering into a deal with them would give the stamp of approval to CellTech's patent and quite frankly, have others lining up for the technology."

Raul leaned back in his chair and took a moment to

appreciate not just her comments, but the lady herself. Amazingly, despite the intense exchange, she looked as cool, calm and collected as she had before the discussion had even commenced. Her chestnut-colored hair was still perfectly in place. Her pad had nary a doodle or stray note and he wondered if she was always so composed and level-headed. For a second, his own mind strayed to picture what she might look like if she really let herself go. The image that formed in his brain was one he didn't dwell on for long. It was too alluring and admittedly, inappropriate for the time being.

He forced himself back to the topic at hand. "I gather Pharmavax will relent on the exclusivity issue?"

Rebecca confirmed it quickly and Andrew seconded it, but with a cautionary, "But only for the right price."

They launched into a discussion of money. While it took a great deal of haggling and a call to the CellTech partners shortly after seven that night, they had an agreement on the price. A price her client would be very happy with, Rebecca thought. They had authorized her to spend up to ten million total as initial payments for both contracts without getting their further approval. She had secured the rights far below that in initial payments, and the additional payment options needed to be well supported by the profits earned by Pharmavax. All in all, she had reduced their risks while getting their rights.

By eight o'clock they had finished conforming all the remaining terms to mirror those in the first contract and a fax was soon on its way to all the parties involved to secure the final approvals.

Once all the facsimile machines confirmed that the agreements had gone through, Rebecca and her colleagues packed up to leave.

Raul stood by Rebecca in the conference room. While he would see her in the morning to finalize the deals, he was reluctant to limit their time to just that. "Now that we've mutually benefitted our clients," he teased, remembering her earlier words to him, "would you like to go get dinner?"

Rebecca glanced over at Andrew and Sheila, who quickly refused. "I'd like to make it an early night," Andrew replied.

"But there's no reason you can't go," Sheila tacked on and Rebecca would have been a fool not to see that they intended to make it an early night together and that they wanted her alone with Raul.

She faced him once more and begged off. "I think I'd like to get ready for tomorrow. Get my bags packed and stuff."

Raul raised one eyebrow. "Stuff, huh? A very vague term for—"

"Packing. Taking a bath—"

"A bath, huh?" he jumped in, his eyes warming and causing heat to flow through Rebecca at the thought of him picturing her in her bath.

"Personal stuff I'd rather not discuss," she hastily replied to cover up her gaff.

She was even more interesting when she wasn't in control it occurred to him, noting the flush of pink rise to her cheeks with her embarrassment, and imagining a similar flush all over her body from the warmth of a nice, hot soak in the tub.

His body began to respond and he gritted his teeth and took a long deep, breath. "Well, then. I'll walk you to the hotel in any case and then let you go."

"It's not necessary," she stammered and finished shoving the papers into her briefcase, looking down at the insides of the leather case the whole time as if to avoid him.

"But it is," he replied, reached out, and helped her snap close the bag when she fumbled with the latches.

Rebecca finally looked up at him. She was so close he could see the varied hues of brown in her eyes. He had thought them very dark at first, but now he detected tones ranging from light gold to shades as dark as the black of night. "No, it's not," she said softly and pulled her briefcase from his hands.

"My subway stop is beneath the hotel." Color stained her cheeks again at his comment, and with a resigned sigh she nodded, accepting that she had no choice but to allow him her company as far as the hotel.

"Let me get my things and I'll meet you by the elevators," he said and when he walked out, Rebecca turned her gaze on her colleagues, giving them a murderous glare.

"Early night? No reason you can't go. Traitors," she complained, but it did nothing but earn amused laughter from them.

She left the room, walked to the closet and bundled herself up, all the while dreading the thought of heading out into the cold night. Throughout their meeting, her eyes had strayed to the windows, where the steady sleet continued to fall, making her wonder whether it would stop in time for them to make it home.

Pulling up the collar of the coat, she fastened the topmost button, hoping it would keep the wind from whipping down her neck as it had that morning. When Raul came out a second later, he took one look at her, shook his head and pulled off his own scarf. "Take this," he said, and without waiting for her reply, he wrapped it around her neck, immediately creating warmth and not just from the scarf. The heat of his body clung to the scarf as did his aroma. His very masculine and compelling scent, a potent pheromone calling to her.

"*Gracias,*" she replied, her voice a little shaky.

"*De nada.* I'd hate for you to spend your holidays in Miami with a New York cold."

She smiled at him and walked to the elevator. With most people gone from the building, it came up and went down quickly, opening onto a lobby that was empty except for the security guard.

Beyond the revolving doors, there was a whirling

mass of white, well beyond the freezing rain and sleet the forecasters had described earlier. Taking a bracing breath, she eased into a gap in the revolving door, Raul and her colleagues following behind her. She moved slowly out of the doorway and onto the sidewalk for the comings and goings of other pedestrians had served to alternately turn the freezing precipitation she chose to call snow into either slippery slush or hard, icy patches which were even more slick.

There was no getting away from it any longer. It was snowing. As she looked up at the night sky, the fat flakes were illuminated by the street lights and reflected back that brilliance, making the night brighter. She squinted against the flakes landing on her face and noted that the sky was filled with dark charcoal grey clouds. Ominous clouds.

"Beautiful, isn't it?" he asked, looking all around and smiling.

Rebecca wanted to growl at him, but instead said nothing and proceeded to slowly trudge up 42nd Street, Raul walking beside her with Andrew and Sheila following. As she neared one intersection, she hit a hard patch and nearly lost her footing, but Raul reached out, steadied her and then offered his arm. "Not that you can't handle it or anything. It's just that sometimes four feet are better than two."

She looked up at him, unable to resist the charm he seemed to be able to turn on so easily. None of them had bothered to put up their umbrellas for the short walk, and crystalline flakes sparkled in his hair and clung to his sleek eyebrows. She reached up, brushed them away and then took hold of his arm. In an unsteady, shuffling gait, they made it to the hotel in one piece. One damp and very cold piece, however.

As he held the door open for her and they all walked into the lobby, Andrew and Sheila quickly excused themselves, leaving her alone with Raul, awkwardly trying to find a way to say good night. It was made even harder when her stomach gave a loud and very obvious rumble, alerting him to her hunger.

He raised one brow and said, "Are you sure you don't want to get a quick bite? The Oyster Bar is a New York landmark and it's right in Grand Central. We wouldn't have to go far."

As he stood there, expectantly waiting for her answer, she wondered if maybe she hadn't already aspired to the ranks of stuffed shirtness, as her colleagues had alluded to that morning. After all, here was a very handsome man, one with whom she had probably just concluded business, asking her to share a meal. What would probably be a very good meal and she was hesitating? Could she seriously be considering refusing this invitation from the first live man who had captured her attention because he was charming and witty and well . . . too handsome to describe?

Her mother hadn't raised a fool, she thought as she inclined her head and said, "Dinner would be great."

# Eight

The Grand Central Oyster Bar and Restaurant was located on the lower level of Grand Central Station right past what had once been a lower level waiting room and was now home to a large food court. The restaurant was a cavernous, noisy place. It had earned a reputation for having some of the finest seafood available from around the world on a regular basis. Whether one wanted raw clams and oysters, urchins from the Mediterranean, or the more mundane salmon fillets, the Oyster Bar had it all.

The eatery was enormous with several different sections. The walls were panelled with a darkly-stained wood. High-reaching archways and columns supported tall vaulted ceilings. Both the archways and ceiling were covered with shiny, cream-colored ceramic tiles. The tiles bounced around the sound in the restaurant. Occasionally, the rumble from one of the trains at a nearby track intruded.

Raul chose to sit in one of the smaller sections of the restaurant where there were a number of long white counters where patrons could sit and order a quicker meal. At this one counter, which was perpendicular to the longer ones in the center of the space, waiters served up all kinds of raw shellfish and the oyster pan roast for which the restaurant was famous. Following his suggestions, and since it was too late to have anything too large and heavy, they both ordered the pan roast. It was fascinating to see the chef behind the counter prepare the dish right before her eyes.

He placed the cookware on a steam jacket device beyond the counter area and quickly whipped up the dish that consisted of fresh oysters cooked with chili sauce and cream and a number of other ingredients she couldn't quite get due to the speed with which he prepared the stew. The oysters, freshly shucked before her eyes, went in just long enough to warm them through and then the server whisked the plates off the steam jackets so that the oysters would not become rubbery. The oysters in the creamy sauce were served over a think slice of bread that greedily soaked up the liquid.

When the steaming plates were sitting before the two of them as they sat knee to knee at the bar, Raul looked over at her, grinned and picked up his spoon. "Ready?"

Rebecca mimicked him and said, "Go."

She spooned up some of the rich brownish sauce, the bread and an oyster, placed it into her mouth and the most heavenly of flavors exploded. Creamy and sweet. Slightly spicy from the chili sauce and with the kind of consistency that only clams, oysters and other similar shellfish could claim. For Rebecca, it was fantastic and the heat of the pan roast seeped into her, driving away some of the chill from the outside weather.

As she went for another spoonful she said, "This is very good."

Raul smiled and likewise dug into the plate for another mouthful. "Nothing quite like it, Becca. It's always my favorite here."

She suspected he had many favorites amongst the local restaurants. After all, he was a successful lawyer with a cadre of clients who were bound to be visiting and needed to be wined and dined. Still, he was taking the time to wine and dine her, and their business was nearly concluded. She appreciated having a friendly face to share the meal. "Thanks again for taking the time for dinner with me."

He paused in his eating to look up at her and smile, the spoon suspended with a plump cream-and-chili-covered oyster inches from his mouth. "I should be thanking you, Becca."

"Why?" she wondered, confused.

"For finally relenting and deciding to go with me." He quickly ate the spoonful of oyster roast. After he swallowed, he gave her a grin that bespoke a myriad of emotions, some which had her insides doing that funny little rumble again. "I know how hard you are to convince when you have your mind set on things, Counselor," he teased.

"And you're a very worthy adversary, Raul. I'm glad we had this opportunity to meet." As the words left her mouth, she realized that it was more than just a platitude. New York might be dreary and cold and inhospitable, but somehow this time with Raul had changed that a little.

The remainder of the meal passed easily, with them talking about an upcoming conference they were both planning to attend and some colleagues they had in common. Safe things, she said to herself, sensing that if they crossed that line . . .

He was telling a story about a lawyer's league softball game against a rival firm, not that she was really hearing what he was saying. There was something almost . . . hypnotic by the melody and rhythms of his voice, and the way his mobile lips moved. The way the goatee framed that mouth and the dimples that peeked out when he smiled.

She took a deep breath and told herself to listen and actually managed a laugh as he described sliding into home and afterwards realizing that the slide had torn an immense hole in his shorts and briefs, exposing most of his butt to the spectators. Problem was, after the chuckle came unbidden images of that part of his anatomy, causing her face to warm and flush.

"You okay?" he asked, reaching out and barely grazing his thumb across the stain of color on her cheek.

She waved a hand in front of her face and fanned it. "Just a little warm in here, and the pan roast did a nice job of driving away the chill," she lied.

He examined her, seemed concerned for all of a second and then his mouth broadened into that too enticing smile. "You're not a good liar."

The flush on her face deepened as his grin grew even broader. She turned her attention to folding her heavy cloth napkin and laying it next to her empty plate. "Some might find that statement amusing. After all, how does that joke go—how do you know when a lawyer's lying?"

"When his lips are moving. Notice it's in the masculine. Maybe only male lawyers can lie," he offered in consolation.

She glanced upward. His hazel eyes, more green tonight from the lighting in the restaurant and the dark olive color of his suit, were glittering with humor and something else. Something inviting. "Somehow I don't see you lying very much."

Raul searched her very expressive face and found emotions no one had ever shown him before. Dangerous ones for he reminded himself that their business was nearly over. She would be on her way back to Miami tomorrow. He attempted to defuse the situation. "Well, especially not at this time of year. I don't want to end up on the naughty list and not get what I want for Christmas from Santa."

Grinning, she inclined her head and her demanding gaze kept his attention. "And what do you want for Christmas, Raul? I mean, you're a man with everything."

Up until the moment she walked into his office that morning, Raul had certainly thought he was the man with everything. Now he knew better. "I'm a man with a lot of responsibilities. I guess a day off would be a great gift under my tree."

Rebecca considered him. His lips were moving . . .

and lying. It was his eyes that were telling her the truth, letting her know that maybe there was more for which he was wishing. Maybe even what she was suddenly thinking about—someone special to share this very special time of year. Despite that, or maybe because of it, she found herself agreeing with him. "*Sí*, when you're life is crazy busy, free time is an amazing gift."

"Mmm," he murmured in agreement and then in a sudden flurry of motion, he placed his napkin on the table and nervously rubbed his hands on his pants legs. "Speaking of time . . . I think it's time that we called it a night. We both have to be at work tomorrow, and I'm sure you have to—"

"Do all that personal kind of stuff," she remembered out loud. "Thanks again for dinner."

"Don't thank me yet. I still have to walk you home." He motioned to the waiter with a signing gesture and the young man quickly brought over the tab. Without a moment's hesitation, Raul whipped out his corporate American Express card and slipped it into the small, black portfolio. The waiter whisked it away, came back with the bill that Raul signed.

He rose and held out his hand. The instinct for survival, both as a woman and as a lawyer, screamed at her to just avoid it. Something even more compelling, almost primordial, urged her to take it.

Raul smiled as she did so, linked his fingers with hers and that simple connection reached deep within her. Even as they navigated the stairs and passageways in Grand Central, where pockets of people were scattered about or racing for trains or subways to take them somewhere else, that unifying touch made everything else around them disappear.

When they came up out of the labyrinth of the station and did the short walk to the hotel, the snow had stopped and Rebecca pulled free of him and like a child, twirled around, holding her hands out and smiling. "It stopped. It finally stopped."

Raul paused to appreciate the almost child-like wonder in her and then sadness set in, for her joy stemmed from her desire to leave New York . . . and him. And he wondered how his emotions had gotten so entangled with her and why her leaving would suddenly create a void in his life. A void that hadn't been there that morning.

Or had it? As she smiled at him, came back and took his hand again and they walked the last few steps to the hotel, he wondered whether the closeness of his family, the way he allowed them to be so active in what little personal time he had, wasn't a way of avoiding the truth. A way of hiding to himself that there was a part of him that was lonely and hadn't quite found what it took to make him happy.

Like the way that enigmatic, hesitant smile of Becca's sent a little thrill through him when it shouldn't have. He drove that thought away as the elevator swept them up to her floor and they strolled to the door of her room.

Rebecca slipped the key into the slot on the door and the green lights signalled its acceptance. She cracked the door opened just a notch, turned and faced him. *"Gracias.* I appreciate all you've done to make me feel . . . welcome."

Raul nodded and gave her a tight smile, unlike those inviting grins he had bestowed on her earlier. He was uncomfortable and she could understand why. She'd sensed them crossing the line from professional colleagues to . . . She wouldn't go there, couldn't go there until their business was concluded. And even after, it made no sense. The holidays, Miami and her family called to her. It was her favorite time of year.

"I'll talk to my client in the morning and then meet you at eleven as planned. Thanks again," she said and opened the door behind her just a crack more.

"I . . ." He swallowed hard, took a step back and shoved his hands in his pockets. *"Mañana,* Becca. *Buenas noches."*

He turned suddenly and stalked off down the hallway.

Only after the elevator doors had closed on him did Rebecca walk into her room and wish it could be as easy to close her mind against her unexpected attraction for him.

Think Miami, she told herself. Think hot and sunny. Think of going home to her family and friends and the only place to be for the upcoming holidays. But even as she forced herself to do so, the memory of Raul's smile stole into her thoughts. It made her think of cold winter nights and how to warm them up.

# Nine

The morning telephone conference with her client went relatively well. In retrospect, surprisingly better than she had imagined. She and her colleagues left the hotel, this time to a bright, clear morning. A morning of promise, it occurred to her. The promise of completing this deal and maybe cementing her partnership. The possibility of enjoying time with friends and family at home during the holidays and a much needed vacation away from work. But away from Raul as well.

Raul, she whispered to herself, her face flaming as she recalled a portion of her dream from the night before. Raul was an unknown commodity she hadn't counted on. And one she wasn't about to let deter her from the goals she had set and which were within reach. She needed to focus herself again this morning, put herself back into that tunnel she had imagined the other day. Raul was an unwanted and unnecessary detour out of the tunnel.

The streets were as crowded this morning as the day before. The sidewalks only slightly less treacherous. The occasional patch of ice forced concentration along the brief walk to Raul's office. Despite the sun and brilliance of the morning, the cold remained brutal outside and grew worse as the wind whipped around on the thoroughfare.

Pulling the lapels of her coat tight against her, Rebecca put her head down and trudged the final half a block to The News building. Once again she spun through the revolving doors and into the unique lobby, but today she and her colleagues didn't stop. There was too much to get finished in too little time if they were going to make one of the nighttime flights to Miami. It hadn't taken long to get into the frenetic Manhattan routine, Rebecca realized. Too much work and too little time to enjoy the sights.

In Raul's office, the receptionist got them settled in the main conference room and advised that Raul would be with them shortly. On the credenza, coffee and sodas once again waited, and as Rebecca prepared herself a cup of coffee to ward off the nip in the air, Raul entered the room.

She turned to face him, bid him good morning as he too walked over to the coffee urn to make himself a cup. *"Buenos dias,* Becca. I trust it is a good day, right?"

Rebecca nodded. "Just a laundry list of things I think we should be able to work out."

"Good to hear that." Raul looked over at her colleagues. "Andrew. Sheila. How are you this morning?"

"Fine, thanks," Sheila replied with a smile and Andrew echoed that sentiment.

"Well then. We should get going if you are all going to make it home tonight. We're expecting a storm later this afternoon," Raul advised.

Rebecca walked to the windows in the conference room, examined the bright, winter sky. "It doesn't look that bad."

Raul came to stand beside her, his shoulder brushing up against hers as he leaned toward the window and looked out as well. "There's a storm front that was supposed to pass, but it's gathered strength. They're talking a few inches by the morning, so we should try to wrap things up soon so that you can avoid the weather."

His voice was low, starting a sympathetic vibration deep inside her. Although they were barely in physical contact, she was too aware of his presence beside her. Of the smell of him—a light, crisp cologne and the underlying scent of Raul. Out of the corner of her eye was the perfectly ironed and pressed light blue of his shirt, which matched the dark navy blue suit he was wearing today. "Tunnel," she reminded herself silently and sidestepped to leave him. She softly said, "Then let's finish this."

As his gaze met hers, Raul was aware that she meant more than just the business at hand. She was almost skittish this morning, clearly uncomfortable around him. He didn't doubt the reason for it. Their attraction to one another had been obvious last night. But this morning, their primary objective had to be work.

He sat beside her at the large, mahogany table once more, and they went over all of their clients' concerns. In reality, the greatest hurdles had already been cleared. These obstacles were minor and dealt more with the logistics of making the payments, auditing the royalties and things of that nature.

Things were sailing along smoothly, and they were nearly ready to finish up the agreements a few hours later when a call came into the conference room for Rebecca.

Rebecca picked up the phone and was immediately filled with concern as Simon Langleis' secretary announced that he would be with her in a second. She couldn't imagine why he was calling, but had no expectations that it would be something good.

"Ms. Garcia," he said a moment later and after she had acknowledged him, he went on to describe the conversation he'd just had with Pharmavax and the suggestions he'd made to them regarding the second deal for the lipid-based vector. The chill outside was nothing compared to the way her blood cooled inside her as he indicated that he'd convinced the client that they required an exclusive given the consideration they were paying.

"Mr. Langleis," she began to protest, but he cut her off and made it quite clear she was to carry out his instructions without dispute or further discussion.

Rebecca laid the receiver back into the cradle, took a deep breath and turned to face the conference room table. As she did so, she noted that outside, a light snow had begun to fall and thought it appropriate. If things were going to go wrong, why not have every possible thing explode in her face at the same time and get it all over with. "My client has had further discussions with management. They have concerns about the lack of exclusivity given the amount CellTech has requested."

Raul was shaking his head and as she glanced at Andrew and Sheila, they ducked their heads down. All knew that on this one issue, there had already been long and detailed discussions and little room for movement on the part of CellTech.

That it would be difficult was clear as Raul raked a hand through his hair, tossed down his pen and rose. He slipped his hands onto his hips, drawing open his jacket as he faced Rebecca. "We've been over this already—"

"But I have clear instructions from my client, Raul. Maybe you should talk to yours again as well," she suggested and he dropped his hands down and nodded.

"I will, Becca, but I doubt they're willing to budge. You know that, don't you?" he urged, obviously hoping she would relent and spare him the call and discussion.

She held out her hands, almost in supplication. "I'm sorry, but—"

He shot up his hand, not needing to hear anymore. With two angry strides, he was out the door of the conference room, leaving Rebecca to deal with her own confused colleagues.

Andrew rose and came to stand beside her, laid a commiserating hand on her shoulder. "Becca, what happened?"

Becca slowly shook her head from side to side and hoped the disgust wouldn't be apparent in her voice. "Simon Langleis. He spoke to Pharmavax after our discussions this morning. Convinced them they needed exclusivity."

Andrew muttered a curse and walked away from her, rubbing a hand across the back of his neck. "Damn. He doesn't know a thing about how hard we worked to get this deal done. How could he do this?"

Rebecca shrugged and made herself another cup of coffee. Her hand shook as she held the cup, a testament to the state of her nerves. She forced herself to take a calming breath and considered the possible ways in which she could salvage not only this deal, but her career.

"Why would he possibly meddle with something he's never been involved in?" Sheila questioned.

Rebecca brought the coffee cup to her lips, took a sip and walked back to the table. She laid the cup on the table with nary a tremble and calmly replied, "He and I had a discussion before I left. He's concerned about Pharmavax and technologies like this."

Andrew stalked over. "So he would jeopardize this deal for personal reasons?"

Rebecca's head shot up to silence Andrew. "This is not up for discussion, Andrew. We know what we have to do, so let's sit down and wait to hear what Raul has to say. After that, we can decide how to proceed."

Andrew shook his head, bent and leaned down close to her, so that only she would hear. "You know that's what he did, but you're too much of a team player to say so. Still, are you willing to let him put the kibosh on this and everything you've worked so hard for?"

She calmly lifted her head and softly answered. "Whatever the reasons, I need to follow his instructions, but I will get this deal for Pharmavax. Somehow."

"And the partnership? You know if you defy him—"

"My first priority is to my client, Andrew. Whatever else happens, I can deal with it," she replied harshly, and regretted it as soon as the words left her mouth. "Andrew, I'm—"

"Sorry," he finished for her. "I am too, Becca. You deserve better, even if you don't know that yet."

With those softly uttered words, he returned to his seat across the way from her. He plopped down into the chair, and as he did so, Sheila laid a hand on his arm while shooting Rebecca a commiserating look. "We will be able to work this out," she reassured, but there was no resounding agreement from anyone at the table.

Rebecca laced her fingers together, placed her hands on the tabletop and just sat and waited, her coffee growing cold as time passed. There was silence all around until Raul came back into the conference room. His stance was tight and unyielding, his face grim. "You want exclusivity. Fine. CellTech wants one hundred million. Fifty as payment for signing, another fifty—"

"We can't go back to Pharmavax with those figures," Rebecca replied calmly, trying to temper the anger she sensed coming off him in waves.

"Fine," he replied sharply. "Then I guess we'll have to settle for just one deal, because CellTech isn't going to budge, Becca. You knew that yesterday, so what brain child at RLL decided to try and press on this point? You're too smart to go back and recommend something like this to your client."

Rebecca grabbed the coffee cup as a way of keeping her hands busy and glanced uneasily at her colleagues. "The who of it doesn't matter, Raul. What matters is what we can do to try and salvage this for both of our clients because I think you believe as I do that both can benefit from the deal we had worked out."

Raul admired the spirit she was showing in what had to be a very difficult situation. He nodded and approached the table, but instead of sitting beside her, he grabbed his pad and pen and took a position at the head of the table. There was no doubt things were not going to be easy.

As the storm grew stronger in intensity outside the windows of the conference room, a similar tempest went on inside as they battled back and forth on the possible ways of garnering exclusivity for Pharmavax and the requisite compensation for Celltech. Finally, after a number of hard won concessions, they had reached a stalemate and it was clear there was nowhere else to go.

Rebecca glanced at her watch. It was nearly five o'clock, but her client would be waiting and hopefully Langleis would be available as well. She asked Raul for some privacy and he acquiesced, advising that he would be in his office until they needed him again. He left and she regretted the distance that had sprung up between them on more than one level.

She dialed, got Langleis on the line and then her representative at the client. Putting on the speaker, she detailed the terms and the stalemate they had reached and a discussion followed. Andrew jumped in time and time again to offer his comments and support of Rebecca and after close to an hour, her representative at Pharmavax relented and Langleis confirmed that it made sense to agree to the terms at that point.

At Langleis' comments, Andrew gave a harsh laugh and Rebecca hoped it hadn't been picked up by the speakerphone. "Can you get approval for this tonight?" she questioned and the Pharmavax representative advised that he would need to make some calls, but could get back to them within the hour.

Rebecca thanked everyone and for the first time since Langleis' earlier call, relief settled in until she glanced out the window and it registered for the first time just how bad the weather had gotten. Big, fat snowflakes whirled around outside the window. The sky was a dark, uneven grey and down on the street below, there was already an accumulation of snow on both the sidewalks and the streets. It certainly wasn't looking good and even if they could reach an agreement, they would be lucky to make a flight out tonight. Rebecca faced Sheila. "I'm going to get Raul back in here. Could you find a phone and call the airline? See what's happening with them and whether there's any space on the last plane?"

Sheila rose and came to stand beside Rebecca at the window. "It's bad out there, Becca."

It had been bad in more ways than one for hours, but she didn't voice that thought. "Let's try to salvage not only this deal, Sheila, but our holidays as well. I really don't want to have to call my mom and tell her I won't be there for *Noche Buena*."

"Well, even if we can't get out tonight, we might be able to tomorrow morning," Sheila said, returned to her spot and grabbed a pad and pen. She walked outside, asked the receptionist to let Raul know they were ready for him and inquired where she could use a phone to call the airlines.

Rebecca looked through the glass window of the conference room. Sheila was sitting on the Queen Anne sofa in the reception area, making the calls as requested. Raul stepped into the hallway a second later and he stopped short, met her gaze through the glass. She motioned for him to enter and he did.

"Pharmavax will get back to me within an hour. Can you wait for the answer?"

He nodded and surprised her by muttering a soft, explicit curse. "I'm sorry it came to this, Becca. For a lot of reasons. And I want to apologize for my anger, but . . . whoever interfered at RLL—"

"Did what he thought was best," she jumped in, still defensive despite the predicament it had put her in.

"I don't think you believe that for a second, but I admire you for your loyalty. RLL is lucky to have you there," he said, and with those parting words, he left the conference room.

Rebecca took a moment to use the ladies room and when she returned to the conference room, it was obvious from the looks on the faces of her colleagues that the news about their flight was not good. "We're not getting out tonight are we?"

"And maybe not tomorrow either, Becca. They're diverting a lot of flights tonight because of the weather and unless it gets much better, they may not have the equipment tomorrow morning. There's a later flight that will probably be fine—at two. I've already got seats lined up for us on that one," Sheila replied while perusing the notes she had taken as she spoke to the airline.

"That's still good, Sheila. If you two don't mind, I'm just going to make the dreaded call," she said and proceeded to dial her mother. She closed her eyes, silently prayed for the answering machine to pick up and breathed a sigh of relief when it did. She left a quick message for her mother and father, explaining that she would call in the morning as soon as she had further information about what flight she would be on.

"Dodged a bullet, huh?" Andrew said as Rebecca hung up the phone.

For the first time all day she was actually able to experience some small measure of relief. "Why is it that even as adults we dread the disapproval of our parents?"

"Hey, some day it will be our turn. Remember that," Sheila kidded.

All of them jumped when a second later the phone rang. Rebecca snatched up the receiver on the second ring. "Rebecca Garcia," she answered and tensed as Simon Langleis came on the line.

"Ms. Garcia. I must say I'm impressed with what you've managed to accomplish," he replied, but Rebecca received no pleasure from his compliment and said nothing in response except, "Has Pharmavax approved—"

"Yes, they have. They're actually quite pleased to have three years of exclusivity, even if it is costing them more," Langleis advised.

Rebecca thanked him for the news, hung up and finally, slowly released her breath. "We have a deal," she said under her breath, as if to convince herself.

She turned and faced her colleagues, grinning from ear to ear. "We have a deal, can you believe it?"

Andrew came over and gave her an effusive hug. "Congrats, Becca. You deserve it."

Sheila joined them and the two women embraced. "You may get your gift after all, Becca. They'd be fools to hesitate after you managed to pull this one off," Sheila commented as she stepped away from Rebecca and her eyes widened, tipping Rebecca off to Raul's entrance.

She swung around to face him. There was a tender smile on his face that broadened as he gathered a celebration was in the works. "Can I assume, Counselor, that our clients will both be pleased."

Rebecca grinned, nodded, and held out her hand for him to shake. He elected to grasp her fingers, bring her hand up to his mouth where he placed a gentle kiss across her knuckles. *"Felicitaciones,* Becca. Are you going to catch a flight tonight, or do you want to finalize the draft and send out the agreements for signature?"

"We're stuck for the night, Raul. We might as well finish it up so that we can have peace of mind tomorrow," she advised and slowly, reluctantly pulled her hand from his.

She was certain that while she might have business peace of mind, her personal peace of mind would never be the same.

# Ten

It took only a matter of minutes to remove the redlining and strikeouts from the last draft. Sheila copied the file to a disk and left to use a printer and make the necessary copies for all of them to review.

All in all, it took them another hour to make sure the amendments were in order, and afterward, they faxed copies to their clients. The originals would go first to CellTech for execution and then to Pharmavax.

Sheila placed the two copies of the original into a Federal Express envelope and immense relief washed over Rebecca.

"Pleased?" Raul questioned, as if reading her mind.

"You can't even begin to imagine," she replied and sat back in her leather chair. "Now it's time to think about getting home for *Noche Buena.* How about you?"

Raul's shoulders went up and down in an indifferent shrug. "The same pretty much. *Mami* and my sisters are taking over my house in the morning, and I'll have to try to survive another Christmas Eve of being bossed around."

Amazingly, she could picture him in his home, a prisoner to the mother and siblings he had described, basically because it was not much different from her own holiday. In a way, they were like two peas in a pod, although they were decidedly two geographically distant pods, she surmised. "Well, I understand and hope that with this business finished, it will be easier for you."

Raul stood, held out his hand to help her rise when Sheila returned to the room. "I'll walk you back—"

"And there's no dissuading you from that. After all—"

"The subway is right there. And dinner if you're hungry," Raul offered and Rebecca considered that this time, with their business concluded, the playing field had drastically been altered. And she didn't know if she was ready to take part in this new game. Didn't know if she had the requisite protection to keep her heart safe if things got . . . well, out of hand. Despite that, she knew she couldn't go back to Miami without at least being able to say that she'd given it a try. That she'd explored the attraction that had been building between them since the first day they'd met face to face. "I'd like that. How about you, Andrew? Sheila?"

Although she asked as a matter of courtesy, she knew that their answer would be no. They probably had their own plans for the cold and snowy evening. Plans that she was certain would go well beyond just dinner. At their polite refusals, they once again prepared to go out into the wintry night, and Raul wrapped his arm around her waist once they were out on the sidewalk. Her pumps were no match for the snow-covered streets.

He leaned close and whispered in her ear, "You are going to have to buy yourself a pair of pants and boots—"

"I brought some. I'll probably wear them for the flight home tomorrow," she said and met his gaze, noting the hesitancy that crept into his eyes at every mention of her departure.

"I don't want to be the Scrooge in your holiday plans, Becca, but—"

"I will be home for Christmas, Raul. I really don't want to think about spending the holidays stuck here without my family," she replied earnestly. He nodded, tucked her in closer to his side as the wind picked up and sent snow whirling all around them, nearly obliterating their view of the sidewalk for a moment until it settled down.

Rebecca appreciated the bulk and warmth of him beside her, for it gave her some stability on the uncertain walkways. It was slow going, and took nearly twenty minutes to go the short two blocks back to the hotel. Once inside the lobby, they bid Andrew and Sheila goodnight, and in light of the bad weather, Raul suggested one of the restaurants in the hotel.

They walked up the stairs together and to the small dining area located in the structure that hung over 42nd Street. "It'll be interesting to see what's happening out on the street below," he said, apparently not realizing that the snow held little appeal for her. On the contrary, each flake that fell was just one more reason for concern about tomorrow's flights. Still, once they were seated next to one another at a table right next to the greenhouse-style windows, she had to admit there was some charm to being inside the warm interior of the hotel with the snow falling all around. It was almost as if she was in one of those childrens' snow balls, and someone had shaken it up to move all the flakes around.

"This is nice," she confessed as the waitress poured her a glass of red wine from the bottle Raul had ordered.

Raul glanced all around. The snow was beginning to cover even the glass-topped structure of the restaurant. The last weather report he had checked before leaving his office had warned of possibly large accumulations. For Rebecca's sake, he hoped they weren't so large as to strand her in Manhattan. "It's relaxed and easy-going in here. Great for watching people on the street when the weather is better."

Rebecca leaned in her chair toward the glass, stealing a peek up and down 42nd Street, but there was little activity going on, both due to the time and the weather. "Definitely something I will keep in mind for the next time I'm in New York."

"And when will that be?" he pressed as he picked up his glass and held it up for a toast.

*"Salud,"* she replied as she clinked her glass against his and took a sip. She shrugged at his question. "Whenever the next conference or meeting happens to be in town. In a few months, I think," she replied.

He told himself that it shouldn't upset him that she could be so cavalier about it when he had been wondering since last night how he would see her again. Her next question helped take some of the sting out of her response.

"So when can we expect you down in Miami?" She glanced at him over the rim of her glass, took another sip, and commended him on his choice of wine. "Delicious."

*"Gracias."* He sipped his own drink and replied, "Maybe if the cold and snow and ice get to me I'll take a few days off to visit your sunshine." In fact, now that he had voiced that comment, it seemed like an immeasurably good thing to do, especially given the smile that she bestowed on him.

"That would be nice. I'd be delighted to show you some of the sights," she offered. He fully intended to head to the office after the holidays and check his schedule to free up some time. In the back of his mind was the possible merger with the other firm that would give him a great excuse to be in Miami. But that might be a long way off and he couldn't wait for that possibility.

In the meantime, he wanted to prolong the night as long as he could. "Have time for an appetizer?"

Rebecca placed her half-empty glass on the table and finally looked at the menu for the first time. She was in no rush. Her plane wasn't until the afternoon and things were quiet at the office. That came as no surprise. Most of Latin America and many parts of Europe closed for the week between Christmas Eve and the Epiphany. The lull in activity overseas always made it an easier time of year since she did most of her work in those countries. "I'm in no rush, so order away," she confirmed and he did just that, choosing two appetizers for them to share while they made up their minds about the main meals.

The waitress came over a short while later, placed the dishes in the middle of the table and took their dinner orders.

Rebecca examined the plates. The restaurant's theme for the moment was Middle Eastern, something with which Rebecca was thoroughly unfamiliar. That turned out to be a good thing she discovered. Raul explained that the one dish was hummus, a mash of chick peas seasoned with sesame seed paste, garlic, cumin, and olive oil. He took a pita bread from the side of the plate, broke off a piece and scooped up some hummus, held it out for her to eat.

She leaned toward him and he fed her the morsel. She chewed, savored the garlicky and nutty taste of the paste. "This is good. What about those?" she inquired, pointing to the dark green rolls, like little logs sitting on the other plate.

"It's a rice mix inside, wrapped in grape leaves," he explained, grabbed one and again offered it to her, raising it up to her lips.

The striations and edges of the leaves wrapped into a roll were clear. The dark olive green log was roughly the length and thickness of a thumb. She bit off half, found that the outside was slightly salty, while the rice inside was a little on the sweet side, probably from the raisins in the mix.

"Like?" he asked and popped the other half into his own mouth, chewing slowly and then grinning at her as she acknowledged that the flavor had pleased her. She grabbed a piece of pita and as he had done earlier, broke off a piece of the bread and scooped up some of the chick pea paste. Gripping the bread between her thumb and forefinger, she extended it to him.

He grasped her wrist, easily encircling it with his larger hand and steadied her as he plucked the morsel from her fingers. When he released her, she reached down, grabbed another grape-leaf wrapped roll, bit off half and offered him the rest. He didn't hesitate and afterward, they traded off feeding each other from the appetizers and sipping the wine, which was going down very smoothly and very quickly.

By the time the main meal came, the first bottle of wine was gone and the second was ordered. The waitress placed the dishes before them, and it was appropriate somehow to feed each other samples of their respective suppers.

Rebecca cut a piece of the lamb from her shish kebab, forked it and picked up some saffron-flavored rice. She held out the forkful to him and he closed his lips around it. His lips were full, mobile as they pulled away with the food. Again she admired the way the goatee framed what had to be one of his sexiest features. It wasn't difficult to make the imaginary leap from the way his lips closed over the fork, to how his lips would close over . . .

*Dios,* but she stopped that nasty, naughty thought before she visualized it in her brain and instead concentrated on eating a piece of Raul's moussaka, which he explained was a type of eggplant lasagna.

Raul examined her face as she sampled the creamy, but slightly tangy flavor of the dish. Her enjoyment of it was clear, her eyes bright and inviting. Her cheeks bore a slight flush, likely from the warmth of the restaurant and the wine they had consumed. He leaned his elbow on the table, placed his jaw on his fist and anticipated her feeding him something from one of the plates.

She grinned, forked up some of his moussaka and fed it to him. "Let me ask you something?"

"Mmm," he murmured, swallowed the mouthful and then scooped up some food off her plate.

"Do you always treat your opposing counsel so nicely?" she wondered aloud and accepted the bite he had prepared.

"Only if they're beautiful, charming and intelligent.

Not to mention damn tough. I hate an opponent who's a push over."

Rebecca searched his face for some sign of dishonesty, but there was not a one, which raised her temperature up a notch. She was certain there was a very noticeable flush to her cheeks and she ducked her head, toyed with the napkin in her lap to avoid his all-too-knowing gaze. He clearly wasn't about to be dissuaded. Placing his thumb and forefinger on her chin, he applied gentle pressure until she was facing him.

"Ready for dessert?" The question hung in the air between them, for Rebecca had no doubt that he was talking about more . . . but she wasn't quite ready to go that far, especially considering the wine she had imbibed. They had just finished the second bottle, and her mind was decidedly muddled, having entered into that pleasant state where the edge was off everything and nothing was a bother.

Except him. He was definitely bothering parts of her psyche that hadn't been quite so alive in a while. Better to curb those impulses and leave them to be explored some other day. "I really need to get to that packing—"

"And other personal things," he finished for her. "I understand, Becca. More than you can imagine."

Once again, with the kind of connection she had been making with him since the day before, his meaning was clear. She waited quietly while he settled the bill and afterward, he walked her to the room, much as he had the night before, and again waited until she had opened her door.

He leaned his forearm on the jamb and smiled sadly. "I guess this is good-bye for now. I'd like to think that next time you're in New York for whatever, you'll look me up."

She met his gaze and the want in his eyes warmed and teased her insides, making her wish for a moment that they might have more time together. Tomorrow, however, would likely find her on a flight to Miami. Back to her home, her parents and hopefully, her partnership. "Next time I come, I will definitely call. And maybe,

when this New York weather is on the verge of making
you crazy—"

"I'll visit Miami," he said. He shook his head, grinned
and cradled her cheek. "I think it's more likely that
what'll make me crazy is thinking that I let you leave
without doing this," he said and leaned close, waiting for
her to refuse him.

She didn't. Meeting him halfway, she brought her lips
to his, met his mouth with her own, exploring what had
been making her crazy since yesterday—the fullness of
those luscious lips. The brush of hair against her skin
from the goatee which teased her, making her ache to
have it against other parts of her body.

The kiss deepened as he opened his mouth. She didn't
hesitate, for kissing him was better than anything she
had ever experienced before. Leaning into him, he
brought his arm around her back, loosely held her, not
pressuring or pushing. Letting the moment build slowly
until she brought her body flush to his, her mouth continuing to enjoy the pleasure of his.

She was clinging to his shoulders, his hand spread
across the small of her back, when an insistent, persistent sound intruded. Rebecca pulled away from him, her
breathing rough and her body vibrating with her need.
The phone was ringing insistently. It stopped for a moment, then began again and Rebecca had no doubt as to
whom it could be. Only her parents could be that annoying. "I need to answer that," she said, her voice husky.

He nodded, followed her in as she rushed to the
phone, picked it up and launched into an explanation. It
was almost funny, he considered, listening to the slight
change in her voice that made her sound younger, repen-
tant. He recognized it well for buried in those tones were
reminders of his own, giving into his mother or one of
his sisters. When she finished with an attempt to reassure
her parents that she'd be home tomorrow, he glanced out
the window and grimaced. He had spent too much time

in the Northeast not to recognize the weather had the signs of blizzard all over it. In the short time since leaving the restaurant below, the flakes had gotten bigger and were falling faster.

Rebecca tracked his gaze. There was a whirling mass of snow outside. She walked to the windows where she quietly stood for a moment until he came up behind her, laid a hand on her shoulder. She looked up at him. "I'm not going to make it home tomorrow, am I?"

He shrugged. "It could stop but—"

"It's not likely, is it? You know, the limo driver who met us at the airport told us his knee said it would be a bad storm. I think he called it better than all those meteorologists," she said and let out a sad sigh.

Raul wanted to comfort her, and so he did the only thing he could think of. He encircled her waist with his arms, drew her back up against his chest and leaned his face close to her hair. "I promise, Becca. You'll be home for *Noche Buena*," he offered. She said nothing and they stood there for a while, high up in the New York sky, watching the world go white around them.

When she finally stepped away, she turned, cupped his cheek and gave him a smile. "I'm very glad I met you," she said.

He took hold of her hand, linked his fingers with hers and walked to her door, knowing it was time he left. "I'm glad too," he said, but couldn't resist giving her a parting kiss before he left. A kiss that promised that this would not be the last time they saw one another.

# Eleven

Once again the hotel alarm went off at 5:30 A.M. and was followed fifteen minutes later by the ring of the phone with a wake-up call. By the phone call, Rebecca was already up, but she wasn't getting ready for her flight. Instead, she was staring out the window at the snow that was still busy falling and blanketing a city already covered in what she guessed was at least two or more feet of snow. It was difficult to tell from her view a good ten or more stories up, but that's what she guesstimated from the way the mailbox at the corner was buried and the large cement planter she had passed on her way to the hotel was nearly obliterated by the white stuff.

The first call she made was down to the front desk to confirm that she and her colleagues could keep their rooms for at least another three days, even though she hoped it would be less than that. She reserved them just in case. Then she called the airline, which confirmed that all flights for that day were cancelled and that they should check back the morning of Christmas Day, although the airline representative was doubtful they'd be flying on that day as well. Apparently the storm had blanketed the entire Northeast with accumulations ranging from two to three feet, and snow was still falling in many locations.

Rebecca didn't need to be told that. A look out her window was enough to confirm the storm was not yet over. When she finished with the airline, Rebecca phoned the front desk and in deference to the early hour, asked for the voice mail systems for both Andrew and Sheila and left them messages about their predicament. She asked them to contact her once they were awake. As she was hanging up the phone, there was a knock at her front door.

It was six o'clock and time for the continental breakfast she had ordered. She was surprised that it was ready and when she opened the door, the young man barged in with the cart and her breakfast, a cheery grin on his face. "Merry Christmas Eve," he greeted and quickly served up her breakfast.

As Rebecca signed off for the room charge, she looked at him and had no choice but to smile at the eagerness on the young man's face. "Happy are we?"

"You bet," he confirmed. "A bunch of the people from the next crew can't make it in and they asked for volunteers to stay and work the extra shift at double time. That'll mean I have a way to pay for all those gifts under the tree this year."

Rebecca nodded and wished him a happy holiday as he headed out the door. At least some people would be happy with the turn of events caused by the weather.

She returned to the table by the window, where the snow continued to fall and dust the edges of the buildings with white. Her mother had begun collecting a Christmas village several years back, and many of the ceramic buildings in the collection had been similarly decorated, with odd motes of snow along the extremities. Well, now she was here to experience it up close and personal, thousands of miles away from her mother and the village.

She sighed, thinking of the call she would have to make a little later once she was certain her parents would be awake. It would not be easy, not only because she hated disappointing them, but because she despised the thought of spending her *Noche Buena* all alone, or in the company of Andrew and Sheila, who would likely prefer to be alone.

The holidays were a time for family and friends. She regretted that she would miss at least the one day this year. As she turned on the television and report after report came in on the blizzard blanketing the area with snow, there was no doubt her Christmas Eve would be spent in Manhattan. Maybe even Christmas Day, although that holiday usually had been one of little activity in her home.

Still, she couldn't be stranded for more than a few days, which meant that New Year's Eve and *Reyes* could be salvaged. She made herself her first cup of coffee, drank a little of it down while watching the newscasts. Finding one with the familiar face of a former Miami newswoman, she settled on that station and ate the remainder of her breakfast slowly, trying to kill some time in what she suspected would be a very lonely day.

She was just stepping out of the shower when the phone rang. Wrapping a towel around herself, she raced to grab it and stood dripping water on the floor of her room as the sound of Raul's voice came over the receiver.

"You okay?" he asked, concern apparent in his tone.

"As okay as any girl who's never really seen snow can be when faced with yards of it," she tried to joke, still not quite over the realization that she was stranded in this inhospitable place.

"I'm sorry about the weather, Becca. I know how badly you wanted to be in Miami," he offered in apology although all of the circumstances that had resulted in the current situation had never been within his control.

"I'm a big girl, Raul. I can handle it, but thanks for thinking of me," she replied and struggled with the towel as it slipped, exposing her wet skin to a nip in the air which sent shivers all across her body. Goosebumps erupted all over and she fumbled with the towel to keep it in place.

There was silence on the line and then he surprised

her by asking, "Would you like to come to my house for *Noche Buena?* We always have room for one more at the Santos Inn."

She was touched by his offer, but didn't want to intrude on his family's gathering. "Raul, it's a really nice offer—"

"I'm doing it for a bunch of selfish reasons, Becca. And besides, I promised you that you'd be home for *Noche Buena* and was hoping my home would count," he quickly countered. She responded to the humor in his voice by smiling, but then the towel slipped further down. She had to juggle the receiver and the towel for a moment, and Raul called out, "Becca? You there?"

She tucked the towel under her armpits, but it fell free across her backside, chilling her even more. "Raul, listen. I have to go. I just got out of the shower—"

"And you're naked as we speak?" he asked with a fairly loud, audible gulp, pulling a chuckle out of her. A very mischievous part of her came to life. "Buck naked," she replied and smiled to herself.

"Listen, Becca. Now you definitely have to say yes and let me do a good deed," he said huskily. The tone of his voice sent a shiver through her, warming and chasing away the nip of the air.

*"De verdad?* And why is that, Counselor?" she replied, her own voice low and inviting.

He laughed and she pictured it, with those full lips of his and that deliciously ticklish goatee. Then he answered softly, his tone intimate and revealing, "Because the thoughts I'm having right now would definitely put me on Santa's naughty list. I need to do something really good—"

"To get back on the nice list? So you do have an ulterior motive for inviting me," she kidded.

"Oh, Becca, a bunch of them. You can't even begin to guess how many," he answered sexily, stirring her with just the sound of his voice and the promise of time with him.

"Then I have little choice but to try and help you get

on Santa's good side as my deed for the holidays," she replied, intrigued by him and relieved that she wouldn't be spending *Noche Buena* alone. And then it suddenly occurred to her that Andrew and Sheila would be by themselves. "Listen, would you maybe have room for two others?"

"Of course," he replied without hesitation and after thanking him, they agreed on a time when he would come by to pick her up at the hotel.

She hung up, pulled the towel tighter around herself and for the first time in a long time, a sense of wonder filled her, coupled with an equal amount of dread. In a little over four hours, he'd be there to take her to his home. She didn't know what to wear and she had to get something to bring as a present for Raul and his family. Given the weather, both might prove to be a problem, but she knew she had to give it a shot, as well as calling Andrew and Sheila to invite them along.

It was a nice thing he had done, she thought, smiling as she went to the bathroom to dry her hair. Definitely enough to get him on Santa's nice list.

And more than enough to get him on her lists, both naughty and nice.


Andrew and Sheila begged off on Raul's invitation. They had planned on spending the holidays with their respective families in Miami, a few hours at each house that would be fun, but tiring. The blizzard was therefore giving them the rare treat to have some time alone and they intended to take advantage of it.

Rebecca was a little surprised therefore when a few hours later, just as she was finished getting dressed, there was a knock on her door. She opened it to find Sheila there.

"Hi. I thought you guys weren't coming?" Rebecca said and poked her head out the open doorway to look for Andrew, but Sheila was alone. "What's up?" she asked, clearly confused.

"Well . . . I know you and I are kind of friends," Sheila began hesitantly. "And friends watch out for each other, right?"

Rebecca placed an arm around the other woman's shoulders and gave her a reassuring hug. "Sheila, I won't say anything about you and Andrew. You have my word about that."

Sheila smiled and held out a small box wrapped in bright red paper dotted with little gold stars. "It's not about Andrew and me," Sheila said and Rebecca took the box in her hand.

It was surprisingly lightweight. She nervously moved it from hand to hand, wondering what it could be and what had prompted the other woman to do it. She gave her a quizzical look and Sheila quickly tried to answer.

"It's about you and Raul, and well . . ." Sheila stammered uncomfortably and Rebecca shook her head, clearly not understanding. Sheila pressed for her to open the box.

Rebecca undid the side opening on the wrap and slid out the small box inside, lifted the lid and promptly turned as bright red as the wrapping paper when she realized what was inside—condoms. A strip of about a half dozen of them.

"Just in case, you know. We didn't think you were . . . prepared," Sheila explained, her face as bright pink as Rebecca imagined her own must be. She didn't have the heart to tell Sheila that she had a few in her cosmetics bag. A few that had been there for quite some time. She wondered for a fleeting moment whether condoms had an expiration date.

"Thanks, I think," she finally managed to get out as she tucked them back into the box. "I really wasn't planning on—"

"Sometimes that's the best way, Becca. Too much

thinking, too much worrying and fretting . . ." Sheila shrugged her shoulders, reached out and gave her a hug.

"This was meant to be, Becca. The weather. Me and Andrew. You and Raul," she said, gesturing to everything around them. "It's like a holiday gift for all of us, even though I know you were hoping for something else. Not that it isn't going to happen soon," she was quick to clarify to ease Rebecca's mind.

Rebecca tightly gripped the box in one hand, nearly crushing it. She believed in many things, including Fate or Kismet or whatever it was respectively called in a variety of cultures. She certainly thought that sometimes there was a grander scheme that resulted in things such as the blizzard outside. But she didn't believe that was the case this time. This was just a snowstorm. Nothing life-changing. Still, while it might not be Fate working overtime on her behalf, there was nothing to say that maybe it wasn't laboring on her friends' behalf. After all, the weather had stranded them and given them time to be alone.

Her hold on the box lessened and she looked down, juggled it and smiled at Sheila in an attempt to reassure. "Thanks, Sheila. You may be right, and in any case, it's always good to be prepared."

Sheila nodded, but it was apparent she didn't believe Rebecca's sudden change of heart. "Have a good holiday, Becca and . . . listen to your heart for a change. It won't steer you wrong."

# Twelve

Rebecca thanked the room service attendant for his promise that a platter of fruits and cheeses and an iced bottle of champagne would be waiting in Andrew's room once they returned from their dinner. She hoped it would help set the right tone for a romantic Christmas Eve with Sheila.

She walked to the bathroom, took one last look in the mirror, hoping that her black trouser pants and beaded black sweater fit the bill of what Raul had described as "dressy casual" to her over the phone. She smoothed the pants and sweater one last time and returned to the main part of the suite to wait for Raul.

She paced a little while, walking by the window and gazing out at the snowy drifts that had covered the concrete, brick and mortar of the city. There was activity out on the street, but it was minimal. People trudged along, some bearing bags filled with gaily wrapped gifts. Others stopped to grab handfuls of snow that they made into missiles to launch at friends who went running and sliding along the street. For the first time, she realized that there were no cars or other traffic along Lexington Avenue and that the pedestrians were actually walking up the street rather than along the sidewalks, which had yet to be cleared in many instances.

The street had been plowed in the early morning hours. The loud rumbling noise had surprised her at first and she'd gone to the window. The bright yellow snowplows had moved by slowly, their lights flashing and blinking as they did their first pass along the street. The snow had flown off the plows, flying up into the air creating a snowy rainbow from the sun rising over the East Side of Manhattan. The man-made blizzard had settled on the sides of the street and sidewalks, covering the vehicles that hapless drivers had abandoned when they became impossible to drive due to the weather.

The stranded cars and buses combined with the snow made Lexington Avenue impassable except by the pedestrians who were taking advantage of the situation to gambol along the New York thoroughfare.

A knock came at her door. She pulled away from the wintry scene below and strode to the door, opened it to find Raul there, waiting. "Hi," she said, smiling at the sight of him. He was dressed in a bright red ski jacket and black jeans whose bottoms were dusted with the snow he had walked through. On his head he had on a striped ski hat and his cheeks bore a flush from the cold. That smile, the one she had thought about in her dreams was brilliant against his olive skin.

"Hi, yourself," he replied, ripped off the hat, and stepped into the room as she motioned for him to enter. He nervously smoothed his hat hair, trying to comb down the locks suffering from being contained in the cap and the static it created.

She reached out and ran her fingers across one errant lock, flushed and moved away from him as she realized the intimacy of the act and how wonderful that head of silken, wavy hair had been beneath her fingertips.

"I want to thank you again for inviting me. It was really nice of you," Rebecca stammered in her haste as she walked over and grabbed her coat off the bed, where she'd laid it in anticipation of his arrival.

He came behind her, took the coat from her hands and helped her put it on, resting his hands on her shoulders when he was finished. She looked up at him, met his gaze and the intensity was unnerving. Sidling away from him, she grabbed a large box from the bed and handed it to him. "I got this for you and your family."

Raul took the box with the distinctive Godiva golden wrapping, the blue, silver and gold ribbons and matching holiday decorations. "This wasn't necessary," he said, but his gaze confirmed how much he appreciated the gesture.

Rebecca shrugged and buttoned up her coat. "I couldn't come to your house empty-handed."

He juggled the box in his hands. "*Gracias*, but I'll wait and give it to *Mami* when we get there. She and my sisters are choco-holics and will truly appreciate it."

She nodded, shifted her hands nervously against the wool of her coat. "Should we be on our way?"

Raul held out his gloved hand and she grasped it with her own and grabbed her purse. After leaving her room, they rode the elevator to the main lobby of the hotel and then walked down to the lower level of Grand Central Station. She strolled beside Raul as he guided her to the entrance to the subway, pulled out a Metrocard from his pocket, swiped her through and then himself. Once inside the subway station, there were tunnels and signs for a number of different things, and had it not been for Raul, Rebecca would have been totally lost. She held onto his hand tightly, walked beside him as he skipped a few stairways and then led her to a long, rising walkway that finally opened up onto a number of tracks.

"What's this?" she questioned, for in this area there was a greater amount of activity than in the station they had just left.

"It's the shuttle to Times Square. You catch it to connect to a whole bunch of different subways, including a number of lines which take you over to Penn Station," he answered and waited until a small electronic signboard advised on which track the next shuttle would arrive.

As soon as the track number came up, she followed him along with dozens of others headed for the same platform. No sooner had the subway come to a stop and emptied its passengers, the new passengers were hurrying on, racing for seats or for what seemed to be prime standing areas. Raul gently steered her toward one section and grabbed hold of a stainless steel pole with his free hand. She grabbed it as well, and after an electronic tone signaled that the doors were closing and some latecomers rushed on, the doors shut tight with a space-age whoosh and clunk, much like that of a rocket ship door closing on its astronauts, Rebecca imagined.

As the subway pulled out of the station, it was almost as if she were one of those space explorers, heading off to mysterious places for here she was, in a totally different place and facing the great unknown with the man standing across from her.

A moment later, there was a high screech and hiss of the air brakes as the subway came to an abrupt halt.

The sudden stop had her rocking back and forth, but Raul exerted pressure on her hand to help keep her upright. He smiled at her and some of her earlier concerns about the unknown dissipated. "First time?"

"Nope, not a subway virgin. But the first and only time was three or four years ago and very unpleasant since I got my pocket picked," she replied and glanced around at the various ads adorning the walls of the train and the amazing lack of graffiti. She recollected that last time there had been a number of "tags" as someone had explained they were called, from various individuals who used the cars as canvases for their names and logos.

"Things have improved a lot since then, but you still have to be careful," he confirmed, almost as if sensing what she was thinking, but they had little opportunity to say anything else as the train moved again and then came to an abrupt stop at the next station. Once more the motion jerked her around, but Raul was her point of stability.

He smiled at her, gave her hand a reassuring squeeze and they joined the stream of people plodding along the platform, their movements slow due to the numbers of bodies crammed onto the relatively narrow space between the two tracks and the large, painted metal girders.

A few individuals were battling the current of the crowd, trying to make it to the train she and Raul had just gotten off of so that they could do the return trip to Grand Central Station. It was like watching salmon battling to make it upriver as they darted and moved through the crowd in their desire to reach the subway.

"Do you do this every day?" Rebecca asked, thinking she'd go crazy both with the crowds and the sense of being confined in the underground warren of tunnels and stairs.

He shrugged, gently pulled her out of the way of one particularly aggressive man who was trying to force his way in the opposite direction. "Not every day," he finally replied once they were in a more open area that led to the various subways at this station. Glancing at her over his shoulder, he explained, "I get in early, so the crowds are not bad and I walk sometimes, either all or part of the way."

Rebecca looked around at the masses of people. "Is it always this crowded?"

"No, this is lighter than a typical rush hour. Actually, it's normally pretty empty on weekends and holidays, but with nothing moving above ground on the streets, I guess people decided to use the subways," he answered.

Rebecca was surprised to hear this wasn't even a peak crowd, for it was busy with people running from one spot to the other. At one newsstand they passed, there was a line of two or three waiting to pay for papers, while some just tossed their fifty cents into a dish on the counter and grabbed the daily paper. She wondered if it was yesterday's paper or if the dailies had worked their miracles and gotten out an edition.

Raul guided her up some steps, past that newsstand and then down a longer flight of stairs. As she followed him, she noted the signs denoting this was the way to the two and three trains, with the numbers enclosed in bright red circles which identified the lines for the riders, she guessed. They were near the bottom steps when there was the flush of warm wind out of a tunnel and onto the platform, and the clackity, clacking sound of something coming in on the tracks.

"Come on," he urged and gave her hand a tug. She quickened her pace and they hit the platform at the same time that the train pulled in and opened its doors, disgorging its riders. Passengers quickly rushed off and up in the direction from which she and Raul had just come and as a space opened in the sea of people, they jumped onto the train, and grabbed another pole. Poles seemed to be Raul's preferred choice although she noted how others scurried into corners by the ends of the cars and forced themselves into the gaps between other passengers on the seats.

Raul leaned closer to her, having caught her watching as one man eased himself into a tight spot and whispered in her ear, "Get even a small piece of your butt in the gap and work your way back."

He chuckled and she joined in his laughter, amazed at the actions and brass of the rider. Those next to him were unperturbed and she guessed that this was just subway riding as usual.

A few stops later, they left the subway and headed up to the street level. The neighborhood they entered was quite different from that of the Midtown she had come to know in the last few days.

There were less office buildings. A college, assorted residences, apartment buildings and small stores made up most of the landscape. On the side streets off the avenues and closer to the East Side, beautifully maintained brownstones lined the relatively narrow streets. She walked with him along one sidewalk that had been plowed, but then as they turned onto the side street lined with brownstones, they were forced back out onto the street, for most people were still trying to dig themselves out of the mountains of snow created by the passing of the plows. "This is nice," she said, getting a distinctive feel here, as if this was a place people could call home, especially as one person after another on the street shouted a greeting to Raul as they passed.

"Nice neighbors, at least the couple that I know," he admitted and waved to one man who was just finishing up with the steps of his home. The man stopped and called out to Raul, "You were out early today."

Raul nodded. "Had guests coming," he explained and stopped in front of one large pile of snow where a path had been cut from the sidewalk to the street between two parked cars. Or at least what she assumed were cars given their size and shape. They were still buried beneath mounds of snow.

"Let me help," he said and took the first step through the narrow pass. He held out his hand and she took hold, slowly inched behind him until they were both on the sidewalk. Snow clung to the sides of her coat from where it had rubbed up against the large drifts on the bumpers of the cars.

Raul bent to brush off the snow and after, led her up the steps of the brownstone. As they neared the door, Rebecca peaked through the large window that opened onto the street. There was a tree right by the glass, gaily decorated and lit, and beyond that, a number of people milled about in the room. Obviously the company Raul had been expecting had already arrived.

She hesitated on the last step, wondering what she was getting herself into once again. It was Christmas Eve and she should have been back in Miami with her family. Instead, she was about to enter a strange home, with a man she barely knew. Granted however, that he was a very bright, attractive, and intriguing man. And she was a liberated, independent woman more than capable of taking care of herself in any situation. Except maybe those involving her parents and siblings and their annoying attempts to interfere in her romantic life, that tiny, but demanding little voice in her head reminded. As he also paused on the top step, he turned and gave her a nervous grin, as if he too wondered what it was that they were doing here together.

"I don't know who's crazier, *sabes?* You for agreeing to come with me into this bedlam, or me for inviting a very beautiful woman to meet my very nosy and match-making mother," he admitted, and having him voice concerns so similar to her own made her relax.

"I was just asking myself the same thing, Raul. You know it's not too late to back out and avoid the twentieth century version of the Spanish Inquisition," she responded. He chuckled, but it was obviously too late as the door swung open and a tall, handsome teenage boy boomed out in a deep voice, "Hey, Uncle Raul. What are you doing out here on the stoop? Do you need some privacy?"

Raul chuckled, but gave the boy a warning glare which had the young man smiling and slapping his uncle on the back as he passed by with her in tow. "Brendon, meet my friend Rebecca," Raul said as Rebecca held out her hand to the youth, who was at least six foot four and had the husky build of a football player.

The young man grinned, shook her hand, and then leaned close to his uncle to whisper, *"Tio,* you know us guys we need to stick together, so I want to warn you that your friend has been all they've been talking about since you left."

Rebecca smiled as Raul reached up—a very long reach with his nephew's great height—and patted the young boy on the back. "Thanks for the warning, Brendon. I know how *Abuelita* and my sisters can be—"

"Except for Alicia," Brendon clarified. "She's been trying to rein them in, but nobody wants to listen to her. After all, they're still trying to find her a husband as well."

Raul groaned and shot a glance at Rebecca. "Are you still sure you want to go through with this?" he asked and craned his neck to look out from the foyer into the living room where the activity seemed to be happening for the moment.

Rebecca considered him and his nephew, who was busy contemplating her and his uncle, clearly wondering at just what their relationship was. She thought about running for a second, then recalled the promise he had made her the day before about being home for *Noche Buena.* "I was worried I'd be alone for the holiday, *sabes,* but instead, you're giving me the chance to have a wonderful meal, some nice company and the opportunity to have my personal life dissected and probed in front of everyone."

Raul grinned uneasily and asked, "Does that mean you're bailing on me?"

His nephew added his own pained and concerned look on behalf of his uncle as they both waited for her answer.

"Heck, Raul. It's going to be just like home, I think. So, are you ready to get this night going?"

Raul smiled at her and offered his arm. She looped her arm through his and walked into the living room where most of his family had gathered, his nephew following behind like an eager puppy.

She sensed as she stepped through the threshold, that her life was never going to be the same.

# Thirteen

As they walked into the room, every head in the place snapped to look at them.

Raul had faced many an adversary in court and across the conference room table, and none sent a wave of fear through him they way these women did, much as he loved them. But when his mother and his sisters were determined to accomplish something, there was no deterring them. And for the course of the last year, they had been set on finding him a girlfriend. One who he would eventually decide to settle down with so he wouldn't become a lonely, old hermit before his time, as his sister Grace had proclaimed at the last family dinner.

He glanced at Rebecca out of the corner of his eye. She was smiling, looking as calm, cool and collected as she had the other day in the conference room, but the hand on his arm twitched slightly, confirming that she was equally as uneasy about this as he. He reached up, gave her hand a pat and the eyes of all of his family fixed on that subtle movement. He imagined he could hear all the gears clicking in their heads, a cacophony of sound as loud as the plows that had rumbled past the house that morning.

Drawing a deep breath, he addressed his mother first. "*Mami,* I'd like for you to meet Rebecca Garcia. She's a business acquaintance who unfortunately got stranded by the blizzard," he said and winced. In his heart he knew Rebecca was more than just a business acquaintance and he didn't for a moment regret the storm.

His mother was too shrewd to believe his statement for a second, but had the grace not to say otherwise. "Ms. Garcia—"

"Rebecca, *por favor,* Mrs. Santos," Rebecca jumped in and held out her hand.

His mother took Rebecca's hand and drew her away from him and into the fold of women who were such a big part of his life. "It's too formal for you to be calling me Mrs. Santos all night long. Especially on a night like this when we're all family here. So, *por favor,* call me Maria. And meet my daughters," she said, and proceeded to present Rebecca to Grace, Erika and Alicia. After, her two married daughters introduced their children and husbands.

Rebecca had already met Brendon, Erika's oldest son, and now she met Lauren and Jonathan, his younger siblings. They were gorgeous children, with brilliant eyes ranging in shades from ice blue to a deep hazel green, like Raul's. The resemblance to both their mother and to their uncle Raul was strong. Erika's husband, Mike, seemed like an affable, easy-going guy and despite the children's resemblance to their mother, she detected much of their father in them as well, especially the boys.

Grace was the youngest sister, Maria explained, and her two kids were the little ones in the family for now. The youngest girl, Deanna, was barely months old and her brother, Peter, was an adorable two year old toddler, who quickly took a liking to Rebecca. He came over, grabbed her leg and smiled, asking that she pick him up. She did, bending to raise him and place him on her hip, much as she did with her own little nephews. The little boy leaned his head against her shoulder and stuck his thumb in his mouth, obviously in comfort mode. "I have a little nephew just like you, Peter. I bet you like to play with trucks and dirt and watch Blue's Clues. Am I right?" she asked and the little boy grinned at her around the thumb in his mouth and nodded.

His father Bob, a man who appeared to be about a

decade older than Grace, came over to take him back, but the boy protested, and Rebecca insisted that it was all right. "Once he's a problem, let me know," Bob said, obviously worried about how his son was imposing.

Rebecca nodded, and with one hand holding the child against her hip, she met the gaze of Raul's middle sister, Alicia. There was an immediate connection, as if this woman was a kindred spirit. She knew from Raul that Alicia was a determined career woman, so maybe that was part of it. She held out her free hand and it was instantly taken in a strong and firm grip. "Nice to meet you, Alicia."

"The same, Rebecca. I'm glad Raul brought you. It's good that he's not alone finally," Alicia replied, clearly surprising her brother by her apparent defection to join her mother and sisters.

*"Mami,"* Raul jumped in, ending further comments. He stepped forward to hand his mother the large box of chocolates Rebecca had bought. "This is from Becca for the family."

His mother smiled. *"Mi'ja,* you shouldn't have, but it is appreciated. The Santos women, like most, just love chocolate."

"You're welcome, Maria. And thank you again for having me here," Rebecca replied.

With the introductions and initial gift-giving finished, the family erupted into activity, his mother, Grace and Erika heading into the kitchen to bring out some appetizers, their husbands in tow to help out. Alicia headed off with Brendon, Jonathan, and Lauren to a lower level of his home to play some video games so the adults could have a chance to talk. "You and I can chat later," she said to Rebecca.

The kids traipsed off behind Alicia like the rats chasing after the Pied Piper. It was funny since at her home, she was the one usually charged with a similar role. Which, she guessed, was the reason why Peter had settled himself on her hip, in no hurry to go. She was a natural child magnet.

She looked over at Raul and realized he had been given responsibility for Peter's little sister. Walking over, she leaned toward Raul and glanced down at the gap between the folds of the blanket to see the face of the baby. She was sleeping peacefully, her mouth moving occasionally as if in dreams of her *mami* and what was probably her favorite pastime—eating.

"She's beautiful," she said and glanced up, finding herself all too close to Raul and all too tempted. It was only natural to move the few inches closer to him and bring her lips to his, give him a gentle kiss that spoke of the happiness she was suddenly experiencing, surrounded by his family.

"Thank you," she said again as she moved away.

He raised his hand, brushed the back of it against the flush of color on her cheeks. She was sweet looking and all too tempting when she blushed. "Don't thank me yet. The night is young and the tribe is on its best behavior for now. I don't know how long that will last."

She chuckled as he intended and glanced down at his nephew on her hip. It seemed so natural, her holding the toddler as if it were her own and the image took shape in his mind of Rebecca with his child on her hip and him holding another. He imagined her round and swollen with his baby growing inside. A little one suckling at her breast and he stopped right there, curbing the impulses that had suddenly arisen.

His mother came in from the kitchen, bearing a platter laden with assorted cheeses and crackers, and his sisters were behind her. The plates they held were piled high with various treats. Miniature *pastelitos,* those savory meat pies from his favorite bakery in Union City where Alicia lived. *Cangrejitos*—flaky, crab-shaped pastries with a mix of ham and chorizo inside. Best of all, the small finger sandwiches cut into triangles and spread with a deviled ham mixture his mom had been making for as long as he could remember.

As Erika walked by with the sandwich plate, he snagged one and popped it into his mouth, earning an annoyed glare from his sister. "Wait for the guest, Raul. You don't want her to think you have no manners."

The glare turned into a bright smile as she faced Rebecca and offered her a sandwich. Grace's little son beat her to the plate, grabbing a sandwich in each hand, and holding one out to Rebecca. "*Gracias,* Peter," she said and took the treat from his hand. He gave her a gap-toothed grin and quickly crammed the other morsel into his own mouth.

Rebecca took advantage of the moment to sit down and Peter made a natural adjustment in his position, settling himself on her lap, his head leaning back against her breasts. It was as if he knew he would have the best place in the house since as a guest Rebecca would be offered first dibs on everything.

Raul joined her a second later on the sofa, using the one edge to rest his arm and support the football hold in which he rocked his little niece. He turned and looked at her, gave her a smile that kicked up her pulse a notch and made her think of what it would be like if the little tableau they were presenting were real. With the two of them sharing a couch, their own little ones tucked in close to them.

She forced herself to tear her gaze from his and met the interested glances of all around them, whom she surmised had been busy thinking similar thoughts. This was bad, she thought, for she knew this night was just an aberration. A product of Raul's holiday spirit that had inspired him to offer the warmth and comfort of his family for this one night and one night alone.

Tomorrow she'd be alone again and that thought brought a painful ache to her heart for it was too easy to imagine herself in a family such as this, with a man like Raul. No strike that, with Raul himself. He had intrigued her like no one else had, and she confessed to herself that part of the reason, beside the ghost of Christmas Present spreading warmth and cheer, was the man sitting next to her.

He was accepting a glass of wine from Mike, whose assigned chore was that of bartender, for he had come in from the kitchen with several bottles and had taken them to a small dry bar in one corner of Raul's living room. Mike offered her a glass of red and she accepted it.

Across the room from them, Bob was busy tending the fire that was cheerfully blazing in a large, brick fireplace. He opened the glass door of the brass fireplace screen and tossed in another log. Sparks flew up as he did so and the fragrant smell of wood smoke wafted from the opening and out into the room.

She inhaled the scent deeply, storing it in her memory banks for it was one that wasn't all that common-place in her life. "Smells nice," she said and glanced at Raul.

"Mmm," he replied and took a sip of his wine, leaned back into the comfort of his sofa. "I love a cold, winter night and having the fire going. It drives off the chill and smells so . . . inviting." He met her gaze and in his eyes was a vision of just how truly inviting. It was all too easy to picture the two of them before the fire, the warmth invading their bodies, the scent wrapping itself around them. Their bodies intertwined in the act of loving . . .

There was sudden heat on her cheeks and she ripped her gaze away, took a sip of the wine to calm her. On her lap, Peter bounced his head against her breasts playfully, grabbed a *cangrejito* as Grace passed by with that plate.

She smiled at the youngster's antics and settled back into the sofa as well. The others all took seats around the sofa and the low coffee table on which they had placed the appetizers. It was clear everyone was settling in for some talk and snacks before the main meal. In her home, this was generally the part of the holiday she liked best.

It was when she got filled in on what was going on in everyone's lives and how they were doing.

It was no different here, she discovered. She sat back and listened as everyone traded stories about what was going on in their lives and asked about the next person. Rebecca tucked away the bits of info, trying to remember that Mike was an actuary and Erika worked out of her house as a computer consultant. That was the reason Erika had time to manage her brood of three.

Grace was on maternity leave, but would be returning to work as an accountant in another two months. Her husband Bob worked at one of the large New York pharmaceutical houses as a product manager for one of their new drugs.

Maria, the maternal head of the whole clan, had recently retired from a teaching position and was busy enjoying herself in Manhattan. She lived just a few blocks away in an apartment Raul had purchased for her so that she could be close by to both him and Grace.

Erika and her family lived in New Jersey, which made her wonder how they had made it into Manhattan given the snowfall, until Erika explained that with the weather threatening to be so bad, they had packed up all their gifts the night before and headed to their mother's place to spend the night. They hadn't wanted to risk missing the holidays with their family. "And I'm sorry to remind you that you're not home, Rebecca. It must be difficult," Erika commiserated.

"And different," Grace chimed in. "Miami's still hot at this time of year, right?"

Which prompted a whole round of questions about her holidays in Miami and her family as well as the expected inquisition about where she worked and what her future plans were.

Rebecca tried to answer each and every question but adeptly steered the conversation away from her career and back to the holidays in Miami and how different things were and yet how similar.

As she sat with his family, there was the familiar smell of the roast pork coming from the kitchen, and the appetizers they were sharing were those that would have been served in her own home. Things like the meat pastries and *cangrejitos*. The small, corn-husk wrapped *tamales* that came out a little later.

She held the plate with the corn meal cylinder filled with small, tender chunks of pork in one hand and fed herself and Peter tidbits of the treat. *"Te gusta?"* she asked the little boy and he nodded and asked for more.

Together they finished off the *tamale* and after, Maria brought out octopus swimming in a garlicky olive oil sauce. The little toddler in her lap made a face at the bits of boiled octopus with its large suction cups. Rebecca looked over at Raul, offering him some, but he made a face so similar to that of his nephew that she laughed.

"Never developed a taste for it," he offered in explanation.

Rebecca nodded and as his mother sat, conversation resumed again for a little while until Alicia came up with the kids who were complaining about being hungry. Maria, Erika and Grace gave their seats to Alicia and the youngsters, explaining that they had to go finish the main meal so all could eat dinner.

Rebecca rose, offered to go help out but Alicia was quick to point out that she was a guest and should enjoy herself. With Alicia's arrival, Peter decided it was time for a new roost and held his hands out to his *tia*, who took him from Rebecca and settled herself in a wing chair adjacent to the couch. The younger kids grabbed some plates and made themselves snacks, and then split for parts unknown again, leaving only Brendon, Alicia, Raul and Grace's little ones, still ensconced in the arms of their *tio* and *tia*.

With Peter gone from her lap, it seemed suddenly empty until Raul handed her his little niece who was getting antsy. "Hold her while I get a bottle," he said, offering her no chance to refuse.

Rebecca cradled the baby, soothing her with a gentle rocking motion. The baby turned its head, began to root for a moment and then opened its eyes and gave her a quizzical look, as if saying, "You're not my mom!"

She chuckled, looked up and met Alicia's amused gaze. "Amazing, aren't they?"

Alicia nodded. "Yes, but of course you know what's even nicer about these two?"

"What?" Rebecca questioned as Raul returned and handed her a bottle of warm milk. She placed the bottle near the baby's lips, let her get accustomed to the nipple and then latch onto it greedily. She smiled and met Alicia's gaze once more. "So, what's so nice about these two?" she prompted again.

Alicia considered her carefully, then grinned and answered, "They go home with their parents."

"Aw, come on, *tia*. You miss us when we're gone," Brendon teased back and it was clear to Rebecca that Alicia adored her nieces and nephews and that the feeling was mutual.

She glanced back down at the baby in her arms, then up at Raul, who had shifted closer to her on the couch. His arm was around her shoulders, his thigh brushing hers. As he bent to examine little Deanna as she ate, the silk of his hair tickled the side of her cheek. When he looked up, his gaze was tender.

She wanted nothing more at that moment than to cradle his cheek, turn his head her way and kiss those lips with their half-smile that spoke of a contentment she was experiencing as well, but hadn't thought possible.

Luckily, the baby's noisy cry shattered the moment, reminding her that she had been neglecting her duties. As Raul laid a diaper across her shoulder and took the bottle, Rebecca picked up the baby and held her up to her shoulder, gently tapping her back until she emitted a loud, gurgly burp.

She chuckled and Raul helped her get the baby settled once more. His sister teased, "Don't let *Mami* and the others see how natural you are at this, *mano,* or they'll never let Rebecca get away."

Rebecca's face flushed at Alicia's comment and beside her, Raul shifted uneasily, moved away back to the far side of the sofa. He glared at his sister and softly said, "Let's keep my personal life just that, Alicia. Please convince the others to leave me and Becca alone. I'm sure it must be embarrassing to Becca, right?" He turned and faced her.

Rebecca nodded and rocked the baby who had finished the bottle and was now happily doing its second favorite pastime—sleeping. When she picked her head up, she realized Alicia was considering her carefully. "I'm sure you understand how hard it is to have a career and find time for any kind of relationship," Rebecca said.

"What's a relationship?" Alicia teased and grinned, looking like her brother. "I more than understand, Becca."

"Yeah. *Tia* just got picked to be the trainer for the New Jersey Maulers," Brendon piped in enthusiastically, the pride evident in his voice. "Does that mean you'll get us free tickets?"

Alicia smiled at her nephew. "I will definitely get all of you tickets and maybe you'll get to meet some of the players."

Rebecca wasn't much of a baseball fan, but she had read about the new expansion teams the league had just approved. "It sounds very exciting. Will you be heading down my way for spring training or any games?"

"Definitely. I think with all this interleague play that we'll be either in Tampa or Miami during the course of the season," Alicia answered.

As Rebecca asked her question after question, Alicia gave her a run down on when the season would begin and what she would be doing. She listened with interest and also slightly in awe of Alicia's schedule and responsibilities for they were much more daunting than she could have imagined. "You have your hands full, Alicia."

"*Sí*, but I'm sure you understand, Becca. Contrary to this very homey scene, I doubt you have much time either and a lot of responsibilities as well," Alicia countered.

The baby in her arms shifted and sighed in her sleep, dragging a smile from Rebecca as she answered. "No time at all, even though this definitely is right somehow."

She stopped short and looked up at Alicia and Raul. "I can't believe I just said that."

Raul reached out and patted her arm. "It's the power of the baby at work, Becca. If you're a woman—"

"Over thirty," Alicia chimed in.

"Still months away from thirty," Rebecca corrected.

"Close enough," Raul jumped in and continued. "Get a baby in the arms of any woman thirty or over and the power takes over. The next thing you know, they're thinking booties and babies of their own."

"Really?" Rebecca questioned with a laugh. "And this mystical power only affects woman, huh? You big manly men are immune?"

"Men are harder to classify, Becca," Alicia began. "Some men run in fear. Others like Raul—"

"Are real comfortable and totally unafraid," Rebecca proposed, having seen Raul with his little niece earlier.

"That's only because she's number five. I'm immune by now," he joked and met her gaze.

Despite his comment, she had seen the tenderness in his gaze before and knew he was not as immune as he proclaimed. She said nothing, especially since his mother entered to announce that it was time for dinner.

# Fourteen

Raul rose and stood before her. He reached down to take the baby from her arms so she could stand. The transfer went smoothly, the baby missing not even a moment of sleep.

Across from them, Alicia rose with Peter still plastered to her side. The other nieces and nephews who had been drifting in and out of the room all went running ahead of them to the back of the brownstone.

"Hungry?" she asked Maria as the grandmother smiled at their haste.

"Impatient," she answered. "Once we finish dinner they get to open their gifts."

Rebecca nodded for they had a similar tradition at her own home. The exchange of gifts came after the main meal and before dessert. The kid's Santa gifts were tucked away to be put out for the next morning and another session of opening presents.

Following his mother to the back of the house, Rebecca realized they had to go down a level to where the kitchen and dining room were located. Once on the lower level, she noted the French doors along the one wall of both rooms. The doors opened onto a courtyard surrounded by a high brick wall. Like most things in New York on this day, the small courtyard was piled high with snow, but there were the odd bumps and taller shapes of what she assumed were trees and bushes.

The snow had drifted up against the glass of the French doors, at least two or more feet high.

Raul paused beside her in the doorway, following her gaze. "Looks cold out there, doesn't it?"

Rebecca didn't get a chance to answer as Erika's littlest one came up to them and tugged on Raul's arm, demanding attention.

Raul glanced down patiently. "What is it, Jon?"

Jon pointed upwards and they both looked up at the sprig of mistletoe hanging from the jamb of the doorway. "You have to kiss her, *tio.* That's the rule."

"I think you mean 'tradition', *hijo,*" his mother corrected. Erika came over and took Grace's little Deanna from her brother's arms, chiding Raul as she did so. *"Vamos,* Raul. You wouldn't want to be the one to break tradition, would you?"

Raul faced Rebecca and raised an eyebrow in question. "Becca?"

She half-glanced at the little bit of green with the tiny wax-like berries and bright red ribbon affixing it to a nail in the jamb of the door. "It's not a Cuban tradition, you know."

Raul grinned, shot the sprig of mistletoe a glance then gazed back down at her. "When in America—"

"Do as the Americans do?" She shrugged, rose on her tiptoes, and rested her hands on his shoulders as she leaned close to whisper, "You sure you want to add fuel to their fire?"

He laid his hands on her waist and turned his face, said in a low whisper, "I'd rather build our own fire, but maybe later."

She looked up at him and he smiled. She did what she had wanted to do since earlier. She brought her lips to his, savored the textures of that smile against her lips. Of the soft brush of his goatee and the fullness of his lips as he plucked at her lips for too brief a moment.

She pulled away, dropped her hands from his shoulders as he reluctantly released her. His family, who had all apparently been watching them with keen interest, quickly erupted into a flurry of activity, laying out assorted dishes with food, scurrying around to seat themselves around the elegantly set table.

Fine china graced each place setting, even that of the kids. Ornate glassware, with a very Mediterranean pattern in gold and maroon added rich, jewel tones to the pristine white of the tablecloths. Cheery red and green plaid runners ran the length of the long table and little brass angel napkin rings held red and green linens. The angels were placed at the center of each place setting.

Raul's spot was at the head of the table and in deference to Rebecca's presence, the spot to his right opened up for her to sit. She reluctantly accepted the seat, wishing that Raul's generosity in including her in his holiday celebration wasn't causing him so much grief. As she sat however, he grinned at her in an attempt to reassure. "Don't worry about it, Becca. I can deal with them," he said softly.

Rebecca nodded and settled into her seat to enjoy the marvelous meal his family had prepared and the conversation and banter between all the adults and the kids. The meal was a long affair, beginning with the first few courses which were served by Raul's sisters.

After the shrimp cocktails and avocado salad were consumed and the plates cleared off, Maria asked for a few minutes so they could finish laying out the buffet in the kitchen.

Rebecca rose, offering her assistance, but again it was refused since she was a guest.

She reluctantly sat down and Raul took hold of her hand, gave it a gentle squeeze. "You know you would insult them if they put you to work," he said, twining his fingers with hers.

Rebecca nodded and took comfort from the solid weight of his hand linked with hers. She told herself it was just a by-product of the whole holiday thing and his

incomparable gift of including her in his family's celebration. That was the reason for wishing they were back
under that door jamb with that sprig of mistletoe over
their heads.

It was the reason, she told herself, that when everyone
in the family dashed out to the kitchen to fill their plates,
she hung back with Raul, letting him draw her close and
into his arms.

She needed no mistletoe to guide her as he wrapped his
arms around her waist. She encircled his shoulders, met
him halfway as he bent his head and took her lips with his.

The taste of her was as sweet as he remembered.
Maybe better, he thought as she answered the demands
of his lips nibbling at hers, drawing a sweetness and sus-
tenance from them that fed his soul. Her presence in his
life was like nothing he had ever experienced before. Although he should have had some small measure of guilt
from taking pleasure in the fact that she was stranded in
New York away from her family, he couldn't summon
even the littlest twinge. He was enjoying her presence
too much. If that was the only gift he got on this holiday,
it would be more than enough.

There was a loud cough and Raul broke away from
her, met his nephew's amused gaze as Rebecca pulled
away from him, a becoming flush on her cheeks.

"I guess I should tell *Abuela* that it was a waste to go
around and buy all that mistletoe. You two don't need it,"
Brendon teased, laying his plate down at the far end of
the table.

Raul stood behind Rebecca and laid a hand on her
shoulder. "They sent you to buy—"

"Yep. Look all around, *tio*. There must be a dozen or
more of those stupid little plants hanging all over," he answered and motioned to the staircase, where sure enough
there was another sprig hung directly above the first step.

Rebecca turned and faced him, but there was no anger
on her face, but rather amusement and understanding.

"They must love you a lot, Raul. Don't be annoyed with them," she urged, laying a hand on his arm and giving their entwined hands a gentle tug. "Come on. Let's go get some food."

Raul nodded and acquiesced. He followed her into his kitchen where the main dishes for the meal had been laid out on the kitchen table. Waiting for Becca to grab a plate, he then grabbed his own and followed her all around as she placed food on both their plates, serving him as they went around. Succulent, slow-roasted pork. Black beans and rice. Both ripe and green plantains. There was still a small spot on their plates as they neared the baked ham and yuca and Rebecca turned and looked at him inquiringly, since only one of the two would fit. "The yuca, *por favor.* I like to leave the ham so *Mami* can make Cuban sandwiches tomorrow."

"Me, too," she confirmed and spooned up some of the boiled yuca with its topping of sauteed onions with the juice of bitter oranges to offset the sweetness of the onions.

With their plates laden with the holiday fixings, they returned to the table, sat and once again enjoyed both the food and the company. When Rebecca was nearly done and wishing she had worn pants with an elastic waistband, she offered her compliments to the chefs. "Please don't tell my *mami* or sisters, but this is the best *Noche Buena* meal I've had."

Her comment brought broad smiles to the faces of all the women. Raul seemed pleased with the way the night was progressing, she thought, noting the contented look on his face. She had to admit she was likewise in a mood she hadn't expected. While this wasn't her family, it was easy to be here with them, enjoying their company. It wasn't home, but it had certainly turned out to be the next best thing.

As Raul and some of the men helped themselves to second helpings from the buffet, she helped out Grace by taking little Peter once more. He was getting antsy next to his mother, interrupting the meal she had barely touched since Deanna had awoken, demanding to be fed.

Peter didn't hesitate to sit with her, plopping himself in her lap as he had done before. Only this time, within a few minutes, he was restless, bouncing his head back against her off and on while shifting in her lap, as if trying to get comfortable. The longer he sat, the more fidgety he grew until finally, Rebecca bent her head close to his little face to ask him what was wrong. It was then she felt the warmth of his little cheek and looking down, saw the flush there.

"He's really warm, Grace," she said, prompting an immediate response from his mother, who came over, put her hand on his forehead and started fussing, the new mother in her going into overdrive.

"Easy, Grace," her sister Erika advised and came over as well, placed a hand on Peter's forehead and confirmed Rebecca's sentiments. "We can give him a little Tylenol, take off that sweater to cool him off."

"I knew he wasn't right this morning," Grace said, her tone one of both concern and self-chastisement. "We were so busy with the holiday—"

"And he's probably just got a little cold. My nephews get them all the time," Rebecca offered and her words and those of Erika's joining in with a similar comment relaxed Grace a little.

Grace walked out of the room with Peter, just as the men were returning with their plates and sat down. Grace's husband was about to go after his wife, but the others assured him that all was under control. He sat back down, but his mind was clearly elsewhere and his second helping of food was barely touched by the time that the remaining kids began to carry on about opening presents.

Maria and Erika shooed all of them upstairs, but Rebecca remained behind and insisted on lending a helping hand with Grace no longer available. The two women hesitated at first, but then relented given all that had to be put away and in the dishwasher. Raul came down a few minutes later and also pitched in.

As he passed by her more than once during the clean-up, he would grin at her and she smiled back, enjoying the simple camaraderie of the moment and the company of his family.

The table was clean and ready for dessert within fifteen minutes. It took only a little longer for all the food in the kitchen to be put away, and the plates and glasses, at least those that would fit, were tucked into the dishwasher.

Rebecca was drying her hands with a towel when Raul came up to her, held out his hand. "Ready for the whole kids-running-wild, wrapping paper–flying–everywhere thing?"

"Ready," she confirmed and slipped her hand into his, liking the comforting weight of his hand in hers.

They allowed his mother and sister to precede them up the stairs and back up to the living room where the kids had rearranged the furniture to face the tree and the mounds of brightly wrapped gifts sitting there. All of the seats were taken with the exception of one wing chair close to the fire. Raul offered it to her, but she declined. "Make yourself comfy. I can—"

"Sit on my lap so I can play Santa?" he whispered into her ear, and a warmth pervaded her that had nothing to do with the fire blazing cheerfully just a few feet away. For a moment she considered saying no, but the word wouldn't come out. Instead she surprised him by nodding her agreement to his proposal.

The grin he gave her was better than any gift sitting under the tree. He sat in the chair and once he was settled, she made herself comfortable on his lap, sitting to one side so he could watch as his nieces and nephews ran around, distributing the gifts under the tree like Santa's elves. On their heads they wore red headbands with brown felt reindeer ears. As they handed out the gifts, there was excited and nervous chatter as people took the gifts, sometimes shook them or checked out the gift tags to see who had given the present.

Piles of boxes were soon building at each person's chair and the kids had set aside areas on the floor for their own gifts.

Rebecca experienced a moment of sadness as she thought of all the gifts she had bought and wrapped, and which sat in bags by her front door, lonely as they waited to be opened. She thought of her own tree and that of her parents', and of all the fun they would also be having by now, opening all the presents without her.

It was if he sensed her pain, for he reached up and rubbed her back in a reassuring gesture. She took comfort from that simple motion and tightened her hold on his hand, somehow wanting to communicate her sentiments. A moment later, Jon came over with a present in his hands, but instead of placing it on Raul's growing pile of gifts, he handed it to her.

Rebecca took the bright green and gold box in her hands. It was long and narrow and sported a large bow of springy curls of green, red and gold ribbons. There was a very simple little gift tag with her name in Raul's messy handwriting. She turned to face him, juggling the box in her hands nervously. "You shouldn't have."

He shrugged, reached up and cradled her cheek. "It's just a little something to thank you for joining me tonight."

"I should be the one thanking you, Raul," she replied, but he shifted his thumb, ran it across her lips, the gesture as intimate as a kiss.

"Open it," Raul said softly, tucking a chestnut lock behind one ear as she glanced down and it obscured her face from him. He didn't want to miss a minute of this woman, especially at a time like this, when all her emotions were visible in her very expressive face. The face of the woman and not the calm, cool and collected lawyer he had squared off against in the last few days.

Rebecca grew suddenly shy, hesitating and continuing

to shift the box from hand to hand, but he reached out and stilled the nervous motion. *"Por favor.* Open it, Becca."

She delayed for a just a moment more, and then she was opening the wrapping with her delicate hands. Hands he had watched for days. Hands whose touch he hungered for at night, when he should have been thinking of other things. Deftly she removed the wrapping and then lifted the lid off the box and her eyes widened in surprise and pleasure.

Rebecca removed the scarf from the box, grasped it in her hands. She examined it and he explained that the one side was silk so it wouldn't chafe her skin like the wool could.

She met his gaze and hers was warm and filled with so much sentiment he had to look away. But she laid a hand on his cheek, applied gentle pressure until he was facing her once more. "This is so sweet, but—"

"You won't have much use for it except in the next day or so, but I figured there's no reason why you should be cold," he said softly.

"I'd like to think I may need it more than just for another day or two. Maybe when I come back to visit . . ." she began but her voice trailed off, as if whatever thought she had was still too fragile and new to be said out loud.

"I'd like to think that as well," he replied and wished for a moment that his family wasn't there, all around them, making noise and keeping an eye on them as they opened their gifts and exchanged exuberant thanks and appreciation for what they had been given.

He realized it was time he got to his presents as well. "Help me," he asked her. She nodded, reached down and picked up his first gift. Together they undid the ribbons and wrapping, the action natural and way too comfortable.

The first box held a new shirt and sweater from his sister Erika and he laid it to the side and together they continued opening the gifts. It was easy to imagine her sharing this same moment with him next year, but unfortunately, it was also painful as he realized that there was little likelihood of that happening.

He told himself to temper those emotions and enjoy the now for that was all that he had. When all the gifts were opened, he hung back with her in the chair, waited until all of his family had torn down the stairs to indulge in dessert.

She remained in his lap, gazing down at him and he didn't hesitate to cup her cheek, draw her down so he could kiss her, wanting her to know just how much this moment meant to him.

His lips were warm and soft. The beard of his goatee a ticklish brush against her lips. She smiled at that, pulled away and met his gaze. "You tickle," she nearly giggled and he grinned, sat up and rubbed his face across her cheek and then down to the side of her neck.

His beard was even more ticklish there, and she scrunched her neck up and chided him. "Stop, we have to get downstairs or—"

"They'll wonder about what we're doing up here?" he questioned and cradled her cheek again, met her lips with his, over and over again, inviting her to deepen the contact.

She opened her mouth and tasted the sweetness of him, better than any dessert that could have been waiting downstairs. Her tongue sampled the velvety wet of his, hungered for more. Breaking apart to draw a breath, she returned her mouth to his, nipping at his full lower lip with her teeth and then plucking at it with her lips, until a persistent call intruded on the moment.

"*Tío. Tío,* we're all waiting for you two for dessert," Brendon called out from the back of the house and then came bounding into the room. He stopped short as Rebecca hastily stood, smoothing her sweater in a nervous gesture.

Raul rose from the chair and placed a hand on her shoulder. "We'll be down in a second, Brendon."

She turned and faced him, smiling. "This was . . . nice."

He grinned, bent and placed one last kiss on her lips, whispering against them, "Very nice. We should do this again."

Reaching up to run her hand through the rumpled waves of his hair, she nodded. "Maybe later."

# Fifteen

The kitchen table was now laden with an assortment of desserts, some Cuban and some Italian, the latter compliments of Grace's husband Bob. Raul's mom had made a thick, rich *flan*, swimming in a dark caramel syrup. Erika had contributed a cheesecake, topped with a guava puree and thin slices of guava shells. Alicia had brought an assortment of pastries—guava *pastelitos, panetelas borachas* and *josefinas*—from Union City. The *panetelas* were soaked with a rum and sugar mixture and really gooey. The *josefinas,* with their bright pink stripes were right next to the napoleons that Bob had brought. The remainder of the table was piled with assorted Italian pastries—cannolis, cream puffs and pignoli cookies. The Tollhouse cookies Grace had made had brightly colored M&Ms peaking out of the surface of them.

Rebecca helped herself to small helpings of the flan, cheesecake and split a cannoli with Raul. As she ate, she thought about how similar the night had been to her Miami *Noche Buena.* Even down to the dessert table with its mix of cultures indicative of the mix that was happening in her generation. Two of her siblings had married non-Latinos as well and it wasn't uncommon for their *Noche Buena* table to hold contributions from her sister's husband, also Italian, and her brother's wife, a long time Florida Conch from the Keys who made an awesome Key Lime pie.

The memories of her own holiday fresh in her mind, she excused herself from the table and asked Raul if she could borrow his phone to call home. He rose, led her to a study in the back of the house where she could have some privacy.

The study was gorgeous, a large room lined with mahogany shelves packed with an assortment of books, some surprising, like the well-worn science fiction books from one of her favorite authors. She roamed the room as she dialed and waited for someone to pick up at home and when her mother finally answered, the sounds of music and chatter in the background were loud. Their *Noche Buena* celebration was still going strong. She glanced at her watch. There was still another hour until the crowd would disperse and head to midnight Mass.

She and her mother spoke for a few minutes, her mother filling her in on who was at the house and how all had missed her presence. "I miss you too, *Mami*. I'll be home before you know it," she reassured and strolled to his desk, where she sat down and glimpsed the photos of his family across the far edge. Clearly he was a man to whom family was important, which raised him a notch in her estimation.

"*Hija,* give this man—"

"Raul," she quickly jumped in.

There was a moment of silence on her mother's part and Rebecca wondered if she had given away anything by just saying his name. "Please thank Raul and his family for including you," her mother finally said.

"*Sí, Mami.* I'll be sure to thank him. Give *Papi* my love and everyone else too."

Instead of returning downstairs to the dining room, Rebecca lingered in his chair. There was a stronger connection to him here, in a room that was so obviously his and filled with things important to him. Besides the variety of books on his shelves and the photos, there were some very good original paintings in an Impressionist style, their blurry colors and images even brighter against the dark colors of the mahogany. Interspersed on the shelves were assorted pieces of crystal and pottery of all kinds. An eclectic mix, very much like the man she had come to know in so brief a time. There was a knock at the door of the study and she called, "Come in."

Raul paused by the entrance where above his head hung another beribboned sprig of mistletoe. She couldn't resist the temptation and walked over to him, stood right next to him and pointed up.

Raul smiled and shrugged. "Who am I to buck tradition?"

He bent, wrapped an arm around her waist and hauled her close, wanting so much more than just the taste of her lips. But he knew he would have to settle for that for now, although he wasn't quite sure he could call the way she was kissing him "settling."

She was eagerly meeting his lips, kissing him back, nibbling and drawing his lower lip into her mouth. As he tugged at her lower lip with his teeth, she moaned deep in the back of her throat, wrapped her arms tighter around him. But there was no way this could go further, not with the heavy trudge of steps from downstairs signalling the imminent arrival of his family.

He pulled away from her, dragged a hand through his hair from the frustration. "I'm sorry, Becca, but it's getting late. I was going to take you back to your hotel, unless of course you want to go to midnight Mass with me."

She hesitated for only a moment, but even that small second was an eternity for him. When she answered "Yes," something inside of him broke free, realizing that their time together hadn't ended just yet.

Raul took hold of her hand, guided her back into the living room where his family had once again assembled and was now busy packing up their gifts and things into bags, preparing to head out. She realized as they talked that they were all heading to their homes instead of to Mass because of the snow. They would give it a shot in the morning, hoping the roads would be better then.

"Mami," Raul said, facing his mother. "Can I trust you

to bank the fire and lock up so Becca and I can head out?"

"*Como no, hijo.* We'll make sure everything is just fine. Don't worry and don't rush back," she replied and Raul knew just where she was going with her comment. He chose to ignore it. "*Gracias, Mami.* I'll see you all tomorrow night," he replied and led Rebecca around as she said goodbye to all, taking extra time to hold and hug a drowsy Peter.

Rebecca thought the toddler was doing better, although there was still a slight flush on his cheeks.

When all the good-byes and thank-yous had been given, Raul handed her scarf and coat to her and helped her slip both of them on. The silk of the scarf was smooth and cold at first, but as Raul tucked it in around her neck, it soon began to warm her.

He grabbed hold of her gloved hand, led her from the house and outside, back out into the cold and snow. Only this time she was warm inside from the food and the company, and the man strolling beside her. Many of the sidewalks had been cleared by now, and so they were able to walk, huddled together, talking softly about the night they had just shared and how it compared to one of Becca's Miami holidays.

In no time they had traversed a number of avenues and were up on Fifth, a little over a dozen blocks from St. Patrick's Cathedral. They walked along the East side of the avenue, Central Park across the street from them. Snow hung on the bare branches of the trees and the top of the low stone wall surrounding the park was frosted with snow and ice.

As they walked along, there was still activity on the streets. People milled along the edge of the park and as they neared Grand Army Plaza and the Plaza Hotel, there was even more action. Pedestrians hung out around the gaily decorated fountain in front of the hotel. Lights twinkled everywhere, strung along with garland on the front of the hotel and along all the stores ahead of them.

On their side of the street, people lingered in front of the FAO Schwartz windows with their displays of the latest toys and dolls. Across the way there was a smaller crowd by Bergdorf Goodman and its windows.

Rebecca marvelled at the stores with their windows all embellished for the holidays and the strange blend of shops. Tiffany's and a little further down, the Disney and Warner Bros. stores, side by side on the busy avenue. Designers like Ferragamo and Gucci mixed in with The Gap and an NBA store. A mix that could only happen in New York she thought, considering how much it was like the fusion of people walking along beside them on the street. Younger couples in jeans and casual dress, like her and Raul, blended with women in fur coats dripping jewelry while being escorted by men in tuxes. White, black, Asian and all colors in between. The huge melting pot America was all about, she considered.

Time seemed to be running in slow motion as they walked along, drawn out in a deliciously languid pace. Despite the cold and the snow, she was having a really good time tucked close to his side, enjoying the uncommon sights and listening as he explained about how he and his family had come to live in Manhattan after growing up in Union City, New Jersey.

It was the excitement and activity, not to mention being closer to work, that had prompted him to leave the predominantly Cuban ethnic enclave he had grown up in for the bright lights of the city. For the first time, strolling along beside him and tapping into the excitement in the air, she could understand the attraction of Manhattan.

As they approached the cathedral, the traffic along the street grew heavier and he explained that it was because Rockefeller Center, with its world famous tree, was across the way. From the steps of the huge cathedral, part of the tree was visible as well as the promenade that led to it, packed with people. The lights on the tree were bright, but not as bright as the snowy night and the buildings surrounding it.

Raul stopped as Rebecca paused on the steps and looked across the avenue. He tracked her gaze and realized she was looking at the tree. "Maybe you and I can get together tomorrow so I can show you the tree, the rest of the store windows, New York Christmas kinds of things. What do you think?"

She glanced up at him and smiled, her eyes twinkling and filled with delight, her cheeks flushed a rosy pink color from the cold of the night. "I think that sounds great."

He nodded, tightened his hold on her hand and led her up the steps of the cathedral. She paused to appreciate the sheer size of the immense Gothic structure with its large imposing spires and enormous colorful rose window facing Fifth Avenue.

Inside, there was a crowd of people milling around. Raul removed his hat and gloves and stuffed them into his pocket. When he turned to look at Rebecca, she had removed her gloves as well and was unwrapping the scarf he had given her from around her neck. She placed her hand in his once more, and together they walked deeper into the cathedral, pausing to dip their fingers in the holy water and bless themselves with the sign of the cross as they entered.

Within the enormous space of the cathedral, a huge group of people, at least several hundred if not more, waited for the commencement of the midnight Mass. The cathedral had been decorated for the Christmas holiday, and sprigs of pine and bright ribbons adorned the sides of the pews and hung from the lanterns illuminating the church.

Raul leaned close to her and whispered softly in her ear. "Let's get some seats and after I'll take you around and show you the various parts of the cathedral."

Rebecca glanced around. The pews were quickly filling up. She nodded, followed him as he walked a few feet to the first bench with some space at the end closest to the center aisle. He held out his hand, motioning for her to enter. She stepped in, right next to an elderly lady sitting beside a young couple holding a baby. As it was out on the streets, inside the cathedral there was a wide diversity of people, all gathered to celebrate.

It was warmer within the confines of the church, and she undid the buttons on her coat, let it hang free. Raul unzipped his parka, removed his scarf and stuffed it into one of his pockets. Once he was done, he reached for her hand again and she slipped it into his, twined their fingers together, experiencing a wondrous sense of comfort and peacefulness so at odds with the hustle and bustle of the city outside the structure.

Part of it was him and the connection they had shared from the very beginning. Another part of it was the sense of community and spirituality from being a part of the vast crowd gathered together to commemorate what surely was the happiest of events in their religion—the birth of their Savior. Rebecca wasn't a devout Catholic, having too many qualms about the Church's stand on certain issues, but despite that, it was times like this that kept her faith alive, for in this union of the people there was something special that couldn't be explained by any science or logic. Something that fed her soul and made her acknowledge that there was something bigger than man. Something she had to just trust and believe. Like love, she thought, shooting a quick glance at the man sitting beside her calmly, sharing this bit of his community with her. Sharing so much of himself with her over the last few days.

It wasn't long before there was a change in the crowd, and soon the altar boys and priests were entering to begin the service, followed by bishops and an archbishop. Raul leaned close to her and explained that this would be the first Christmas mass this archbishop would celebrate in the cathedral since the death of New York City's religious leader the year before.

As Mass commenced, years of training took over and she and Raul answered the various calls by those on the altar. In deference to the holiday, the readings and homily stressed the peace and love of the season, and the happiness of new beginnings and births. The songs of the choir echoed those sentiments. Rebecca's spirits were uplifted by the very positive messages and the energy of the crowd responding to that inspiration.

When the Mass was over, the organist continued to softly play, filling the church with music. As promised, Raul led her to the various sections of the church to see the statues of the saints and the marvelous stained glass windows. It was amazing to traverse a dozen different side chapels and the marble Lady Chapel, set off behind the main altar.

At one statue, Rebecca paused, lit candles for her grandparents who had passed away years earlier, and said a short prayer for their souls.

Raul stood by patiently and when she was done, led her back to the front of the church where they once again bundled up and headed out into the cold of the night. As before, he tucked her close to his side. They had gone only a block when he asked, "Would you like to take the subway back, or are you up for the walk?"

If someone had asked her a month ago if she could possibly take any pleasure from trudging through a foot of snow in freezing weather, she would have asked them if they thought she was certifiably insane. Now she knew she was as she said, "I don't mind the walk, that is unless you want to—"

"No, I'd rather be able to spend the time with you," he answered, and she snuggled up against his side and together they continued down Fifth Avenue, pausing occasionally at a window or two, finally making it to 42nd Street. They turned off Fifth and walked the last few blocks eastbound toward the hotel. At a twenty-four hour deli, they stopped for some hot chocolate, continued walking as they sipped the chocolate from the thick paper cups.

Rebecca still hadn't finished her drink when Raul walked her to her door, nor had he. "Care to come in and maybe add a nightcap to what's left of that hot chocolate?"

"I'm not a nightcap kind of guy, actually. But I would like to get warmed up."

She met his gaze and hoped that she wasn't misreading the signal in his eyes. She could think of a number of ways to get warmed up. "Would you like to come in then, and . . . talk. Maybe—"

"Get to know one another better?" he jumped in and leaned close to her, nuzzling his cold nose against the side of her neck.

She laughed, scrunched up her neck in response to the abrupt chill of his skin and pushed him away. "Come in, Raul. Take your coat off, we'll warm up that nose—

"Just my nose?" he teased, rubbing the cold side of his face against hers.

Rebecca chuckled and pulled away from him. "Just shut up and come in before I change my mind," she said, opening the door of her room and grabbing hold of the front of his parka to playfully drag him in.

# Sixteen

She stepped into her room, placed her half-finished cup of hot chocolate on a small table by the door and removed her coat. She gestured for him to make himself at home. He smiled and did as she said, rid himself of his parka over a chair and sat on the couch.

She tossed her coat on a chair, removed her gloves and scarf, placing them on top of the coat. Grabbing her cup, she walked over to the sofa and sat opposite Raul, removed her shoes.

Her toes were cold, some numb even despite the well-insulated boots she had brought with her. She bent and rubbed them. Noticing her obvious discomfort he said, "Put them up here," and patted his thighs.

She raised one eyebrow and gave him a questioning glance. "Part of getting warm?"

He grinned, and the infectious sexiness of it did indeed help her heat up a little. She swung her legs up and placed her heels on the hard muscles of this thighs. He set his own cup of chocolate to the side, gripped a foot with both hands and massaged slowly. His thumbs pressed into her instep and her skin warmed as circulation returned. With it came an achiness from all the walking they had done during the late afternoon and night.

Rebecca moaned and closed her eyes. "That feels good," she said and he grunted a "uh-huh," and kept up the massage, moving to her other foot until it too was relaxed and warmer with the needle-like return of blood circulation.

The soothing sensation at her feet moved upward as he worked his way to her calves, again pressing his thumbs and fingers into her cold, achy muscles. Her dress slacks had done little to protect her from the chill of a New York winter day. As he hit one spot that was particularly tender from all the walking they had done, she uttered an "Ouch."

He glanced up, his gaze hooded beneath his thick eyelashes. "Sore?" he questioned, and moved on the couch until her knees were now covering his thighs. It would take only another small move for her to be in his lap. And now, unlike before in the study of his house, there was nothing to stop them. No one to act as a buffer against his very potent sexuality and her equally powerful response.

It frightened her, since no man had ever moved her the way he did. And she had no time to think about why she felt that way and what to do about it. She only had this night and maybe another day or two in his company before she returned to Miami.

So much had happened in so little time. So many surprises and gifts, like those waiting under the tree on Christmas morning. It was the ones you weren't expecting, the ones that didn't even cost a cent, that gave you the most pleasure.

Like the surprising emotions she was having for him and the unexpected gift of her attraction. And as she met his gaze, the pleasure of noting the way he cared for her.

Rebecca decided she was going to explore this gift, accept it in the spirit of the season and have faith in the miracle of love. She lifted her arm and pointed to the side of her neck and shoulder. "Sore up here as well."

He arched his eyebrows and gave her a knowing smile. *"De verdad?* Then, why don't you come here?" he replied and patted his thigh.

Rebecca pushed off the arm of the sofa, swung her legs so she straddled his lap, facing him. She laid her hands on his shoulders to steady herself. She was staring straight into his face. "Is this all right?" she asked, and suddenly brazen, she bent her head, nuzzled the side of his face with hers and dug her hands into his wind-tousled hair.

"Mmm," he replied, and brought his large hands to her waist, slipping them beneath the hem of the sweater she wore until his fingers were against her skin. "This is definitely all right. Maybe even good."

She chuckled against the side of his face, brought her hands around to cradle it. "Only good? You know, Counselor, I never settle for being only good . . . at anything."

Pulling away from him, she met his gaze and he reached up with one hand, cupped her cheek. His thumb caressed the line of her jaw, then trailed upward to trace the edge of her lips. "Me neither, *querida,* but . . . I normally don't just jump into things either."

Rebecca mimicked his actions, bringing her thumb up to his lips, where he gave it a gentle nip with his teeth, forcing a smile to her lips. "You and I . . . this is difficult for a whole bunch of reasons. We're done with our business, but we may be adversaries again in the future. We're 1500 miles apart normally. We're—"

"Really attracted to one another," he jumped in and silenced her by gently placing his fingers across her lips. "We could logic ourselves out of this, *sabes?*"

She whispered, *"Sí,"* against his fingers. "We could, Raul, but—"

"I don't want to," he jumped in. He brushed some stray tresses off her face. "I've never had these feelings before, Becca. This week, since the day you walked into my office, has been special. And today with my family. Tonight in church and after . . . nothing has ever felt this right. This . . ." His voice trailed off, and she didn't need him to continue.

"This is a time of loving and giving," she said to him softly, and bent to kiss the edge of his lips, little kisses that were tender and enticing. "Maybe that's part of the problem," she said, wanting him to be fully committed to where they were going. "Maybe we're too caught up in all the seasonal cheer."

He chuckled against her lips, moved his hand up beneath her sweater, bracing her back as she continued dropping little kisses all across his lips and face and he returned them. *"Querida,* this is not about Christmas cheer, and as for loving and giving . . ."

Raul pulled away from her, moved his hands to cup her shoulders. "Giving is good, Becca. That is, if you're up to the receiving?"

He half-glanced at her and Rebecca smiled down at him. He'd never seen a more brilliant smile nor a more welcoming one. He moved his hands to her back, urged her as close as their position would allow, which was about as close as two people could get. Her thighs cradled his hips as he leaned into her and nuzzled the collar away from her neck. He opened his mouth on her skin, tasting the sweetness of it. Smelling the unique scent of her that he knew he would remember long after she was gone.

The thought made his heart contract, but he ignored it, told himself to accept what they had been given for the moment. After all, it was more than some people ever experienced. He brought his mouth up, bit her lower lip until she opened to him. As he tasted her, revelled in the way her tongue answered his, he moved his hands down and slipped them back beneath the edge of her sweater, needing the contact with her skin.

Rebecca glided her tongue against his, then along the harder edge of his lips, delighting in the flavor of him and of the desire growing in her. His hands against the small of her back were warm, moving upwards and taking the edge of her sweater with them until he finally pulled it up and over her head.

Beneath the sweater she wore a pale peach camisole and nothing else, which delighted him. He pulled away, cupped her breast and passed his thumb over her nipple. It contracted into a hard nub beneath the fabric. Her breath caught in her throat as he continued moving his thumb against it and brought his other hand up to do the same to her other breast.

He glanced up at her. "Do you like that?" he asked. She nodded.

Raul moved one hand down to the small of her back, urging her upward. He tugged at her breast with his thumb and forefinger. Her breath caught audibly which confirmed to him just how much she liked it. He looked up as he continued playing with her breast and her dark brown eyes grew even darker, widened with her desire. He needed her so much, but he also wanted to savor this for as long as he could. Wanted to relish her myriad responses. He reached for the small strap of her camisole, slowly eased it off and the fabric gaped a little against her skin, exposing the upper swell of her breasts.

He brought his lips to the newly exposed flesh, opened his mouth on her, rubbing his lips across her skin while with his hand he continued to pull at the nub of her breast. She moaned, and it reached inside of him, made his already hard arousal tighten. "Tell me what you want, Becca. Tell me what gift I can give you next," he tried to tease, but his voice was low and way too serious, reflecting his need.

Rebecca cradled his head to her, bent and dropped a kiss near his temple as she whispered, "Unwrap me, Raul. A little at a time. Find out what's hidden underneath," she answered brazenly.

He took her at her word, slowly easing off the camisole to expose her to him. He pulled back, braced his hands on her ribs as he took his time looking at her. In response, her breasts tightened even further, tingled with the need to have his hands and mouth on her.

"Do you like my gift?"

"I definitely have no thoughts of asking for a refund or exchange," he confirmed and met her gaze. "But now that I've received, I think it's time for me to do some more giving. Don't you think?" he asked, but didn't wait for her answer to cup her nipples, rotate them between his thumbs and forefingers. "Raul," she said softly, cupped the back of his head and urged him to her.

Raul closed his lips around her nipple and he had never in his life had a sweeter treat. He suckled her, drawing the hard tip against the edge of his lips, rolling his tongue around it and shivering. She whimpered, then released a husky little moan. He switched to her other breast while sampling the moistness he had left behind with his hand, pulling and pinching while he teethed and bit her nipple.

Her body was trembling against his lips, and her hips bumped against his arousal. He sensed she was near the peak from just this and he wanted to take her over that edge.

He rose with her and she wrapped her legs around his hips, clung to him tightly as he walked to her bed. Once there, he backed her onto the edge of the mattress and lowered her against the sheets. He pulled away from her, gazed down to confirm that she wanted more.

Rebecca stared up at him and couldn't deny the question in his eyes. She sat up and reached for his sweater, needing more of him. Wanting his skin pressed against hers. She had the sweater about half way up and Raul's hands were suddenly there, helping her pull the sweater off and toss it to the side.

He had a beautiful body, lean and lightly muscled, with no hair to mar the deep creamy color of his skin. She tentatively laid her hands on his waist and his skin was hot and smooth against her palms. Bending forward, she buried her head against the skin of his abdomen and teasingly bit a spot just above his navel.

He reached down to pull her into his arms. Her breasts were flattened against his chest and he slipped his arms beneath her buttocks, urging her even closer.

"This is nice. Very nice," he said and Rebecca nodded.

"Very," she acknowledged and met his lips with her own as he lay with her on the bed. Over and over she kissed him, cradling his head in her hands, her tongue joining with his. When he broke away from her, they were both breathless and trembling and she knew there was no stopping now. She wanted him too badly.

Slipping away from him, she removed his pants and briefs and then quickly divested herself of her remaining clothing. She sat on the bed, reclining against the pillows and held her hand out to him in invitation.

"Are you . . . do you have protection, Becca?" he questioned as he crawled up on the bed toward her and lay along the length of her.

She reached over, yanked open the drawer and pulled out the small box with the condoms, handed it to him.

Raul glanced at the wrapping and removed the box from it, chuckling as he did so. "A gift?" he asked and glanced up at her as he tore one envelope from the strip and opened it, removing the condom.

Rebecca smiled and laughed, reached out and took the condom from him. "Sheila and Andrew are very efficient helpers. They wanted to make sure I would be . . . prepared was the way I think she put it."

"Prepared, huh?" he said and then sucked in a breath as she placed her hand over him and slowly, teasingly unrolled the protection into place. "*Dios,* but remind me to lure them away from RLL would you?"

She laughed again, but that merriment soon turned to a gasp as he quickly rolled her over and buried himself in her, his erection creating a deep, profound pressure.

He didn't move at all, just stayed inside her, his own breathing held for a long time until it finally exploded from his chest with a deep groan. "This is . . . so right, Becca."

"*Sí,* it is, *mi amor,*" she responded, reached up and ran her hand through the strands of his longish hair. Grasping the back of his neck, she urged him down to meet her lips. The kiss they exchanged had none of their earlier haste. It was long, slow and so tender that she wished it would never end.

But it did, and they barely separated, pulled in deep lungfuls of air and gazed at one another. He placed his arms on either side of her head, brushed his hands along the edges of her temple as he finally shifted, drawing out slowly and then just as languidly penetrating her once more. He bent his head again, lapped at her lips with his tongue and she opened her mouth, gently nipped his lips, drawing them into her mouth, sucking at them as he inexorably increased the rhythm of his thrusts, until she could no longer deny the waves of desire bathing her body. She whimpered against his mouth, clutched his shoulders with her hands and her nails bit as her desire grew in intensity.

"Raul," she gasped and he dropped a kiss on her lips and lowered his head, using his mouth on her nipples, alternating between each one and reaching down with his arms to urge her knees up against his hips, increasing his penetration to the point that she could no longer hold on.

She arched her head back and her cry of completion nearly sent Raul over his own edge, but he had waited too long to share this kind of need with any woman. He wasn't going to rush it now that it was in his grasp.

He braced one hand on the bed beside her waist, slipped another beneath the small of her back and she arched it in response. A flush worked over her breasts and her soft, mewling cries drove him on as he prolonged her orgasm with the movement of his hips.

Gritting his teeth, he battled against the heat of her. Against the wet of her that made him slide in and out so easily, dampened the root of him as he drove deep and she cried out her pleasure once more.

Inside her, the tightening around him increased, pulled at him and he could no longer ignore it. The force of his release rushed over his body as he came, spilling himself against the barrier of the condom, his own shout of pleasure hoarse in the quiet of the early morning hour.

She wrapped her legs around him then, urged him down next to her, running her hands along his back, answering him with the lingering vestiges of lust which slowly turned into the slow, tender kisses of love and contentment.

Rebecca buried her head against his chest, her arms draped across him lazily, his body buried deep inside, still hard for now. He moved his hands over her back, gently and leisurely, helping bring them back down to earth from the heights they had climbed together.

When he finally slipped out of her, he excused himself, ran to the bathroom and then quickly returned to huddle next to her, sharing the warmth of his body until it got too cool to remain on top of the sheets any longer.

There was no question in her mind that he would stay for the remainder of this holiday night. No question that he would be with her in the morning and they would spend part of the day together.

The only question she had as she drifted to sleep in his arms was whether she would be able to return to Miami with her heart intact, for there was no doubt in her mind that he now owned a piece of it. One she didn't think she could ever get back.

# Seventeen

He prolonged his awakening, enjoying the way her body was spooned against him, their limbs entwined carelessly as if they had spent many a night together. The naturalness of it surprised him. He'd never experienced it before. His morning erection was tucked cozily against the small of her back.

There was a soft little snore and he smiled at that, for it gave him something else to remember about her. To store away for the future in case . . . he drove that painful thought away.

It was Christmas morning, a time for wonder and cheer. He wanted to treasure it and her for as long as he could. In another day or so, she'd likely be gone.

Rebecca shifted against him. She rolled until she was lying on her back, smiling up at him sleepily, his hand splayed across her flat belly. *"Feliz Navidad,"* she said, reached up and brushed a piece of errant hair on the side of his head.

He smiled at her, bent and dropped a quick kiss on her lips before bracing one elbow on the bed, resting his head there. *"Feliz Navidad,* Becca. I hope this is a good Christmas for you even though you're far from home."

"Mmm," she answered, thinking it was her best Christmas morning ever and that she was anything but lonesome for her family and Miami.

He glanced down at her, his gaze determined and inquisitive. "Do you regret—"

"It's certainly not what I imagined I'd be doing. You, me, a white Christmas and the whole mistletoe in Manhattan thing," she answered, but quickly added, "But I don't regret it for a second, Raul. This has been . . . This *is* very special to me."

He rubbed the palm of his hand across her belly, the movement surprisingly one of comfort and not sensuality. "I feel . . . I feel like I'm a kid again and just woke up to the best possible gift Santa could ever have brought. One which I didn't ask for and could never have expected."

Rebecca smiled, totally in synch with him. "Those are usually the best kinds of gifts. I never expected this either, but it's great. Wonderful. Scary," she admitted and turned onto her side to face him and encountered . . .

She glanced down as his hardness pressed against the soft skin of her belly and then looked up at him. His eyes were dark, blazing with heat, urging her on. She laid her hand on him, running her palm over the tip of him, over his head until he groaned and closed his eyes. "This is nice," she said, shifted her hand to encircle him and slowly stroked him.

He brought his hand to her breast and cupped it. Ran his thumb lazily across the hardening nub of her nipple. "Very nice," he confirmed as he bent his head and took her into his mouth.

Her soft, little cry drove him on and they made love, wishing that the morning would never end.


They roused about an hour later, the winter sun weakly throwing its light against their bodies as they cuddled on the bed, talking.

"You have tan lines. From a bikini," he said, tracing the edges of those lines with an index finger.

"A little bikini," she confessed naughtily.

He chuckled. "What else should I know about you?"

Rebecca shrugged. If he was in Miami, they'd date

and he'd find those things out for himself. But he wasn't in Miami and it saddened her to think how unlikely it was that he'd spend enough time there to find them out. "I work at RLL and rumor has it they may make me a partner soon."

"They'd be fools if they didn't make you an offer. Enough about careers. What kind of car do you drive?" he questioned.

She smiled as she thought of her car, a recent extravagance to which she'd treated herself. "A brand new, Sebring Limited convertible. Garnet with a tan top and interiors."

"Not predictable. I like that," he said and urged her on. "Where do you live?"

"South Pointe. Just blocks from South Beach in a large condo complex," she replied and turned in his arms. "Will you come and visit? Stay with me?"

He smiled at that and it reassured her. "When do you want me?"

"All the time," she teased and he embraced her, rocked her in his arms playfully.

"Truthfully," Raul pressed, his tone determined, but she didn't want to do serious at the moment.

"Truthfully all the time, Raul. But about visiting me— as soon as possible. I go back to Miami the day after tomorrow. How about the next day? I have the whole week off for vacation." She laid her hand on his chest, stroked the muscles there as she waited for his answer.

"I think I'd like nothing better than to spend New Year's in Miami, but what about your family? Wouldn't they maybe wonder if this wasn't something serious—"

"Is it?" she questioned, looking up at him and snaring his gaze. He smiled tenderly and cupped her cheek. "I'm supposed to go to my mother's later. The rest of the family will be there, having Cuban sandwiches and the rest of the leftovers. I'd like you to go."

"I guess it's serious, huh?" she baited him.

"Definitely serious. So what do you say? We get ready and see the sights, head to *Mami's*. Are you game?" he asked, rolling over onto her and friskily pinning her to the bed.

"Definitely," was her quick reply before she turned her mind to other, more pressing matters.


They showered together, dressed. Rebecca lent Raul a clean T-shirt that was oversized on her, but fit him just right. After their sightseeing, he'd drop by his house for a change of clothes before heading to his mother's.

Outside the hotel, the morning was crisp and clear with the temperature hovering just above freezing. On the main thoroughfares, the snow had been cleared enough for traffic to finally move, although traffic was still light, probably due to the holiday. Despite that, the edges of snow along the roads were blackened, dirtied by the grime tossed up by the cars with their passing. Along the tops of the piles, the snow had partially melted, refrozen into a hard crust that glistened with the sun's rays.

It was beautiful, she thought, as she strolled along beside him, tucked into his side. They had walked up 42nd Street, crossing Fifth Avenue so that they could detour through Bryant Park. At one time it had been called Needle Park and had been a place to be avoided due to the drug dealers and prostitutes, he said. Now the criminals had been driven out and the park restored to its original state.

Raul explained how in the spring and summer, beautiful flowers flourished in the borders along the edges of the main lawn. People would pause to catch the rays or watch a movie during a yearly film festival and other events. Today, those bushes and beds were packed with snow. The main lawn boasted a number of sculptures of animals, made of pine branches and boughs, surrounded by lights for the holidays.

They continued downward to Herald Square and Macy's, where Rebecca had her first glimpse of the store's Christmas windows. The theme this year was Dr. Seuss's *The Grinch Who Stole Christmas* and the windows were adorned with various scenes depicting merchandise in the store, the Grinch and the Whos from Whoville. Along the Broadway side, it was dioramas of the various Suess characters, depicting the parts in the story where the Grinch whisked away all the holiday gifts from Whoville and after, when he finally found his heart and returned them.

She smiled at the bright colors of the scenes and the faces of the kids and adults who had braved the weather to view them.

After watching for a while, he led her back down 34th Street to Fifth Avenue, where they backtracked uptown so that they could pass by the Lord & Taylor windows. The theme there was decidedly different, more staid in keeping with the image of that store. Starting on one corner, the windows had animated scenes depicting Dickens' *A Christmas Carol*. A larger crowd had gathered and they got on line to view the displays and listen to the music and story pumped out of speakers mounted beneath the green awnings of the store.

The scenes where whimsical, with many little hidden secrets happening behind the figurines portraying various scenes with Tiny Tim, Scrooge and the Ghosts with their messages. A little mouse ran around in a circle, chased by a cat in one. Carolers, rocking back and forth, sang in another. She delighted at each window, searching for the little treasures until finally, regretfully, they had reached the last display.

He stopped, turned to face her and asked, "Enjoying it?"

She gave him a broad smile and relished the answering grin on his face. "Very much."

"Up for more?"

"Definitely," she answered. They took off once more,

staying on Fifth. He paused at one building, stopping to point out a large memorial in the side of the building, almost like a doorway. The bronze plaque, nearly eight feet high and three feet wide, proclaimed that for over seventy years this had once been the home of John D. Wendel, Esquire and his family. "One of New York's eccentricities and reminders of what life used to be like," he said, motioning all around him to the stores and businesses that ran the length of the avenue which had at one time been the tony address for the city's rich and well-connected inhabitants.

Rebecca looked around, tried to picture it as a quaint, Victorian kind of town like the one the gentleman and his family had once resided in. It was difficult to imagine, for in her mind, New York City had always been a large, bustling kind of place, almost as if it and its skyscrapers had been born full grown. She took hold of his hand, gave it a tug. They crossed the street to stand in front of the main library.

There were small gardens in front of each wing, and in the center, a long set of stone stairs bracketed on either side by the famous lions. Each lion sported a large wreath as its holiday motif.

Raul held his hands out, pointing to each immense reclining lion. "Patience and Fortitude are their names I'm told. Unfortunately, the library is closed today, but maybe tomorrow we can get in," he explained and she smiled at the thought of spending another day with him.

"I'd like that. I like books," she told him.

He replied, "I'll keep that in mind. Books are a definite—"

"Turn on. I love to read." Everything and anything, she thought, but especially romances. She wondered what he would think of her reading choices, but decided that was something to be left for another day of discovery.

"I like that as well. Maybe tonight you and I can cuddle by the fire and read," he said, but by the teasing quality in his voice, she doubted reading was the number one activity on his mind.

"Definitely doable," she confirmed and once more they resumed their walk, until Raul stopped at a sidewalk stand, one of the few out on the holiday. The small, metal wagon boasted an assortment of sodas on display, a large grate over a small charcoal fire on which a few large pretzels sat and a number of chestnuts. "Hungry?" he asked, but he was already reaching for money from his jeans pocket and pointing at the chestnuts.

"A pretzel would be good," she answered and he added that to their purchase. The wizened, older lady handed him the pretzel with a napkin wrapped around it and a small bag holding the chestnuts she had plucked from the grate.

Raul handed Becca the pretzel. She pulled off a piece, offered it to him and he reciprocated, cracking the shell of the chestnut while juggling the bag in his hands. Steam erupted from the shell as he split it in two. He pulled the creamy meat of the chestnut from it and held it out to her. She took the morsel from his fingers, blew on it to cool it off before popping it into her mouth. "Good," she said, the flavor reminding her of the *castañas* her grandmother roasted for the holidays.

"Mmm," was all he replied as he munched the piece of salty pretzel she had given him. They walked side by side down the avenue. Ahead of her were the spires of Saint Patrick's. As they neared the crowd grew heavier, so Raul discarded his empty bag of shells in a garbage can at the corner, drew her close.

She went without hesitation, liking the way she fit just right beneath his arm. She walked beside him, their legs occasionally brushing, huddling tighter together as they moved through the crowd. They paused in front of the large bronze statue of Atlas holding up the world, enjoying the simplicity of its lines in contrast to the ornateness of the Gothic nature of St. Pat's across the way.

Afterward, they slipped back into the promenade leading to the heart of Rockefeller Plaza. Small, exclusive stores lined either side of the mall. Down the center ran a long garden. Angels, horns silently trumpeting the season, wore coats of twinkling white lights. At the end of the mall, a throng of people had gathered. They slowly worked their way to the edge as people slowly shifted out of the way to allow for others to stop and enjoy the view.

Rebecca leaned on the brass railing. The skaters on the rink below crowded onto the small piece of ice. There were people of all ages together on the rink. Some barely doing more than an awkward walk-shuffle. Others able to execute more complex turns and even an occasional spin when the space allowed. One skater took a tumble, laughing as he landed on his butt and continued sliding on the slippery ice until a partner came to help him up.

At the side of the rink, other skaters prepared to swirl around on the ice beneath the gleaming golden statue and the enormous Christmas tree. "Who's the statue of?" she asked.

"Prometheus bringing fire to the humans. He might have pissed off the Gods, but he's right at home here," he said with a chuckle.

And he was clearly in a place of honor, Rebecca thought, the sun beaming off him as he loomed above the rink and in the center of it all, proclaiming the victory of the humans over those mercurial gods who would keep them down.

After a few more minutes, he took her hand, led her to side of the Plaza and up a block where they paused to peer in through the windows of the set for NBC's *Today* show. The set was empty for the show had aired hours earlier.

Leaving the studios, they walked to the huge tree. Rebecca paused beneath its wide, spreading branches and looked up at the slightly dizzying height of the tree. Hundreds of lights were strung along its branches and burned even in the daylight.

Raul stood by, enjoying the sight of her face reflecting her contentment. He glanced at his watch. It was well past noon, because they had lingered in bed that morning. The snack of the chestnuts and pretzels had not been much of a breakfast, and his stomach was reminding him that he needed something a little more substantial to keep him until they headed to his mother's later that day. "Hungry?"

She shrugged and looked away from the tree. "A little, but I can wait until later."

"I can't," he admitted and his stomach rumbled, which prompted her to reach out, rub her hand across the mid-section of his parka as if to stop the sound.

"Where do you want to go?" she asked and he grabbed her hand and led her to 51st Street where he flagged a cab. He popped open the door as the cab stopped, and she jumped in with him right behind her. He said to the cabbie, "The Plaza."

The man nodded, pushed the button on the meter and took off. It was a short trip, only about eight blocks or so. He deposited them on the corner of 57th, right by the hotel and Grand Army Plaza.

Raul stepped out onto the curb and assisted her from the cab. She slipped her hand into his and they walked up the short flight of stairs to the ornate doors of the hotel. They pushed through the revolving doors and entered.

The interior of the hotel was an amazing representation of Victorian splendor. Marble floors glinted with the warm glow cast by the many crystal chandeliers overhead. The walls and moldings were gilded with gold paint, opulent and ostentatious.

Before them in the middle of the space was the Palm Court, its edges defined by low planters sporting flowers in keeping with the season and inside the space, low palms and other flowers in larger circular planters.

Raul placed his hand at the small of her back and they entered the restaurant and sat down. Knowing they would soon be headed to his mother's, they opted for steaming cups of tea and scones with clotted cream. As they talked about all they had done that morning, waltz music played softly in the background and a crowd of older ladies with big hair, some of the hair with that un-explainable blue tinge, slowly drifted in. A few had granddaughters with them, and Rebecca smiled as the older women tried to impress the proper manners on their young counterparts. It brought back memories of her own *abuela,* insistent that Rebecca know how to act like a proper young lady.

The light snack restored her energy, and gave her the opportunity to warm up again. Rejuvenated, she was ready to continue their explorations. This time, unlike the night before, they crossed over 57th Street and walked along the edge of Central Park, heading west-bound toward Columbus Circle. They paused at the en-trance to the park at Sixth Avenue to admire the large statues there, many of them dedicated to heroes of vari-ous Latin American countries. One in particular called to her, for it was a statue of Jose Marti, leader of Cuba's fight for independence. "Why here?" she questioned, looking all around.

Raul shrugged, turned and squinted as he looked up Sixth Avenue. He motioned down the avenue, placed his hands on her shoulders and urged her to look. "See that thing hanging from the lamppost. Way down," he said and she detected some kind of small sign hanging from the lamppost and then another on the opposite side of the street even further down. "Those are small metal shields with the emblems of the various Latin American coun-tries. It's why it's called Avenue of the Americas, but only the tourists call it that."

"To youse," she teased, "it's Sixth Avenue, is that it?"

"*Sí.* To us guys it's Sixth. I was going to ask if you're ready to burn some calories?" he said, grasped her hand and gave it a playful shake and dragged her away from the statues, urging her to walk westbound once more.

"Going to ask? So why don't you?" she questioned, glancing up at him.

"I thought you might want to try your hand at some ice skating, but I'm not sure if the rink is open today and if we'll be able to navigate the paths in the park yet."

Rebecca shrugged. "I inline skate down in South Beach all the time. It's supposed to be very similar to ice skating so maybe tomorrow we can give it a try?" she said, her tone questioning. She was almost fearful of what his response would be.

He paused, looked at her, then reached up and cupped her face, the leather of his glove soft against her cold cheek. "I would like nothing better than to spend tomorrow with you. I just need to run by the office early in the morning."

She smiled, joy surging through her at the knowledge that they would have another day together. "That's . . . great. Well, what are we going to do now?"

He glanced around, grinned and leaned close to whisper into her ear. "I'm getting a little cold and tired. A nap in front of the fire might be nice before we have to brave the family, don't you think?"

Rebecca grabbed the front of his parka and shifted upward to nip his ear lobe. "Sounds perfect."

He raised his hand in the air, let out a loud whistle that had a cab waiting at the curb for them in a second. She smirked and shook her head. "You don't waste any time, do you?"

Raul snagged the handle on the door, pulled it open and held it out for her. As she slipped in, he said, "Not if that time involves you, *querida*."

# Eighteen

Back at his house he gave her free rein of his kitchen so she could make some hot chocolate while he lit a small fire in his study. She marveled that he had every gadget necessary and when he came down to see how she was doing, she held up a weird looking utensil, wondering what it was. "And this is?"

"An ergonomic potato peeler," he said, grabbed it from her hand and tossed it back into a drawer. "My sisters think that if they feather my nest enough it will entice some unsuspecting female to roost."

She shook her head and chuckled. "As in the way to a woman's heart is through your kitchen accessories."

He laughed and wrapped his arms around her waist as she moved to the stove to stir the hot chocolate she was making the old fashioned way—with powdered cocoa and milk. In a small pot she stirred the mix with a wooden spoon that looked well-used. He leaned his head on her shoulder, watching as she stirred, his front pressed against her back, warming her with the contact. "How's the fire doing?" she questioned, a little unnerved by the intense scrutiny he was giving her culinary chore.

"You're at home in the kitchen," he said and slipped his hand under the hem of her sweater, nibbled at her earlobe with his teeth.

"Don't get any ideas, Counselor. My best culinary feat is being able to reheat take-out food in the microwave. I have better things to do than spend my time in a kitchen," was her quick rejoinder.

He inched his hand beneath the waistband of her jeans. "Believe me, *amor,* I do too."


The heat from the small fire bathed her back while he warmed the other parts of her body. The empty mugs that had once held their hot chocolate rested on a low coffee table. Their clothes were strewn all over the room.

"I could get addicted to the colder weather, you know," she teased, half-opening her eyes to look up at him as she rested her head against his chest.

"Just the cold, Becca?" he replied, his eyes still closed, his hand rubbing idly up and down her back.

"Mmm. Just that, Raul. Well and maybe the hot chocolate." Or maybe it was the way hot chocolate tasted on his lips, infinitely better than any cocoa she'd had before.

"You are definitely a lawyer, Becca," he said and this time opened his eyes to gaze down at her.

His statement confused her so he quickly clarified, "Your lips are moving and you're lying."

She shook her head and attempted a pinch, but he was too lean and well-muscled to allow her to grab much. Still he reached down to still her hand, force it open against his heart. "We should think about getting ready. I need to be at *Mami's* soon."

Rebecca didn't want to move from this very pleasurable position, nestled against his chest, the fire creating a very pleasant cocoon around them. Unless of course it meant the even more blissful heat from a shared bath.

She raised her head and propped it on an upraised elbow. "Is it time to . . . get cleaned up?"

Raul quickly went into action, standing and pulling

her up into his arms. "Definitely time for a nice, long soak in my tub."

"Definitely," she confirmed.

They barely made it to his mother's on time, having indulged in the bath for too long.

Her hair was still a little damp at the ends when they arrived at his mother's apartment, which was only a few blocks away from Raul's brownstone. "This was a nice thing you did for her," she said as they walked down the hall and toward his mother's place.

"She and *Papi* did a lot for me. What else could I do?"

She admired his attitude, for it spoke of a man who cared deeply for his family and wasn't afraid of owning up to the responsibilities inherent to such relationships. It boded well for whatever woman would be lucky enough to become involved with him. She stopped short as she realized that for the moment, she was that woman.

He stopped as she did, turned and faced her. "Everything okay?"

Rebecca looked at him and smiled, took a step toward him and kissed him tenderly. A kiss meant to convey all her love for him. He answered her entreaty, his mouth gentle and soothing, offering comfort and a sense of rightness beyond explanation.

When they broke apart, he grinned at her, an almost beatific smile. "Time to face the music," he said and she trailed behind him to his mother's door.

He knocked and a second later his sister Grace opened the door, little Peter balanced on her hip. "Well, it's about time . . . Oh, hi, Becca. I didn't know you'd be coming."

Rebecca smiled, reached out and ran her hand along Peter's cheek. He was still a little warm. "I hope I'm not intruding and that Peter is feeling better."

"Nope, not intruding. In fact, I think that it's great *mi hermanito* finally has some sense," Grace replied and led her into the living room where her husband was sitting on the couch with the baby. Alicia sat there as well, her gaze almost inquiring as it settled on her brother. At the far end of the room in one corner was a small artificial pine tree, heavily trimmed with an assortment of ornaments. At the end opposite the tree was a table well-stocked with an assortment of foods.

Everyone was as surprised as Grace to see her, but that surprise quickly transformed to pleasure. His mother came in a moment later, carrying a platter piled high with sandwiches and schooled her features to try and hide her astonishment. "Rebecca, it's so good you came. My son didn't mention it," she chastised, but it had little bite for her delight at seeing her son with someone was apparent to one and all.

"*Gracias,* Maria for having me again. It's so nice to be able to have family to spend Christmas with," she said, and grabbed the platter from his mother and took it over to the table, placing it in the last bit of open space.

Maria hugged her son, came over and gave her a hug, chiding. "*Hija,* take your coat off and make yourself comfortable."

Rebecca slipped her coat and scarf off and handed it to Raul, who grabbed it and walked to another room. As her son walked off, Maria quickly slipped her arm through Rebecca's, guided her to a small sofa and sat her down, leaving a spot next to her for Raul, who came and joined them.

It made for a cozy family scene, Rebecca thought. Everyone was a little more calm and relaxed after the excitement of the night before. Maria explained that Erika and her family spent Christmas Day with Mike's family, who celebrated American-style.

"That makes it easy for us," she said with a sigh. "I would hate not having *mis niños* around for the holidays."

Rebecca looked across the way at Bob, who was gently rocking the baby still. "Is your family in the area, Bob?"

"They're on the other coast, so Grace and I take off for the week and head out to California to spend New Year's with them," he replied. The baby whimpered a little and Grace glanced down at her, wrinkled her nose. "I think it's time for a change," she replied.

Little Peter leaned over as well and grimaced. "Stinkies, mommy."

Everyone chuckled and Grace stood, let Peter loose as she took the baby from her husband so she could change her daughter. "Time to get rid of that *caca, pequeñita,*" she said.

Peter, seemingly bereft without a hip on which to perch, quickly toddled over to Rebecca and climbed into her lap. *"Hola, mi amorcito.* Did Santa treat you right?" she asked as he cuddled against her.

He told her about his toys and all that Santa had brought to his house, even with all the snow and even though they didn't have a chimney in their apartment. Santa had still somehow miraculously found their tree. Peter had played with a lot of the toys that morning until his belly had started hurting.

"You're belly still bothering you?" she asked and he nodded. She glanced up at Maria who gave her grandmotherly diagnosis.

"We think he has a touch of the flu. The fever's been low grade and he hasn't been eating," she replied and rubbed her little grandson's belly as he nestled against Rebecca.

When Maria withdrew her hand, Rebecca picked up where *Abuela* had left off. She rubbed the little toddler's belly, remembering how her *Mami* had done the same to her as a child, singing softly until Rebecca was sound asleep. She wasn't going to sing in the crowd of people in the room, but the belly-rubbing did the trick for in about half an hour, Peter had drifted off to sleep.

Grace returned a long time later. Deanna had required a complete change of clothes, then wanted to be fed, and

finally had settled in for a nap. So that the adults would
be able to talk, Bob picked up his son to take him to a
spare bedroom where he could sleep in peace.

When he returned, Maria herded everyone into helping themselves to the food, much of it the products of
leftovers from the delicious *Noche Buena* meal. The
Cuban sandwiches were still warm and filled with roast
pork and baked ham from the night before, enhanced
with the traditional swiss cheese and Cuban bread. The
boiled yuca had been turned into tasty deep fried chunks
and Alicia had provided a trio of dipping sauces from a
*Nuevo Latino* restaurant run by a friend in West New
York.

"Rey and Blanca send their best," Alicia told Raul as he
spooned one of the sauces onto his plate and he quickly
explained to Rebecca that their friends were related to the
CellTech partners and were expecting a new baby.

"I'm surprised Rey is still letting her into the kitchen,
Alicia," he said and his sister laughed.

"Blanca lives for the kitchen . . . and Rey, of course,"
she replied. "She is doing great and only has about two
months left to go so she's going to keep on working until
the baby is almost due."

"Nowadays that's what women do," Rebecca chimed
in for it was a pattern many of her friends and family had
followed.

"Is that what you would do?" Raul questioned as he
helped himself to some *congri,* a mix of black beans and
rice.

Rebecca couldn't say that she'd given it much
thought. In her mind having a child generally involved
having a husband, so without the one, the other issue
was moot for the moment. "Probably what I would do,"
she confessed, thinking that she hadn't spent all that
time and money on her degrees to toss them all out the
window when a baby came.

"It makes sense," he replied, nodded as if to second

his own statement, and waited by her side as she helped herself to some avocado salad.

Rebecca's plate was filled to the edges with the assorted edibles, so she followed Maria into another room that proved to be a small eat-in kitchen. Shortly, everyone else was seated and conversation renewed, this time around the theme of working women and careers. The problems of the modern liberated woman who sometimes bore more of a burden than her supposedly unliberated counterpart of the last generation.

It became a spirited conversation, one in which the men opted for silence as Rebecca and Raul's sisters raised the dilemmas of coping with multiple responsibilities in addition to their traditional domestic roles. Raul and Bob said nothing, on occasion rose to get additional food from the other room.

It was Maria who finally put an end to the conversation by asking, "Would any of you trade what you do for what women of my generation were allowed to do?"

There was resounding agreement from all of the younger women that they wouldn't trade the freedoms they had, even given the heavier load of responsibilities.

"*Bueno*, now that we have that answer, who's ready for dessert? I understand our gentleman are going to take care of making the coffee and bringing everything out while we clean up," Maria said.

Bob and Raul looked at one another. Rebecca was sure this had not been in their game plan. But despite that, they agreed to help out and with everyone pitching in, the meal was quickly put away and the finishing touches of dessert and coffee were promptly served up. Just in time for Peter to wake up and ask for some food, but he only picked at it as he sat on his *tio* Raul's lap with the small piece of Cuban sandwich.

When the night ended, it was with a touch of regret, for she had enjoyed herself immensely talking to Raul's sisters and mother, and playing with his little nephew.

That regret was tempered by the knowledge that although her night with his family was over, the night to be shared with him was just beginning.

There was no doubt that she would return to his home with him that night and that come the morning, she would wake beside him. After, she would return to her hotel and he to his office to deal with a few things so he could take the rest of the day off, also to be spent with her.

When they arrived at his home, he led her to the third floor where his bedroom was located. The room was elegant and tasteful. The walls were painted a deep wine red and accented with forest green trim along the window sills and mouldings. A large cherry sleigh bed dominated the center of the room, its surface covered with a dark green bedspread that matched the accents in the room. Soft light came from a brass chandelier overhead and bedside lamps. The rich jewel green of the lamp shades softened the light, casting mellow glows all around the room.

She faced him, holding his hand and slightly nervous about the night to come.

Raul turned to her, as if sensing her hesitancy and almost as expectant as she. Having her here, in his home, in his bed, had just raised the stakes in their whole relationship, she thought. He seemed to realize that as well.

He cradled her cheek and with his thumb traced the edges of her face, gently and with almost a sense of wonder.

Rebecca knew they had both been given a special gift for these days, the most special of the holidays she celebrated. A holiday of new beginnings and hope and faith. And more importantly of love.

It was with that special sense that they slowly undressed and eased into the bed together, letting the intimacy build languidly, until they were both shaking from the emotion of it. Mingled cries of completion were followed by a hushed, serene kind of silence. Neither was

ready to take the next step for it had already been so
much and in so quick a fashion.

Sweaty and sated, they soon drifted off to sleep, con-
tent in the company they were sharing for the moment,
thinking of the day to come and how they would spend it
together.

# Nineteen

Raul gave her a quick kiss in the lobby of the hotel and promised to return by noon.

For the first time in who knew how long, Rebecca found herself with nothing pressing to do. She ambled up to her room, checked the voice mails which confirmed that Sheila had already been busy that morning for she had firmed up their flight reservations for the next day. By noon she would be on a jet back to sunny, warm Miami and her family.

It didn't bring a sense of cheer.

She called her office. She and her paralegal Nancy back in Miami reviewed a few bits of correspondence. There was nothing of consequence, except maybe the good news that they had been able to serve the counterfeiter in Argentina and as a result, a hearing would shortly occur on the seizure request.

The success of that victory, small as it was, brought no joy.

Knowing that her mother would be home, she called, got the low down on all that she had missed on Christmas Day and gave her mother an abbreviated and very censored version of how she had spent her own day. With the promise of being home tomorrow and ready to celebrate New Year's, she ended her call home.

There hadn't been a hint of a hidden set-up with a suitor, or any kind of reprimand at having missed the holiday. Her mother had been almost reasonable about her absence.

None of it gave her any sense of relief. None of it was capable of removing the sense of melancholy she had woken with that morning. It was as if the Grinch in the Macy's windows had come alive during the night and stolen all the happiness out of the holiday. Just like he had taken everything out of . . .

She stopped short. The Grinch had taken all the physical trappings of the day, but not the heart of it. Not the soul of it. It was why the Whos could still enjoy their day. Why they could still sing so gloriously about the love that made it special.

The love that she had for Raul. That emotion had made it possible for her to enjoy *Noche Buena* and Christmas with his family.

The upcoming separation, that Grinch in her holiday scene, was what was responsible for her melancholy. And she had just the thing to combat it in the three hours until Raul returned to rekindle the light of her spirit.

A thorough session of retail therapy at Victoria's Secret and a nice long, hot bath so she could be wickedly clean for him when he arrived.


Raul faced his partners and quite calmly told them that he had to abstain on the upcoming vote on the proposed merger of their firm and the new Miami office. He had always been in favor of both, but he now had too many personal reasons clouding what should be only a business decision. He wanted nothing more than to have the proposal approved for it would give him a very real excuse for spending more time in Miami.

More time with Rebecca, he thought as he confirmed his decision to abstain to his partners and excused himself from the meeting.

Rebecca. He breathed her name with a soft sigh as he

returned to his office, sat and leaned back in his chair, smiling the whole time. What a wonderful surprise Rebecca had been and all thanks to Mother Nature and her whimsical moods.

He steepled his fingers before him, remembering how pleasantly they had spent the night and the wee morning hours. Talking. Touching. Making love. And while he wouldn't downplay just how wonderful the touching and making love had been, the talking had been just as good. Maybe even better.

Rebecca was downright fun to talk to. She had a quick wit and a dry humor that made him chuckle often. The question of bright didn't even need to be asked. She was one of the most intelligent women he had met, but she wasn't arrogant or condescending in any way.

She was good with kids and had passed muster with his family. If he had to make a list of her good points, he'd be at it for a long time unless of course he started off with the bad list first. While there was only one bad, it was a big bad and made the making of the good list moot.

She lived in Miami. Had a career and family in Miami. That issue was one they'd have to address sometime tonight, or maybe tomorrow morning, before she left for all those things in Miami that called to her.

But for right now, all he had to deal with was getting her over to Lincoln Center for the ballet for which he had managed to get tickets. His mother and sisters had always dragged him and his father to the Nutcracker during the Christmas season. He'd protested at first, convinced that the last thing he wanted to do was watch a bunch of men in tutus flit around on a stage.

That had been at the age of twelve when his family's finances had finally gotten to the point to allow for that kind of treat. Before then, the days off from school during the Christmas holidays had generally been with his mom at home, or visiting close family or friends. And of course, cleaning up the house and getting it ready for his family's New Year's and *Reyes* celebrations.

It was with much grumbling and protesting that he'd been dragged along and he'd suspected his father wasn't anymore keen on the idea than he. Even at that age he'd known that his father was caving in to his wife's demands as a way of demonstrating his love and in a way, a demonstration of pride that he could now afford such a gift for the family.

Raul had therefore not grumbled very loudly so as to not injure his father's dignity. And of course, it had helped that there had been a neat sword fight between the nutcracker and the Rat King. Plus, much to his relief, it was the women wearing the tutus and not the men.

The leaps and running turns of the ballerinas had impressed him. It made it a little easier to repeat the adventure the next year and ever since then, his family had either taken in the Nutcracker ballet or the Christmas Show at Radio City Music Hall over the holiday season.

Rebecca was a classy lady. She'd prefer a ballet to the high stepping, flashy musical productions for which Radio City was famous.

Plus, it was right near the rink so they could try out the skating and then head to Tavern on the Green, where he had made reservations for an early supper.

With the tickets safely tucked into his back jeans pocket, he slipped on his coat and headed out the door, advising the receptionist that he wouldn't be back. She smiled at him knowingly. He wondered just how many people in the office were busy prying into his private life via a grapevine faster than any mode of communication currently known to modern man.

Once in the lobby of his building, he paused to look at the large globe, admiring just how rare and beautiful a thing it was. Rebecca had mentioned to him one night how she had first thought New Yorkers oblivious to their surroundings and how she still wasn't convinced that they saw even a small portion of the wonders around them. It wasn't something he could argue with her about, for he was certain that he'd been guilty of it more than once. So he took a breath, spent a moment appreciating it and then nearly bolted out the door in his haste to get to Rebecca.

Lincoln Center was still wearing its winter coat of snow and the lights from Avery Fisher Hall, the Metropolitan Opera House and the State Theater shone on the piles of white scattered here and there throughout the large central plaza into which all the buildings faced. The subway ride, or maybe it was better she say "rides" as they had had to switch trains in order to get both uptown and crosstown, had been relatively easy since it was off hours for travelling.

That had left them with plenty of time to wander about Avery Fisher Hall and then check out the inside of the Metropolitan Opera House. Then, along with hundreds of others, they packed the lobby of the State Theater, waiting until the doors opened. When the ushers released the ropes along the entrances to the carpeted stairways leading into the theater, people rushed forward. It was body to body to get through the tight openings.

Raul had somehow managed to secure orchestra seats. They were center stage, barely ten rows away from the pit that held the orchestra. From her seat, she had a partial view of the soft lights from the pit, the musicians and their instruments. They were busy warming up and tuning.

The hall was large. Balconies lined the sides and in the back there were a number of levels that ran high up into the theater. The theater had a very fifties kind of ambience, from the adornments along the balconies to the lights and ceiling fixtures that resembled a bunch of large metallic snow crystals.

As she was busy taking in all the sights, Raul leaned closed to her and asked, "Are you a ballet fan?"

"I occasionally go down to Lincoln Road to check out the ballet. The director there is quite well-known," she answered and settled back in her seat as the lights dimmed. The conductor came out to take his place at the podium in the orchestra pit.

"I hope you like this," he replied and she reached out, grasped his hand and gave it a squeeze.

"I'm sure I will. I really appreciate what you did to get these tickets."

He smiled and even with the lights dimming, she met and held his gaze, wanting him to know just how much all of this meant to her. He understood for he leaned over, placed a soft, gentling kiss on her lips, and twined his fingers with hers.

The music of the overture to Tchaikovsky's *Nutcracker* began and as the lights were lowered, it became apparent that the large theater curtain depicting an angel hovering over a small village had twinkling lights which grew brighter as it became darker in the hall.

The curtain came up and a palpable hush, a sense of excitement scurried through the people in their seats as they became involved in the tale of the young girl and the Nutcracker who came to life and became a prince who lead her into a wonderful fairy tale world.

Rebecca watched and appreciated. The young children playing the various roles were delightful and the two chosen to be the young girl and the Nutcracker had a poise well beyond their years. The remaining dancers exhibited their skills as the story evolved—the dances of the various fairies by the corps; the solo where the male dancers exhibited their leaps, with that amazing sense of *balon* that made it seem as if they were actually suspended in the air for a moment.

In the short intermission they ambled out to the red carpeted hallway to stretch their legs.

When she saw one of the Kennedys there with her family, Rebecca tried to act like a real New Yorker, merely glancing their way to confirm that's who it really was and hanging back, letting the woman purchase a snack at a small stand in the hallway just as if she was anyone else in the crowd.

Raul teased her over it, saying he was impressed with her behavior.

"Why? They're entitled to their privacy," she replied.

He surprised her by saying, "No, because a real New Yorker would have said, 'Hurry up, lady. You're holding up the line' when it took her so long to find the change in her purse."

They laughed and returned to their seats.

Now, with the show over, they were headed back out into the hallway where a large group of people was bolting out a side door. She and Raul followed and found themselves at a side entrance. A long line of limousines waited at the curb and as people hurried over to the cars, she and Raul broke free of the crowd and walked over to the sidewalk.

Raul was holding her hand, guiding her along and she asked, "Are we going somewhere?"

"To the rink, if you're up to it," he said, looking at her as they walked side by side and crossed the street in the direction of Central Park, which was a few blocks away.

"I'd love to try it out," she answered and they leisurely strolled the few blocks to the entrance to the park.

It had gotten dark in the time they had taken in the Nutcracker, and the night sky was clear and filled with stars. The lights had come on in the Park and they walked along the lit pathways until they reached Wollman Rink. Raul paid the entrance fee and the rental for the skates. At another booth they obtained the skates in their sizes and walked over to the bleachers by the side of the rink so they could change into the skates.

Rebecca slipped her feet into the leather boots, pulled

the laces tight to hold her feet and ankles in place. She'd been told it wasn't much different from her in-line skating and in truth, the feel of the boot was similar, although lighter than the padding and plastic boot on her inline wheels. When they were laced, she rose and teetered unsteadily on the thin blades, her ankles shifting inside the boot.

Raul jumped up, steadied her and then bent, grabbed her laces and tucked them into the top of her boot. When he rose and took hold of her hand, he explained, "If they come undone and you snag the blade on them you might take a nasty fall."

Rebecca looked down, nodded and thought that these skates suddenly felt much less substantial than her trusty, reliable Rollerblades. With her hand gripping his tightly, she trudged to the edge of the rink, where she took her first step onto the white, glistening ice and nearly fell on her butt.

Raul encircled her waist with his hands, kept her upright. "I thought you said this was just like in-line skating," he teased. She shot him a glare, allowed him to lead her further onto the ice where together they executed a very inelegant, but purposeful step-shuffle around the rink. By the time they did a lap around the crowded ice, she was a little steadier on the blades and could take a moment to revel in the experience.

As in Rockefeller Center, skaters glided all around, a motley crew of all ages, sizes and skill levels. With the rink being substantially larger, they regularly had to go around one group or another, not an easy task given the way the blades ran away from her. If it hadn't been for Raul supporting her for the first lap around the ice, she would have certainly fallen.

As they neared the spot where they had left their shoes, he relaxed his hold on her as if he recognized she was getting the hang of it. She hesitantly tried to skate away, using a stroke similar to that she used with her in-line skates, her only contact with him the slight touch of his fingertips on hers as he skated beside her.

She had gone only a few feet when one skate snagged on a gash in the ice, putting her off balance. She attempted to compensate and found she had overdone it. A moment later she landed on the ice on her rump with a solid thump and a little bounce. *"Carajo,"* she muttered under her breath as she laid her hands back on the ice and glanced up at him as he came to stand before her, an amused grin on her face.

"You find this funny, huh?" she questioned as he held out his hand, accepted his boost up and his holding her upright until she could stabilize herself.

He chuckled, slowly gave a shake of his head. "I thought you said you in-line skated all the time."

She nodded, stroked with one foot and skated away from him. He followed just behind her. Braving a quick glance behind her even though it might put her off balance, she said, "I skate all the time along the path in Lummus Park. It's quite . . . refreshing," she said, a mischievous and sexy tone to her voice that she didn't recognize.

"Really?" he said, hastening his pace so he was almost right behind her. "And why is that?" he whispered, close to her ear.

She turned her face slightly and teased, "Because I skate in that tiny little bikini you—"

He lost his balance, his feet flying out from under him. He landed on his rump heavily and muttered a curse beneath his breath.

Somehow Rebecca managed to turn and stop, returned to where he sat on the ice, looking up at her. "How little?" he asked, one eyebrow arching upward.

She smiled, bent at her waist to lean toward him so he might hear her better. "Teeny, or have you forgotten the tan lines?"

Raul closed his eyes and groaned. "You are an evil woman, Becca, to tease me like this."

When he opened his eyes, they were blazing with golden fire, heating her with their intensity. "I want to see you in that, Becca. I want to skate beside you—"

"So let's do it," she said and offered her hand out to him.

He glanced up at the proffered hand, grinned and shook his head. "I guess you know that isn't what I meant, but I guess it will do for now."

He took her hand, and although he made a show of letting her think she was helping him out, she knew he was more than capable himself. Still she appreciated the gesture, just as she reveled in having him slip his arm around her waist and skate beside her, their legs working in unison, building up speed as they did this lap around the ice.

The greenery of the pines in Central Park flashed by her and in the night sky there were the bright, twinkling lights of the stars and of the city. Up beyond the pines and the bare branches of the other trees, rose the sky-scrapers, reaching for the heavens with their tall peaks. Competing with the stars for control of the night sky with the muted glow from their windows.

Rebecca took it all in, breathed in the flavor and essence of the city, and the frosty, biting air that was clean here of exhaust and fumes. If it was possible, she would say it smelled of the ice, a crisp, biting scent she was hard pressed to describe. It smelled from the pines scattered here and there around the periphery of the rink, of the wet wool from scarves, coats and mittens, and of the man skating beside her. Of all, his was the scent that called to her, worked its way into her mind and heart.

She breathed deeply of his aroma, drawing it into her lungs and mind so that she might savor it later, once she was gone and back in Miami. So that she could recall it to keep her company until he came to visit, or she returned to New York.

With that in mind, she did another few laps with him, talking softly and infrequently for this moment of con-

tentment needed few words. Finally, reluctantly, Raul
mentioned that they needed to stop so they could make
their dinner reservation. They skated over to the bleachers once more and switched into their shoes.

After returning the skates, they took a short walk
along the quiet, faintly lit paths of the park to Tavern
on the Green. They entered and for a moment Rebecca
was taken aback for it was like stepping into a child's
imagination and entering Santa's North Pole with all its
magical wonders. From the doorway, through the halls
and into the large room where the hostess guided them,
the restaurant was bedecked in its holiday finery. Yards
and yards of festive ribbon, multi-layered bows in a
rainbow of colors, and pine garland hung along the
hallways, chandeliers, rafters and draped the multitude
of windows visible which allowed glimpses of the park
beyond.

And if that wasn't enough, in addition to the ribbon,
bows and garland, dozens of wreaths made from an assortment of glass ornaments lined the hallway.

"This is too much," she leaned close and whispered
to him.

He shot her a quick glance. "Just wait."

The host led them into the Crystal Room and Rebecca
knew then just what Raul had meant. The room was immense, capable of sitting a few hundred people. Glass
walls provided glimpses of the trees beyond, which were
strung with hundreds of blue lights and sparkled in the
clear night. Huge crystal chandeliers shimmered and reflected light on the dining area, the vast array of poinset-
tias decorating the tables, and on the large, fourteen foot
tree gaily decorated with twinkling, multi-colored lights
and ornaments.

They were seated at a table near the glass window. As
Rebecca sat, she glanced outside. In addition to the trees
decorated with the hundreds of glittering blue lights,
there were smaller miniature Christmas trees outside.

She laughed at the wonder of it all and smiled at him. "Does it matter what the food tastes like with all this?" She motioned with her hands to everything around them.

Raul appreciated the sight of her, her face flushed from the cold outside and her eyes glimmering with her excitement. Her hair was a little mussed, from the skating and the walk. She had never looked quite so appealing for there was a wonderment in her eyes that spoke of the hidden spirit in her. The one that had attracted him from the moment he had stepped into the conference room and she had snagged his attention. He memorized her like this, taking a mental snapshot. It was a picture he would pull out in the future, hold in his mind and appreciate for it would never fade or crinkle. Never lose its vibrancy because of his love for her. He knew that now after only a few days with her. He was in love and he couldn't imagine what he would do come tomorrow.

And because the night was so wondrous, he drove that thought away and somehow found the strength to act as if there was nothing wrong with the picture they presented, that of two people in love.

He ate the meal he ordered, trying to appreciate the creaminess of the lobster bisque. Trying to savor the creamy, apple-spiced mix of barley and risotto the chef had created to accompany the pork loin he had chosen for his entree.

And while he did that, he attempted to carry on a conversation with her about things that suddenly seemed mundane compared to what he really wanted to talk about, namely, what would happen tomorrow and the next day. What their lives would be like once they stepped out of this magic time that had been given to them and returned to their real lives. Lives that were 1500 miles apart.

He was just finishing up his meal when he sensed a sudden change in her, as if she too had somehow just woken up to the fact that the clock was rapidly running away with the time they had left. When the waiter came over to ask about dessert, it was she who quickly answered that they didn't want any and could he bring the check.

She glanced at him uncertainly, but he reached out, grasped her hand and smiled, confirming his agreement with her decision.

Rebecca let out a long, drawn-out breath. While she was enjoying herself immensely with the wonderful sights of Manhattan, she wanted to be with him and him alone, somewhere private, where she could show him just how much he meant to her. She was relieved with the efficiency of the waiter therefore as the tab was settled and they walked out into the gardens surrounding the restaurant. Again there was more to catch her eye, for in addition to the trees with their twinkling lights, there were a dozen of small topiaries in animal shapes.

The touch of whimsy in them made her grin and draw close to him. She wrapped her arm around his waist and dropped a quick kiss on his cheek. He eyed her curiously.

"What was that for?" he asked, slipping his arm around her shoulder and giving her a playful hug.

"For nothing and for everything. I can't even begin to tell you—"

"Then don't," he jumped in, his tone suddenly serious. "Don't . . . you don't need to tell me, Becca. I feel the same," he said, turned and faced her. He cupped her cheek, ran his thumb over the arch of her brow tenderly. Bending slightly, he brought his lips to hers, the warmth of his mouth a tantalizing contrast to the chill of the night air. The brush of his goatee teased her skin and she rubbed her lips back and forth against his, enjoying the textures of his lips and mouth, and the taste of him, more flavorful than the gourmet meal she had just consumed. She could have stood there all night long, with her lips biting and meeting his, her tongue doing a dance of intimacy, and his hands cradling her face as if she was something infinitely fragile and special.

It was the sudden jangle of bells against leather and the heavy clomp of hoof against asphalt that jolted them apart.

The carriage was barely a foot away. The young man driving it was leaning toward them on the bench, grinning. He wore an old, black top coat and on his head sat a bedraggled and battered black bowler. "I can offer you a much more comfortable locale for those kinds of activities," he said, and spread his arm wide to point to the large back seat.

Raul chuckled and glanced down at Becca. "Sounds like a good idea, but I know you might need to get back to do packing and other things, personal stuff you know," he razzed her.

"You know the best thing about being an anal, over-achiever attorney is that you never leave anything to the last minute. My 'stuff' is all ready, so—"

"We'll be taking that ride. Through the park and then over to 66th and Second," Raul instructed the young man, whose smile brightened at securing the fare. He leaned down and opened the small door of the carriage.

Raul held his hand out and she took it and his assistance as he boosted her up the long step from the ground. She settled onto leather bench, waited for him to step up, close the door behind him and then sit next to her.

The driver tossed a large, woolen blanket back at them, and it landed in Raul's lap. He looked back at them, gave a knowing look. "It can get . . . cold once we get moving."

Raul turned to face her. "Well in that case, maybe you'd like to come on up here," he said and patted his lap. "So we can conserve that all important body heat."

She arched a brow in disbelief, but relented, allowing him to slide over to her side so she could sit up on his lap. When she was comfortably settled, his arm braced against the side to cushion her back, Raul grabbed the blanket and tossed it up over them.

The driver snapped the reins against the horse's flanks, the bells on the harness jingling as the horse took its first steps, pulling away from the doors of the restaurant.

The motion jarred them closer together, but Rebecca wasn't complaining. Beneath the wool of the blanket there was a small cocoon of warmth and as the driver predicted, the slight wind from the passage of the carriage through the night increased the chill in the air.

She shivered, huddled closer to him, laying her hand over his heart. It beat strong and steady beneath her palm, like the man she had come to care about. She wanted him. So much, so badly. Inching up, she kissed the line of his jaw, ran her face against the soft, springy hair of his beard.

He bent his head, nuzzled her face with his, traced the upper slope of her lips with his mouth, his motions slow and deliberate. Patient and yet with an edge beneath that was enticing and . . . demanding. She answered, leaning into him, sliding her fingers up into the silky waves of his hair, holding him close.

Finally they broke apart, both breathing heavily. "I wish I had skipped work this morning so we would have had more time for this," he said softly, ran his thumb along the edge of her lips, wet with the evidence of their kisses.

"No, I don't think so," she replied and gave this thumb a gentle nip with her teeth.

"And why not?"

She reached up, nibbled on the edge of his jaw and then moved up to whisper in his ear, "Because you would have missed the little gift I bought for you this morning."

He pulled away from her, arching the fine, dark line of his brow in question. "A gift for me?"

"Another *little* gift for you," she clarified.

"Really. And I thought Christmas was over," he reminded, his tone playful.

"Well, I recollect that the Twelve Days of Christmas are those between Christmas Eve and *Reyes,* so if that's true—"

"No partridges or pear trees, I hope," he questioned.

"No, *querido*. I'm hoping you'll find this much, much sweeter," she replied without hesitation, eager for him to explore her offering.

"Hmm, so where would you be keeping it?" he questioned, clearly getting into the spirit of her game.

She grasped his hand, the one beneath the blanket resting on her thigh, and guided it to the buttons of her coat. "You may need to unwrap it a little, like the other night," she warned. He groaned low in his throat, but did as she asked, undoing the buttons on her coat, his fingers fumbling with his haste.

Raul slipped his hand beneath the folds of her coat and his hand encountered the cashmere of her sweater, slippery and satiny beneath his fingers. He itched to move his hand up, cover her breast, relish its fullness, but she seemed know his intent for she warned, "You're not quite there yet, *mi amor.*"

He looked down into her smiling face, and the night stars were reflected in the dark brown of her eyes. She glittered like those stars, bright and alive. Her smile warm and inviting. Teasing. Tempting. "Really? So maybe I have to unwrap a little more?"

"Maybe," she confirmed and he slipped his hand beneath the edge of the sweater and encountered the fine satin of a camisole. He stroked it softly, moving the back of his hand across the fullness of one breast and beneath his fingers, her nipple beaded. He continued to rub, his pace languid and unhurried as the cab bounced along, the clip-clop of the horse's hooves loud against the quiet of the night.

"Do you like?" she questioned, running her fingers through his hair, smoothing a lock blown loose by a wintry gust of air.

He bent his head, nipped at her full lower lip with his teeth and whispered, "I like."

He turned his hand, cupped her and she exhaled a shaky breath against his lips, then a moan as he took her taut nipple between his thumb and forefinger. "I guess you like too."

"Too much," she admitted against his lips before she deepened the kiss. They lost themselves to their passion and to the night, the horse blanket providing them a little haven from the eyes of the driver as they travelled along the dark, winding paths of Central Park. The stars glimmered overhead. The bare branches of the trees and verdant green of the pines created a canopy of privacy beneath which they touched and kissed.

The brighter glare of lights eventually intruded and she took a deep, quivering breath and met his intense gaze.

"We'll be there soon," he said, his voice shaky.

"Good," she replied and he smiled, moved his hand from beneath her sweater and smoothed it back into place.

Rebecca cuddled up against his chest for the remainder of the ride, enjoying the warmth of him. The reassuring and invigorating experience of being in his arms, tucked tightly in his embrace.

By the time they arrived in front of his home, her heart had only just begun to slow from the caresses they had exchanged. Her body had an inner glow going that was just primed and waiting for his touch to ignite it once more.

While his movements in helping her out of the carriage and opening his door would appear unhurried to the casual observer, there was an energy she sensed as she waited patiently for the snick of the lock opening, the beeping of the alarm within until he disarmed it, and the second beep signalling that he was resetting it for the night.

After that there was no waiting as he turned and swept her up into his arms, carried her up the stairs and into his bedroom, where he brought her by the bed, and then let her slide down into his arms.

There was an edge this time as they quickly disrobed, each movement almost poignant as they knew that after tonight, it might be a while before they saw one another again.

Rebecca had no doubt she would be with him again she thought, as he sat on the edge of the bed and eased her sweater up and over her head. She stood before him in the maroon camisole he had explored earlier and the matching tap pants that hugged her hips, made her legs look long and sleek.

He rested his hands on the curve of her hips, right below the hem of the camisole that exposed her flat belly and navel. He moved his thumbs slowly back and forth across her skin, the slide of them so erotic she wished he would move them up, glide them over her hardened nipples which were just waiting for the touch of his hands.

Raul had never seen anything so beautiful. She stood before him, the deep wine color of her gift a perfect foil that accentuated the creaminess of her skin and her marvelously sleek shape. Not too thin. Not too toned. Definitely all woman. He met her gaze and her want reached deep inside him. His erection tightened, pushed against the fabric of his pants, eager to be stroked and touched with those fine, aristocratic hands she had with their long fingers and soft palms.

But he knew she was waiting for his touch as well. It was in the half glance she shot his hands as he moved his thumbs against the silken skin at her waist and the heat of her skin, the slight damp beneath his fingers. He could smell it, her arousal, and it was a potent perfume.

He raised the hem of her camisole up, bent and tongued her navel, dipping into that sweet indentation with his tongue. He moved his hands up, slipped the balls of his thumbs up over her nipples and she gasped lightly and reached for the camisole, pulled it up and over her head.

Her breasts were full and as he cupped them with his hands, they fit there perfectly, as if made just for him. He reached one hand behind her to the small of her back. Her skin was damp there. With just the gentlest of pressure he urged her closer, whispered against her breasts, "I know you like this, *querida*. You're trembling and you make that little sound in the back of your throat—"

She let out a little moan then, and he encouraged her. "Like that, *amor mio*. You make me hurt with that sound," he said as he playfully nipped at her breast with his teeth and then soothed it with a long, wet lick of his tongue. She whimpered a little.

"Touch me, see how hard I am for you," he urged, took her hand and guided it to his lap. She encircled him and he let out his own, quick little rumble of passion.

"You make that sound when you like what I'm doing," she said, her breathing growing heavier as she stroked him through the fabric of his pants while he suckled her nipples, played with them with his fingers as well.

"It's your sound, Becca. Just to let you know how you excite me. How much I want you," he said, the breath coming heavier in his chest. As she stroked him forcefully, he groaned, reached down and slipped off her panties, and a second later, he had turned her so that she lay down on the bed.

He took off the rest of his clothes, removed a condom from his back pocket and slipped it on. She shifted on the bed, opening her thighs a little, seducing him with a view of the sweet core of her, wet and glistening. As much as he wanted that, he wanted something else more.

He placed one knee on the bed, crawled toward her and when he was at the juncture of her thighs, he bent his head, nuzzled the soft curls of hair and braced a hand on either side of her as he slipped his body between her thighs and brought his mouth to her.

Rebecca nearly came off the bed as he kissed her clitoris, sucked and nibbled at her lips until she was drenched with the juices he was wringing from her. Her insides were clenching, a demanding vibration working its way through her, spreading to her arms and legs until she was coming apart on the bed, her hands grasping his head and holding him there until he shook his head loose and with a powerful surge, lifted himself up into her, driving relentlessly until she was nearly screaming her completion.

When her release came, it was like a bright star, radiating heat and beautiful, golden light all over. His own hoarse shout just after confirmed his satisfaction. He dropped down onto her, his weight heavy, but pleasantly comforting.

There were only the sounds of their breathing and the occasional street noise intruding. No words. Nothing to remind that time was fleeing quickly, but despite that, when they finally pulled up the sheets and comforter, Raul asked what time she had to be back at the hotel and set the alarm.

As Rebecca fell asleep in his arms, she wished the damn clock would never go off.

# Twenty

She woke in the middle of the night with shivers and a pounding headache that quickly became so bad she was nauseous from the pain. She made her way to the bathroom. The lights as she snapped them on were like a bright, angry explosion. She squinted, went to his medicine chest and located a bottle of aspirin. At the sink, she ran the cold water, popped the pills and cupped her hands to have something with which to drink them down.

A moment later her stomach revolted. She hurried to the toilet, threw up not only the aspirins, but part of the night's meal. She flushed and wiped her mouth with some toilet paper, but a moment later she was heaving again and her stomach was contracting painfully.

There was a knock at the door. "Becca? Are you okay in there?" he asked, his voice soft and filled with concern.

She couldn't answer as another wave hit her and an awful dry heave racked her body.

He was beside her in a second, holding a glass of water for her to rinse out her mouth and rubbing her back in a soothing gesture. "I'm here. Lean back and try to let it pass," he said and she did just that, closing her eyes and leaning against his solid bulk.

She took a few deep breaths and looked up at him. "I don't feel very well."

Raul placed his hand over her forehead. It was clammy and she looked pale. "Maybe it's something you ate." When after a few moments she was calm, he picked her up in his arms and took her back to the bed, where he gently tucked her in.

"I'm going to get you some ginger ale," he said, and left her curled up on his bed, shivering and looking miserable.

He hurriedly poured a glass of the soda and returned upstairs to find her with her head hanging over the bowl again, her body racked with spasms. Again he gave her support, helped her back to bed.

It was a pattern they repeated throughout the remainder of the night until Rebecca finally fell into a fitful sleep in the wee hours of the morning. Raul looked at his watch and realized two things—he was too tired to get to work after the rough night and there was no way Rebecca was going to catch her plane.

He called his office and arranged for anything urgent to be sent to his home office. He called Sheila and Andrew, told them that Rebecca was ill and asked that they call and leave her flight ticket open.

"What about her things? We're checking out today," Sheila advised.

Raul had no doubt about what to do. "Check her out and have the concierge have a messenger bring everything to my address. I'll take care of the bill," he said and gave Sheila all the information she would need.

The next call he made was to his sister Grace for he was certain that whatever Becca was suffering from had been transmitted by his little nephew Peter. *"Hola, hermanita,"* he said as she picked up. In the background was the sound of a baby's insistent crying.

Grace's voice as she answered sounded harried and tired. *"Hola,* Raul. It's not a good time."

"I can hear," he replied and winced as a particularly loud wail came over the phone. "How's Peter doing? Is he still sick?"

"That bug really has gotten to him. He's been sick the past two nights throwing up and running a fever. The doctor says there's nothing we can do but wait it out and try to get him to take in some liquids to keep him from getting dehydrated," she replied quickly and in the background, Peter called out for his *mami*.

"I can hear that you need to go, Grace. Let me know if you need anything." She gave him her thanks and told him it was better he stay away lest he wanted to get sick as well. Raul bit back a comment that it was a little too late for that. Obviously whatever bug it was had been busy incubating over *Noche Buena* and Christmas. Poor Becca had gotten it from being with his family.

He headed back upstairs to find that she was still asleep, but had tossed off some of the covers in her restlessness. He tried to straighten them and tuck them back in without waking her, but she opened one eye and rolled over onto her back, holding the sheet up across her breasts to hide her nakedness. "I feel like hell," she said.

He reached out, brushed back a lock of her hair, and passed his hand over her forehead. She was still warm and yet clammy at the same time. Her face was pale with not a tinge of color in it. "Typhoid Peter has the same thing. I'm sorry, Becca."

She shrugged, reached out and grasped his hand. "Don't worry. My nieces and nephews have done their share of contaminating. It's to be expected, only—"

"You wanted to be on your way home today. I called your friends and had them make arrangements. Your stuff is on its way over from the hotel."

She didn't argue with him. *"Gracias.* I don't think I could have gotten on a plane feeling like this."

"Think nothing of it, Becca. Just rest. When your things get here I'll bring them up—"

"Don't you have to get to work?" she asked.

"I can work out of the house for the next day or so until this passes," he said and flinched at the look on her face.

"Another day or so? How do you know—"

"I called Grace. Peter has been sick since Christmas

night apparently and is still sick," he answered. She turned a sickly greenish color before his eyes. "Becca?"

She didn't answer. She didn't have time to as she bolted from the bed and to the bathroom. He assisted in whatever way he could and then helped her back into bed, where she settled beneath the covers. "Try to get some rest. I'm going to bring up some ginger ale and crackers. Maybe you'll be up for some soup later," he said and she nodded, curled up into the fetal position on the bed.

"Raul?" she said as he walked away.

He turned and faced her, wishing there was something he could do to make her better. "What is it, *querida?*"

"I need to make some calls," she said. He knew she was concerned about her parents and the upcoming holidays. Holidays she hadn't wanted to miss. He walked to his side of the bed, grabbed the portable phone and handed it to her. "Make whatever calls you need to. Leave this number for them."

She nodded, rolled over onto her back and shot him a quick glance as she nervously handled the phone. Finally she said, "I'm sorry to be sick, Raul, but in some demented way, I'm glad to be here with you."

And in some demented way, he felt the same way too.


Becca spent the next two days and nights sick as a dog, Raul patiently by her side, a willing and capable nurse. And a delightful sleeping companion, she thought, thinking of how right it was to curl up next to him at night, talk about the day's events and the cases he was working on that the office had either faxed to him or sent over by courier. It was somehow right that they were sharing this time together.

But it was just an interlude, she reminded herself, thinking about the call that had come that afternoon from her office, asking that she confirm her availability for a meeting the day after New Year's Day. The day she was due back in her office from her holiday vacation break.

She was ready to head back the next morning, the worst of the bug behind her.

That was of course until she woke to an empty bed and the sounds of Raul in the bathroom, suffering from the same malaise that had clobbered her over the last day or so. It was inhuman to leave him she told herself and her parents. Surprisingly, her mother hadn't put up much of a battle and hadn't even asked why it was that Rebecca was in his home and being cared for by a virtual stranger, nor why Rebecca thought it her responsibility to care for him in turn.

It didn't bode well for she knew that upon her return to Miami there would be an inquisition about Raul.

That didn't dissuade her from canceling her flight plans yet again and staying with him until he was well. By the time the flu bug had run its course, it was already the morning of New Year's Eve. It made no sense to go home that day, especially when Raul offered to take her to a fancy party in Times Square. After all, how often did one get to do it up big time in Manhattan on New Year's Eve.

Not often she knew as she slipped into the tub with him that morning and they just lazed in the hot water in the whirlpool bath big enough for two. She was nestled close to his chest, his arms and legs wrapped all around her as she soaped up a big washcloth and ran it across his forearms, depositing big, fat pinkish clouds of suds on him.

He took the lather in his hands, brought them up across the front of her, moving his hands up and down her arms languidly and then to her breasts, where he cupped them, slowly shifted his thumbs across her nipples until they hardened.

Against the side of her face came the brush of his beard as he whispered, "I could get very used to this."

"Mmm," she murmured, enjoying the slight, abrading motion of his thumbs. "Baths?" she questioned.

He nipped her ear lobe playfully. "You, *querida*," was his low, urgent reply.

"*Ay*, Raul. You know—"

"You have to go back tomorrow," he jumped in, cognizant of the command performance that had been scheduled by her partners for her return. He hesitated, stopped the motion of his thumbs and then softly said, "Fate is conspiring to keep us together. First the negotiations your partner tries to screw up. Then my little nephew and his very big germs. But now, Fate isn't tossing anything else at us."

She glanced down at her hands which were below the surface of the water and were gripped around the washcloth in a stranglehold. "Let's not do this right now, Raul."

"Let's not talk about you staying, is that it?" he countered and his body stiffened behind her.

She nodded, half turned in his arms and cupped his face. "We both know we have separate lives over a thousand miles apart. And yes, Fate has done its best to keep us together the past week."

"But now you need to make the decision, Becca. Do you want to stay here? Do you want me to go there?" he pressed, thinking of the proposal his partners had yet to approve. He held his breath as he waited for her answer.

Rebecca looked down, took a deep breath and said, "I want to be with you, Raul. Right now, I don't know how to accomplish that. We've only known each other what? All of a week?"

He placed his thumb and forefinger under her chin and exerted gentle pressure until she was facing him. "Sometimes that's all it takes, but I do understand you have another life in another place. And I think we both know why the partners want to meet with you on Monday, right?"

She nodded for with the rumors and the recent success in the negotiations, she was hopeful it was to talk partnership. "You've made it in your own world, Raul.

You're a name partner in a well-known, reputable firm. Give me my chance to make it as well."

While Raul recognized she had a point, it was hard to reconcile it with what was in his heart for he wanted her with him. Still, if he didn't give her that chance, he'd never know the truth of how much she cared for him and she would always be wondering "What if . . ." Neither was a good way to get a relationship off the ground.

"I won't say that I wish it could be different right now, but . . . I want you to be happy, Becca, more than anything. And I want you to be sure. Logic says this has happened too fast and we should take a step back. See if in a week or two, we are still—"

"Feeling the way we are now. I think we will be, but we both need time to think and make some decisions about what to do," she confirmed and laid back in his arms.

Raul pressed her close, needing the contact so that when she was gone, he could remember it. When she turned in his arms, kissed him and straddled his legs, he willingly went along for the ride, his need for her greater than any logic or sensibility.


At mid-day they finally roused themselves out of bed and went shopping at Bergdorf's for a dress for Rebecca. The party that night was formal and she had nothing suitable for the occasion.

He had always dreaded the shopping expeditions his mother and sisters dragged him on, and yet this time, he found it more than amusing to watch her parade in and out of the dressing room in an assortment of gowns, some of them so outrageous they were both giggling over the style. The last gown Rebecca took into the dressing room she refused to show him and when she came back out in her street clothes, she was smiling. He knew she had found the one.

The young lady at the register had already wrapped

and hung up the gown by the time Rebecca went to pay. Raul was left holding the hanger, wondering what was beneath all the plastic and how Rebecca looked in it.

After another quick foray in the store for shoes and the necessary accessories for the dress, they were back in a cab and headed for his house, carrying an assortment of bags. "Are you sure you need all this?" he questioned, worried she had been forced to spend way too much in order to go to this party with him.

She arched one brow elegantly. "You don't want me to be underdressed, do you? What kind of impression would that make on your client?"

"They are friends as well, so there's no need to worry. We all went to school together—"

"And I don't want them to think I'm some little *guajira* from Miami," she said with an unexpected and very feminine little huff.

He didn't press further and hours later after a quick nap during which they did little sleeping, they were both getting ready for the party. Rebecca insisted on going to another bedroom, wanting a little privacy she said. He knew it was because she wanted the dress to be a surprise, and the thought of it made him warm a little, building the anticipation of how she would look. When she came out of the bedroom in her coat, he knew he'd have to wait a little longer.

At eight they flagged a cab to drive them as close as they could to Times Square. When he dropped them off on the corner of 42nd and Fifth, the streets were already teeming with people headed to await the coming of the New Year. They walked up 42nd and Rebecca noticed the library and Bryant Park from their earlier excursions. They continued up past Sixth and to the corner of Seventh. On one side of the street was an elaborately decorated subway station. Bright neon lights identified the lines which could be accessed there.

Above it, there was a micro-brewery over which hung

a huge model of a British Airways Concorde. On the corner on which they stood was a large, brightly decorated ESPN Zone. In the center of the street in a block of its own, was a triangular-shaped Warner Bros. Store. Across the way on the opposite corner, colors burst from the facade of a Disney Store. From all the shops and businesses, bright lights and highly visible displays colored the streets.

Raul took her by the hand and led her up the block. As she walked, Rebecca looked at all the neon and glittering signs on the buildings. It was an amazingly garish and totally unbelievable sight. One only possible in New York, it occurred to her. Along the crowded sidewalks, people were clamoring for position and at one point, she and Raul had to walk single file, body pressed to body through the crowd. In some sections of the square, people were crammed into pens, and Raul explained that once you were in there, you couldn't get out until after midnight. The pens were some of the prime standing spots to witness the various shows going on during the course of the night and of course, the famous dropping of the crystal ball at midnight.

It was slow going through the crowd, but eventually they made it to a doorway and ducked inside to the lobby of a hotel.

"Talk about crowded," she said, letting out an exhausted breath.

"*Querida,* you ain't seen nothing yet. That crowd's just starting."

Raul led her to an elevator and they entered and went up to the fifteenth floor and once there, to a large corner suite. At the door of the suite was the name of the company with a sign that proclaimed it a private party. The company was known to Rebecca for she had recently heard the buzz about the development company behind some of the Internet's hottest dot coms. "Nice clients," she told him as he knocked on the door.

"And friends. One of my younger sisters went to

school with them. We all kind of hung out together," he explained as the door opened and a very handsome young man stood there, dressed impeccably in a tux and holding a glass of champagne.

"Raul, it's about time—" he began and stopped short as he saw that Raul had a guest.

"*Bueno chico.* I can see why you're a little late," he said and held out his hand to Rebecca. "Ramon Suarez. Nice to meet you."

"Rebecca Garcia, and I hope I'm not imposing."

"No, not at all." He turned and shouted out to someone in the room. "Hey, Ricardo, get your sorry butt over here." He motioned for Rebecca and Raul to enter and closed the door behind him.

Rebecca was surprised as another young man, clearly Ramon's identical twin, rolled over in a wheelchair. He smiled at her and it was a carbon copy of his brother's. The only differences between the two men were the fine, fairly new scars on this man's face and the wheelchair.

He held out his hand and she shook it, introduced herself. Grinning, he winked at Raul and advised, "I'm Ricardo Suarez. The better half of the team. I'm glad you could join us tonight. I know Raul has been a little under the weather, but it's obvious he's better now."

Rebecca quickly glanced at Raul out of the corner of her eye and noticed the smile work across his face. "I am thanks to Becca. I understand things are going well for you too, Ric."

The smile on the other man's face was brilliant now as he pointed to his shoes and wiggled his feet. "*Mira, chico.* It's just a matter of time now, *sabes,*" he said and Raul reached out and clapped him on the back.

"I'll have to get out on the court then and practice my serve so you don't kick my butt," he said and after a few more minutes of friendly banter between the two, Ricardo motioned for them to make themselves at home. Raul escorted her further into the suite.

Waiters and waitresses walked around with hor d'oeuvres and sparkling glasses of champagne. One end of the room boasted a bar, where bartenders poured other drinks for the large crowd of guests. At the other side of the room, a buffet table was covered with platters of food and nearby, a DJ spun CD's to provide the music softly playing in the background. At the entrance to what might be a bedroom, a young lady was busy taking coats and they walked over.

As Rebecca swept off her coat, Raul's surprised exhale reached her ears and she smiled, pleased at the results from the dress. "Are you sure you aren't going to be cold?" he asked, leaning close to her ear, his voice a gravelly whisper.

Coyly she looked over her shoulder at her back, bare to the waist due to the cut of the gown. "Oh, no. I think you know just how to keep me warm."

He groaned in her ear and she turned, previewed the front of the bright red dress. It had small straps holding up the deep V bodice which ran to below her breasts, exposing her cleavage. The sequined fabric hugged her slender waist and hips, flowing to the ground flawlessly.

He stepped close, placed his hand on her waist and brushed his lips against her forehead as he whispered, "You are perfection, *querida*."

Removing his own coat, she had no choice but to acknowledge he was no slouch either. The color and cut of his tuxedo emphasized his good lucks and lean physique. "You're not too shabby yourself," she replied, slipped her arm through his, and followed him through the crowd, meeting some of his other friends.

The night passed too quickly as they sampled the food and champagne the Suarez brothers provided. As it was nearing midnight, people jockeyed for spots along the windows lining the one wall of the suite, waiting to witness the spectacle of Times Square on New Year's Eve.

Raul had been right before, Rebecca thought. The

street below was packed, the pens that had been so clearly visible before now lost in a crush of bodies. The glittering, blinking lights of Times Square showered their rainbow of colors onto the crowd, which was growing more animated as the hour of midnight drew closer.

Rebecca snuggled up to Raul, who wrapped his arms around her waist, nestled his head next to hers. In the background, the DJ shut off his system and turned up the volume on the projection television in the corner as Dick Clark announced the time and went into a spiel about how many people were gathered for the celebration.

A waitress came by, handed them glasses filled with champagne and another young lady followed, handing them gaily wrapped little bags with grapes. Rebecca was familiar with that tradition, for her Spanish grandparents had always insisted on it—one grape for each month of the year and each gong of the clock on New Year's. Moments later the countdown began and the noise from the crowd was audible even as far up as they were from the street. When the large crystal ball atop the former Allied Chemical building lit up, a sudden hush came over the crowd. Then came the excited chatter which slowly crescendoed to a deafening roar as the world welcomed the new year.

Rebecca turned and kissed him. His taste was better than any champagne or grapes. He kept on kissing her as all around them people were clapping and hooting, exchanging hugs and kisses. The DJ powered up his system, launching into a loud, Latin salsa mix.

Finally Raul pulled away, held up his glass and she clinked it, took her first sip and juggled the bag to open it, removed a grape and fed it to him. He did the same and before long they had finished all the grapes and returned to kissing, sweetened by the juice of the grapes and the fine, smooth taste of the champagne.

"Do you guys ever come up for air?"

She abruptly broke away from him and met the amused gaze of Ramon, who slapped Raul on the back, leaned close to him and whispered something. Raul's face split into a broad, endearing grin and his gaze as he settled on her was hot. Nearly sizzling. Funny thing was, she knew just why.

"Ramon, I want to thank you for having us, but I have an early flight in the morning—"

"And we really need to get going," Raul finished, grabbing hold of her hand, and wishing his friend goodbye.

Ramon smiled, slapped Raul on the back once more as the two of them walked away to get their coats. It wasn't hard to do. Most of the party had moved to the end by the DJ and people were busy moving to the salsa beats of the music, clearly just getting into party mode.

Rebecca was already in being alone mode, knowing their time was limited. Haste was an inappropriate term to apply to the way they hurried out of the hotel through a side door to avoid as best they could, the Times Square Circus. A cab was out of the question so they hurriedly walked back toward Grand Central and the subway.

For once Rebecca appreciated the mass transit system she had bemoaned a week ago. A train came within a few minutes of their getting to the platform, hastening the trip to his home.

There wasn't a moment's pause on her part as they walked into his brownstone. She headed upstairs, slipping her coat off and tossing it on a chair in his bedroom as she waited for him by the edge of the bed.

The lovemaking that came had an edge to it. One of upcoming loss and separation. One of want and hope which they conveyed with softly spoken words and the meeting of their bodies. As they lay together afterward, Rebecca nestled against him, wanting to memorize every little detail of him. How the side of her face fit perfectly into the smooth hollow between his pectorals, right over his heart. The smell of him and of course, the wonderful delicious tickle of his soft, curly beard against her lips.

Memories she'd hold onto until they were together again.

# Twenty-One

Boarding the plane back to Miami was one of the hardest things she had ever done, but she did it.

Just as she somehow managed to go to work the next day, sorted out the pile of papers and files which had accumulated on her desk during her absence, and prepared for the lunch time meeting with the equity partners of the firm.

The call asking her to meet them in Mr. Langleis' office came shortly before the lunch time hour. Rebecca went to the other floor, but the walk was like that of a prisoner approaching the electric chair and for good reason. The meeting could be about a number of things, some of them not good, although as she and Raul had discussed, it was more than likely about offering her a partnership.

When she reached the anteroom to Langleis' office, the secretary smiled and motioned for her to enter. "They're waiting for you."

Rebecca nodded, knocked and walked in. The six equity partners of the firm were within, talking companiably. As she entered, they all turned and smiled, their mood obviously upbeat. For the first time, she was able to draw a deep breath and quell the nervous flutters in her stomach.

The meeting was for exactly what she had hoped. The delayed Christmas gift that had been on her list for so long. They explained to her the terms and the increase in her salary, indicated a written contract would be on her desk by that afternoon so that she could read and sign it.

Funny thing was, as much as she had wanted this before, after the negotiations in Raul's office and noticing the way he ran his firm, and the days after when they had become lovers, a partnership with these men seemed not quite as good as before. She knew the reason for that wasn't them, but rather herself and the recent changes in her life.

She also realized that the actions she took now would impact on a number of people at the firm. She needed to carefully consider what she would do. "I'm honored by being offered this opportunity, gentleman," she began, but Langleis cut her off.

"As well you should be. This is quite an offer for someone like you," he said. As she quickly glanced around, she saw some of his fellow partners cringe at his choice of language.

"What Simon means is, someone as young as you," one of the men tried to clarify, but as she looked from one face to the next, she knew there was more to it than just that. More to it unfortunately than the skill, effort and labors she had shown over the last four years with the firm. And she had to reconcile that fact as well with all the other new things in her life. "Again, I'm honored. As you can imagine taking a step such as this is something that shouldn't be taken lightly. I trust that I can have a little time to consider the terms, read through the contract and make a decision."

Simon Langleis began to bluster, incredulous that she should even have any qualms, but he was quickly silenced by one of the other men who confirmed that they wished for her to be totally certain about entering into this position and remaining as a long term employee with the firm.

The message couldn't be any clearer to Rebecca that refusing the offer clearly meant she should think about going somewhere else. She didn't even know why she was hesitating she told herself as she thanked them once more, shook all their hands and walked back up to her office.

Instructing her assistant that she wanted no interruptions as she was certain that the rumor mill would have it all over the office and she'd have a line of visitors eager to ask and confirm, she closed her door, sat on the sofa in her office and laid her head back against its edge.

She was never more confused in her life. The tunnel vision she had so carefully perfected had shattered like a fragile Christmas ornament, allowing her glimpses of a life she hadn't really considered before in the fractured bits of glass. Of a man who made her happy in ways that were too tempting to think about. He was either a bump in the road she had to plow over and forget, or a detour that there was no way to avoid. The path not taken Frost would have said.

The problem was, she wasn't quite sure whether to take that detour on the road less travelled.

She called him that night and they talked at length about the offer and Rebecca's misgivings after Langleis' ill-spoken words. It was little consolation to hear Raul remind her that the field of law was oftentimes still an old boy's network. A very Anglo old boy's network in some cases and that having them break that mold was an accomplishment about which she should be proud.

They didn't touch on the subject of what accepting the offer might mean to their relationship until almost the end of the conversation when Raul said, "No matter what your decision, Becca, I'm here for the long haul."

Despite his words she had the very real misgiving that it was only a very rare relationship that could survive that kind of separation for a long length of time. Not to mention that with the responsibilities that both she and Raul had, taking even a long weekend every now and then wasn't generally an option.

Which left her wondering just what she wanted now in her life and whether RLL was the place for her. A small knot of tension and doubt formed in the pit of her stomach. She pressed her hand there, rubbed at it as if that alone would help drive it away.

The knot grew bigger as the week passed, making it difficult to eat or sleep as she pondered what to do. The *Reyes* celebration approached. The unsigned partnership contract sat in her briefcase, coming and going with her everywhere.

The apprehension was in the back of her mind every night as she talked to Raul, missing him more than she had thought possible. He didn't ask about her decision, as if sensing that pressing her would be an issue. With his silence, he gave her his silent support that he trusted she would make the decision that was right for her. Right for them.

Whatever decision she made had to be one she could live with, but the knot inside her stomach didn't subside with that realization. It just grew bigger, almost to the point of making it difficult to breathe as she told her family about the partnership offer as they gathered that weekend for the *Reyes* celebration and the belated giving of gifts to Rebecca since her absence on *Noche Buena.* Her brothers and sisters, while supportive, all thought her crazy for even hesitating. Her youngest sister even went so far as to hint that if she didn't take the position she'd be messing it up for any other woman or Latino who came after her. After all, it wasn't often that the partners at RLL offered to let someone in. The fact that she might refuse was something that hadn't even crossed their minds and wouldn't sit well with them.

It was her mother who offered a small salve to her sensibilities by pointing out to her siblings that of all of them, Rebecca had always been the one to toe the line while they chased after what their hearts desired. "It's your turn now, Becca. Listen to your heart," she urged, fixing her other children with a glare to silence them from any further comments.

It was her heart that was on her mind the next morning as they went to Mass and then afterward to a small neighborhood parade celebrating the coming of the Three Kings to visit Jesus. There were three men dressed in flowing robes and huge papier mache heads who played the kings. They were drawn on a small float made to look like a stable. Huge papier mache camels and smaller lambs, chickens and barnyard animals decorated the float as well. Children dressed as shepherds followed, all of them in a procession through the neighborhood in celebration of the Epiphany.

She smiled at the antics of the children as they followed the float and afterward as her nieces and nephews opened the small little gifts the kings had left for them. One little niece insisted that a huge eye had peeked through her bedroom window and that when she had looked, it had been an enormous camel looking in. She was certain the Three Wise Men had been clopping around on the roof, getting ready to come in and leave their gifts.

Rebecca listened patiently to her explanation, recognizing the melding of Santa with the Three Kings. It didn't surprise her for as they became more and more Americanized, some of their traditions either changed or disappeared entirely. The festival of *Los Reyes* was one such casualty, for in many households and neighborhoods it was a forgotten holiday.

Traditions were important, she knew. It was those things you kept close to your heart so as not to lose that essential part of you. The part that reminded where you were from and inevitably, guided where you were going.

Her traditions had always stressed love and family above all else. But they had also urged hard work and the success it would bring. It wasn't the first time those two things had warred in her heart. The knot in her belly, still insistent and troubling, reminded her that success was within her grasp while the love of her life wasn't. There was no doubt in her mind that she loved Raul after a week away from him and the nightly calls she had come to cherish. They were the one thing that abated the angst inside her.

But despite those reassuring and pleasurable calls, her bed was too big and lonely without him. In the back of her mind, she wished he might be missing her enough to come visit. Had been hoping that he would surprise her and come share the *Reyes* holiday with her rather than just calling to see how she was doing.

Her Monday at work was hectic and a last minute emergency had her staying very late. By the time she arrived home, she was dead tired. After listening to the one message on her machine from Raul saying he was sorry he had missed her, she climbed into bed, the partnership contract still unsigned. Still buried in her briefcase. Her heart torn and undecided. The knot in her stomach growing to painful proportions.

He'd battled himself over it long enough. Picking up the phone, he dialed her number and listened to the ring. A second later she answered, her voice slightly drowsy as if she'd been asleep. "Becca? I didn't wake you, did I?"

"Mmm," she said, making a groany little sound in the back of her throat which unfortunately sounded too much like the sweet moan she made as she was getting excited. "I just fell asleep, but I'm glad you called." There was a moment's pause on the line and then she softly said, "I miss you, Raul."

He expelled the breath he didn't even know he'd been holding in. "I miss you too, Becca. Do you have time to talk?"

That sound came again and then her husky laugh. "With you, always, Raul. How was your day?" she asked, and he went on to tell her. She answered in kind, explaining how her day had gone and why she was so tired.

"So, you're in bed, huh?" he asked, picturing her all

warm and sleepy, wearing something like the ice blue pajamas he had been able to experience in the flesh, or rather in the removal of pajamas leading to the flesh.

"Mmm. And you? Are you in bed, *querido?*" she asked, the pitch of her voice low and incredibly intimate.

"*Sí,* but I wish you were here, Becca. I never knew how lonely my bed could be without you," he replied, wanting her to know just how much her absence was felt.

"Me too, Raul. But . . ." She stopped mid-sentence. There was a deep, indrawn breath before she asked with a throaty chuckle, "What are you wearing?"

He didn't hesitate to answer. "*Nada.* Just my birthday suit."

There was a strangled cough across the line. "Aren't you . . . cold?"

He looked down at the way the sheet and blanket tented over his erection. "No, not in the least. I'm thinking of you and—"

"I've been dreaming about you too," she said sexily.

"Was it a good dream?" he questioned. Her husky laugh across the line stirred him even more, creating a painful ache low in his groin.

"Oh, no, *querido.* Not at all. Tell me," she began, her voice low and exciting. "When you were thinking of me, did it make you hard, Raul?"

He bit back a moan. It took all his restraint and a deep breath for him to be able to answer. "*Sí, querida.* So hard I think I could—"

"I'm needy for you too, Raul. My nipples want your mouth on them and that wicked goatee. And *Dios,* I'm getting . . . bothered, thinking about you and where I'd like for you to be," she answered. He closed his eyes and imagined her, thinking of how the tight nubs of her breasts would be pushing against the ice blue silk of her pajamas. Of how they'd feel in his mouth and taste against his lips.

"Becca, this is getting . . . dangerous," he warned, needing to go and take care of his aching erection.

"Do you want to stop, Raul?" Rebecca asked, surprised by her own daring and the way she was excited about a man who was miles away at the end of a phone line.

He groaned. The sound reached inside her, causing a sympathetic vibration in her most intimate place. "Raul?" she prompted again.

"Can you touch yourself, Becca? Can you imagine it's me there, pinching and pulling those beautiful breasts?" he urged, and she did as he asked, reaching up with her free hand and rolling a stiff nipple between her thumb and forefinger, over and over until a small gasp escaped her.

"That's good, *querida*. Open your shirt," he said, and she clumsily undid the buttons of her pajamas with one hand, letting her shirt slip open, exposing her to the chill of the air conditioning. It tightened her nipples even further.

"I . . ." She had to swallow, run the palm of her hand across both breasts, before she answered. "I'm . . . getting cold, Raul. It's nippy in here."

"My bad. I don't want you cold. I want you hot and . . . are you getting wet, Becca?"

She was but she needed him with her on this journey. "Can you picture it's me, Raul. Touching you. Stroking you."

His heartfelt moan told her of his need. She imagined his big hand encircling his shaft. She softly urged him to move that hand, think of her all around him, taking him in.

"Becca, I can't keep this up much longer, *querida*. I want you with me, coming with me," he pressed, his voice a little rough, his breathing a little choppier. "Am I in you, Becca? Can you feel me? Am I at that sweet spot that makes you moan?"

Becca slipped her free hand beneath the waistband of her pajamas, opened her thighs and gently slipped a finger against the swollen nub between her legs. At her first contact, her breath caught and Raul gave his own rough little cry and urged her on.

"I'm there, Becca. With you, inside you," he urged and she slipped first one finger then another inside and called out his name at the pressure and sensations rolling over her.

Raul stroked harder, faster as he gripped the phone tightly in the other hand, his eyes closed as he pictured her, wishing that he was burying himself within her, the heat and wet of her surrounding him. Hearing her cry and the heat of her breath against his face as she came.

He was close to it himself and knew she wasn't far from reaching her own peak. "Becca, come for me, *querida. Por favor,* so I can go put myself out of my misery," he urged and across the line came her soft, guttural cry. It was almost enough to put him over the edge, but he held on somehow, slowing the pace of his own movements. Unable to finish without hearing her satisfaction.

"Raul, I can't take much more of being without you," she said softly, the anguish clear in her voice.

"We need to be together, Becca. Somewhere, any-where. I don't care where, just say the word," he pleaded.

"I promise, Raul. I'll let you know soon," she said hesitantly, and it was enough to strip away all the desire in his system.

"I can wait, Becca, but ..." He couldn't finish. Couldn't lie and say he could wait indefinitely to be with her again. He couldn't. He'd come to that realization during the week without her. He suspected that she knew it as well.

"I'll talk to you soon, *amor. Te quiero,*" he said, want-ing to reassure, but his voice lacked the tone to be totally convincing.

"Raul, I . . . I love you. Please remember that. I just need some time," she murmured.

"I know, Becca," he replied and hung up, but it was hard for him not to wonder how many more times they'd repeat this scenario. And how many times he could endure it without his heart breaking beyond repair. He knew he could have to make his own decision soon about how to be with her.

# Twenty-Two

He stared out the windows of his office, his hands fisted in his pockets. On his desk sat his organizer, open and waiting for him to sit down and find the free block of time that would let him board a flight for Miami . . . and Becca.

There was a knock on his door. He called out "Come in," and his partner, Antonio Fuentes, walked in.

"Raul. We need to talk." Antonio was clearly concerned, the tone of his voice serious. He stood before Raul's desk, his face hard and his jaw set into a grim line.

"Tony, I've told all of you that I had to abstain from voting on this decision. I've just got something too personal that—"

"Colors your opinion. We all know, Raul and we understand. I guess I should have told you that it's a deadlock, kind of," Tony clarified.

"I can't settle the tie, you know that. Besides, it can't be a tie with five of you to vote," Raul answered as he sat at his desk and faced his partner.

"Brian won't cast his vote yet. The two voting in favor of the merger are actually hesitant as well, but not for the reasons you might think," Tony explained.

Raul grabbed the pen from his desktop, tapped it on his desk in exasperation. "The Mendoza firm in Mexico is a good one. They have a number of clients and connections in Latin America who may produce a lot of business for our firm," Raul pressed, reiterating all the reasons that had made him in favor of merging with the Mexican lawyers. A merger that would give them an office in Miami, the little voice in his head reminded.

"We all understand that, Raul. In fact, the two votes against the new office and the two who are wavering are not due to any belief that this wouldn't be good for us. We've all thought for a while now that an office in Miami would help create more business with Latin America." Tony sat down in a chair and crossed one leg over the other.

"So what's the rub, Tony? If we all agree—"

"We all have family here, Raul. So do you, kind of, but we have wives, kids, houses. We need someone from this firm there to oversee this, but none of us can transplant easily. Well, none of us, but you," his partner said, a broad smile on his face.

Raul shook his head and was unable to control his own grin. "You know I was just looking for any excuse to head down there, don't you?"

Tony chuckled and gestured with his hands. "*Chico*, you have been a bear this week. We all knew it had nothing to do with this merger. Will you do it? The vote will be five to zero with one abstention if you say you'll go. And that you'll round up a few more lawyers to help man the office down there."

Raul closed his organizer. He picked up the phone and buzzed his assistant. "Get Eduardo Mendoza on the line for me."

The cardboard box was nearly full, but there were a few more things left to pack.

A loud knock on her open door grabbed her attention and she turned to find Andrew Waverly standing there. "Hi, Andrew. Come on in," she said, motioning to the office that was hers for only as long as it would take her to pack.

"I was sorry to hear about what they did, Becca. A little extreme given that all you did—"

"Was refuse their partnership? I knew they wouldn't be happy. I guess I should've known from some of their past actions that they might not respond reasonably," she answered, picked up a clock one of her overseas counsel had given to her and placed it in the box.

Andrew walked over and helped her pack the last of her knick knacks into the box. "You deserve better—"

"You've said that before. I think I always knew that some of the things here weren't things with which I agreed. I blinded myself to them and to how I would fit in because I wanted that partnership so badly. But then, when the end of the tunnel was right there . . . I realized I had been travelling down the wrong road and the place where I was headed wasn't where I wanted to be," she answered, the knot in her stomach gone since that realization had come to her.

There was a discreet cough. Both she and Andrew turned toward the door.

Raul stood there awkwardly. "I had wanted to surprise you, Becca. Guess I'm the one who's in for a surprise." He glanced around the office, noting the bare walls and the empty desk. He motioned to the box sitting on the bookshelf. "Going somewhere?"

Rebecca laid a hand on Andrew's arm. He nodded and left the room, closing the door behind him.

Rebecca walked up to Raul, took hold of his hand and led him to the small sofa in her office. "Andrew was just here to offer some commiseration. That's all."

He cupped her cheek. "It wasn't Andrew that surprised me, Becca. I know he's just a friend." He motioned to her office with his free hand. "What happened?"

"I said no. They said, sorry but go," she replied and reached for his hand, twining her fingers with his and giving his hand a playful shake. "So I guess I'm now a lawyer in search of a job."

"Why did you do it, Becca? It was a dream opportunity," he said, drawing close to her and wrapping an arm around her shoulder.

She leaned her head against the fabric of his suit jacket and laid her hand over the space right above his heart. "I thought about it. Long and hard. Finally took a look at things and decided that professionally this maybe wasn't what I wanted for a number of reasons. That was the first reason, but not the most important one."

Beneath her hand, the beat of his heart seemed to stop for a moment as he waited for her to go on. She looked up and met his expectant gaze. "I realized maybe New York and the cold weren't quite so bad if you had someone to keep you warm at night. Figured there were more than enough firms up there who needed an experienced trademark lawyer."

He smiled, a broad, unrepentant smile that lit up his face. "Well, I have no problem keeping you warm, but if you head for New York, we're going to have a big problem again, *querida*."

"Why?" she asked, moving her hand up to trace the edges of his goatee, the brush of that springy hair so familiar beneath her fingers.

"Because you are now looking at the head partner of the newly formed firm of Adamson, Fuentes, Santos and Mendoza. I'm here to set up our new Miami office and quite frankly, I was hoping you'd consider joining our little merger," he replied as he bent his head, brushed his mouth across her lips.

"*Querido,* the kind of merger I had in mind wasn't of the legal type," she whispered and opened her mouth to accept him and all that he was offering.

*Three years later*

Rebecca signed the partnership contract with a flourish. "Don't you even want to read it, Becca? I mean, this is a big step," Raul asked, stepping around her desk to stand beside her chair.

Rebecca rubbed her swollen belly as another contraction grabbed at her midsection. "Raul, *mi amor.* We don't have the time unless you want your new little son or daughter to be born in this office."

He bent down next to her, extended his hand to lay it over hers as it rested on their child. "Considering we made him or her in this office, it's only right," he teased, until she sucked in a sharp breath. The baby shifted strongly beneath their hands.

"Oh, *Dios,* Becca. You weren't kidding," he replied and jumped upright, held his hand out to help her from the chair.

"Nope. There are some things I just don't kid about," she answered as he warped into hyper mode, racing over to her closet to remove the bag they had packed and stowed away.

"Raul," she urged, stood and grabbed his hand, forcing him to slow down. "We have all the time in the world."

He shook his head, wrapped his arms around her waist and drew as close as he could. Between them, their new little child impatiently turned. He grinned, bent his head and brushed a kiss across her lips. Another movement came, like a sharp kick against his midsection and Rebecca groaned, drew in another sharp breath.

He glanced down, laid a hand on her belly. "Becca, we might have all the time in the world, but this little one is ready for his *mami* in Miami," he teased.

Rebecca managed a smile despite her pain and reached into her desk drawer for the dried out little bit of green and white he had given her three years earlier. She held it up over his head, grinning. "Just so long as we don't forget about the magic of a white Christmas and mistletoe."

Raul laughed heartily, grabbed the fragile little sprig from her hand and tucked it back in her drawer. "Never, *querida.* Never," he said and jumped away as another kick came against his belly along with another harsher breath from Becca.

She glanced down and he followed her gaze, noticing the small trail of water on the floor.

It was definitely time to go.

For a look at this month's
other Encanto romance

# *HOLIDAY HEAVEN*

by Victoria Marquéz

just turn the page. . . .

When they turned into Pelican Bay, Gabriela realized that Marcos lived in one of the waterfront apartments she could only ever dream of visiting. She'd seen the models when they had first gone up for sale and they were gorgeous with stunning views of the Gulf of Mexico.

Moments later, Marcos's hand rested on the small of Gabriela's back as he led her into his condominium. The familiarity of his gesture made her straighten her spine to counteract the tingle his touch invoked.

"Nice place," she said casually, despite feeling awe-struck by his elegantly appointed home.

Sleek, minimalist Italian furniture, including a dove-gray suede sofa with pewter legs, rested on glossy pale oak floors. Modern oil paintings in vivid colors graced the pale wheat colored walls. On the opposite end of the living room, oversize sliding glass doors offered a breathtaking view of sea and sky from the eighteenth floor.

"Come on," he said, "I'll see what Carmen left for us to eat."

Gabriela followed him into the kitchen and was imme-diately drawn to its efficient layout and elegant decor. The ultramodern combination of sleek cherry wood cabi-nets, stainless-steel appliances and charcoal speckled granite countertops beckoned her culinary talent.

"Now this is what I call a perfect kitchen," she said, running her hands over the smooth granite.

"Glad you like it," he said, reaching into the refrigerator and extracting a large platter. "It looks like Carmen left her specialty."

"What's that?" Gabriela asked, raising herself on tiptoe to peer over his broad shoulder.

"Argentinean *matambre* and potato salad," he answered, placing the plate at the center of the kitchen table. He opened a cabinet. "Grab a plate and help yourself," he said, opening a drawer and taking out two knives and forks. Utensils in hand, he sat down at the small glass table and pulled out the chair beside him. "Sit down and enjoy."

"I will," she said, serving herself a helping of the rolled flank steak, stuffed with carrots, spinach, peas, and a hard-boiled egg. "This is delicious," she said after the first bite of the savory meat. "Carmen's a good cook."

Marcos nodded. "I lucked out with her. There's only one problem. She cooks only Argentinean dishes and I crave Venezuelan food."

She clucked sympathetically. "Imagine that," she said, secretly thrilled that he didn't get everything he wanted. "I had no idea you were so deprived." With satisfaction, she popped a forkful of creamy potato salad into her mouth and chewed it slowly.

He raised one dark eyebrow. "Do I detect a hint of sarcasm?"

"Sarcasm? Oh, no. I was just sympathizing with you," she said, savoring a morsel of the *matambre*.

Marcos glanced at the clock on his kitchen wall. "Abuelita Coqui should be arriving in about an hour." He ate in thoughtful silence. After a brief pause, he asked, "Should we go over everything I told you about her this morning?"

Gabriela pushed her plate away and gave him a disbelieving look. "I'm going to ignore that question so I won't feel insulted. It's not too difficult for us non-doctors to remember simple details, you know."

"Don't make light of this, Gabriela. Convincing Abuelita Coqui that you're my intended will take a lot more than answering simple questions. She will expect me to be openly affectionate with you." He leaned forward and gently cradled her jaw with his hand. Before she could resist, he covered her mouth in a seductive kiss.

"What—what are you doing?" Gabriela stammered, pulling away. His mouth had felt warm, his lips soft, yet firm against her vulnerable mouth. Her heart raced at the intimate sensations he'd aroused with one simple kiss. What a naïve fool she'd been not to consider for a moment that this charade would include physical affection from Marcos! Just last night she had felt a stirring of passion when his strong arms had led her in the *paso doble*. She had spent most of the evening telling herself that it was the music affecting her and not his intense physical appeal.

But now this kiss . . .

Marcos didn't respond to her question. Instead, he regarded her with a steady amber gaze that unsettled her nerves. She decided she wasn't hungry anymore and didn't wish for him to see her sudden discomfort. Standing abruptly, she gathered the dishes and utensils, then carried them to the sink. In awkward silence, she quickly rinsed and loaded them into the dishwasher.

"Gabriela," Marcos said quietly.

"What?" she said, not turning to face him.

"You'd better not be having second thoughts because it's too late for that." His tone held a warning note. "If you recoil from my touch, she'll catch on immediately. Especially if you act prudish with me."

His last comment really irked her, making her feel like an inexperienced spinster. Prudish? She'd show him prudish.

Slowly, she turned to face him, adopting an air of nonchalance. "I'll try not to recoil from your touch, even though I'm not particularly attracted to you," she said, grinning smugly. "But you are paying me handsomely and you're a pretty decent kisser." She sighed dramatically. "I guess I can make an effort to act like I'm enjoying your attentions."

Marcos's mouth twitched in amusement. "I'll do my best to keep you satisfied," he promised.

For a look at one of next
month's Encanto romances

# TEMPTING DELILAH

by Gloria Alvarez

just turn the page. . . .

Victor paced restlessly in the half-darkness of his study, waiting for Delilah. Light from the street filtered through the blinds at the windows, casting long slanted shadows against his clothes and down onto the carpet.

He walked to the window, peered out of the blinds to the street beyond. Even at this hour, there was a steady stream of cars passing by. But not one stopped to let Delilah out.

And why did he feel so protective of her? She was a grown woman. A woman who'd rebuffed his offer of friendship.

Oh, all right, he wanted more than friendship with Delilah, a lot more. But she'd been pretty clear, even if she wasn't convincing. So why did he still feel as if he had a claim on her?

If he dug a little deeper into his psyche, he could probably find the answer.

Maybe his whole reaction was some primal thing—if he couldn't have Delilah, he didn't want anyone else to, either. Not a particularly modern attitude, but then, relations between the sexes rarely were.

It couldn't be love. He wasn't ready for that. He might never be really ready for that again.

Enough with the analysis. He paced again, away from the window, across the room and behind his desk. He dug his fingers into the back of his chair, squeezed tightly.

Anyway, the reason didn't matter. He knew how he felt, and he wanted her here. Now. Safe.

*So you can change her mind,* an insidious voice in his head suggested. *Bedevil her with kisses and soft whispered words. Break down her resistance. Make her want him the way he wanted her.*

The attraction was there. He just had to get past her reluctance.

But she had to *be* here for him to even try. He couldn't chip away her defenses without her.

The key turned in the lock, a slow scraping of metal against metal. Victor released the chair, crossed the room in four swift, silent steps, held the door open for Delilah as she stepped across the threshhold.

Light from the street spilled onto the marble floor, bathing Delilah in moon glow and street shine. Her face was flushed, her hair tousled, a small smile played at the corners of her mouth.

"Where have you been?" Victor demanded, the question flooding from that primal place deep in his brain.

"Having a good time," she said airily, stepping out of his way. The dress she wore, some body-hugging yellow thing, shimmered with beaded flowers and leaves. It was sexy, plunging to a V in both the front and back. It revealed a gentle swell of cleavage and a smooth expanse of back. The tips of her tattooed angel wings fluttered as she moved, and the skirt swirled sexily around her knees.

A woman in a dress like that . . . Victor growled under his breath. She shouldn't be wearing that out of the house. She shouldn't be wearing that with anyone but him.

"What's the matter?" she asked. "Can't sleep? Or just checking up on me?"

"I was . . . worried about you." He reached for her hand, but she strode over to the steps, mounted the first one, looped an arm over the banister for support.

"How touching." She worked for sarcasm in her voice and got it. "But I'm a big girl. I've been taking care of myself for years."

"I know. It's just . . ."

"Just what? You're my employer, not my owner. When I'm not working, I'm entitled to a life."

"It's just . . . you haven't . . . why tonight?" he asked insistently, walking up to her and looking her straight in the eye.

"Why not the night you kissed me and changed everything?" She met his gaze defiantly, daring him to disagree.

"You should have stayed. We could have . . . discussed this."

She laughed. "Discussed? Maybe for a few minutes. Then you'd have kissed me again. And again." She moved up another step. "So I went dancing. If I got kissed *there,* it wouldn't matter *here.*"

"And did you?"

"Dance? Of course." She threw her head back, swayed a moment on the step, the skirt of her dress flaring slightly, revealing half the length of her trim, smooth legs.

Victor caught her wrist, pulled her down the three steps back to the foyer.

"Dance with *me,*" he demanded and took her in his arms.

He moved easily to a song he heard playing in his mind, with its bright guitars and rhythmic salsa beat. Delilah never missed a step. She was a natural dancer, light on her feet and quick.

Too quick. Every time he tried to catch her face with his hand, to move in closer for a kiss, she'd spin away, grabbing his hand at the last second to dip backward. She'd kick her left leg high in the air before she landed back on two feet and start to move again.

Clasping her shoulder, Victor guided her firmly in the direction of his study. He began to hum low romantic tunes by Tito Puente as they danced through the French doors and around the sofa and wing chairs, past his desk to the bookshelf.

They moved well together. Delilah seemed to know

what he was going to do even before he did, anticipating turns and twists and moves he didn't remember starting.

At the bookshelf, he took his hand from Delilah's waist and pressed a button on the CD player. A second later, the real Tito Puente broke the silence between them with his sexy Carribbean beat.

"Mm-mm," Delilah said, seeming to relax as the soft music washed over them. Victor pulled her closer, and she no longer resisted, closing her eyes and leaning against him. She rested in his arms, solid and real. Waiting.

He only had to seize the moment.

She draped her arms around his neck and swayed against him, moving her body gently against his, her feet stationary. The pressure of her body was exquisite torture, the heat of her skin fired his desire. He waited a second, prolonging the fire, letting the anticipation build. . . .

For a look at next month's
other Encanto romance

# THE BEST GAME

by Hebby Roman

just turn the page . . .

Liana sat beside Damian, pulling her knees to her chest and looping her arms around her legs. They were silent for a time, watching people stroll by them on the bridge.

"So how did you get started? Modeling, I mean." He broke the silence.

Here it was again. He couldn't let it go. Most people couldn't. She really shouldn't fault him. She should just ask to go home.

She'd been prepared to despise Damian Escobedo, remembering him as an arrogant, conceited jock. But he'd changed too. Or maybe she was the one who had changed? Compared with the suave jet-setters she knew, Damian was a homeboy. He didn't intimidate her one bit. In fact, she'd enjoyed flirting with him, just to see his reaction.

And his reaction had been predictable. She was no longer the skinny, four-eyed, braces-wearing teenager of his recollection. She'd grown up and filled out; she had perfectly aligned teeth and wore contacts. He was in awe of her looks, just like all the others. It made her want to spit and hurl and curse and do all manner of unladylike things. If no man saw past her looks, how could she find anyone who really cared for her?

*Might as well humor him,* she decided. Sighing to herself, she asked, "Are you sure you want to hear this? It's really boring."

*"Por favor,* it won't be boring to me."

"Oh, OK." She tilted her head, gazing at his handsome

face from beneath her eyelids, curious to watch his reaction. "During my junior year, I was asked to be on a float for Fiesta. A New York photographer for *People* magazine took my picture and liked my looks. He contacted me, offering to introduce me around. I flew to New York and interviewed with the Ford agency. They liked the way I looked and signed me. Then they put together a portfolio for me. The agency managed to get me some local shoots in San Antonio while I finished high school."

Uncrossing her arms and straightening her legs, she rose from the hard stone bench. "Do you really want to hear the rest of this?" She shot Damian a look.

"Only if you want to tell me."

"Wrong answer, Damian." She tossed her head. "The wrong answer," she repeated. "I really hate talking about this."

"*¿Por qué?*"

His cocoa-colored eyes attracted her. As Audrey Hepburn would have said in the classic movie *Breakfast at Tiffany's,* he might be a rat but not a superrat. And she was tired of evading questions. Damian Escobedo was innocuous enough. After tonight's prearranged date, she wouldn't see him again. And she wouldn't tell him everything. Not nearly everything, just enough to satisfy his curiosity.

Shrugging, she grabbed his hands, pulling him to his feet. "Let's walk while I tell you."

"OK, whatever you say." He followed her, catching up and lacing one arm around her waist.

Leaning against him, she put her head on his broad shoulder and gazed at his profile. He lowered his head. Their lips were a mere two inches apart, if that much. This was known as the defining moment, she knew. But she didn't want it, didn't want him to kiss her. Not now, maybe never.

Pulling away, she skipped ahead, hurtling down the steep, stone-carved stairs. Stopping, she waited for him

on the walk in front of the exclusive hotel La Maision.
When he joined her, she offered her hand.

He grasped it, and she fought the feelings coursing
through her. She tried to ignore the touch of his rough,
male flesh against hers, tried to disregard the pull of his
masculine appeal. Her feminine needs, long suppressed,
clamored, like a Hydra monster, threatening to gobble
her up.

Struggling to put her confused feelings in their right-
ful place, she reversed her earlier decision. She wanted
to kiss him, wanted to find out what this crazy attraction
was about. Too much tequila maybe?

Reaching up, she curled her arm around his neck and
forced his mouth down to hers. At first, he seemed star-
tled by her blatant approach. He hesitated, and his lips
merely grazed hers.

But then he warmed to the task.

His mouth moved over hers, warm and supple, mold-
ing to her lips. His hands came up, cradling her head.
His mouth was like hot velvet against hers, his lips firm
and moist, searing her senses and heating her blood.

Moving with infinite care, he made a song of their lips
pressed together. With each fraction of a second, she expected the questing thrust of his tongue, demanding ac-
cess, suggesting intimacies she didn't care to share. But
he surprised her, his tongue slid over her lips, worship-
ping their contours but not demanding entrance.

It was a full kiss, a kiss of hot and moist flesh, of wonder and awe, of reverence and carefully controlled passion. It was a kiss that was hot and tender and cherishing,
all at the same time. It was a kiss she would never forget
because she'd never experienced anything like it before.

This was her first kiss . . . Her first real kiss, she realized with a kind of awe. Not that she hadn't been kissed
before. She'd been kissed many times, too many times.
But the kisses had been meaningless, a predictable prelude to seduction.

When they were both breathless, they parted, gazing deep into each other's eyes. Taking each other's measure again. A new awareness suffused them and a grudging respect.

He circled his arm around her waist again. She followed suit. "Let's walk," he said. "Finish telling me how you started modeling."

And weak fool that she was, grateful for a kiss that hadn't been a prelude to anything other than the simple pleasure it gave, she did as he asked.